A NIGHT'S ENCOUNTER

"Genny? You are still up?"

She sat in the chair he had just vacated, not removing her hands from where they still lay in his, as he sat on the footstool before her. "I could not sleep," she said.

"Neither could I."

"Xavier?" she questioned again, then went on, her eyes downcast. "Are we friends again?"

"Yes," he answered at once, ardently, squeezing her hands.

Their eyes locked in the dim light, silent messages flying between them. Relief. Pleasure. Renewed trust.

He did not breathe, and did not feel the loss of it. All he knew was that she leaned toward him, her eyes soft and shy but unwilling to leave his. He leaned toward her as well, guiding her closer to him by the pressure of his hands on hers. Closer and closer, so that their mouths were only three inches apart, and then two, and then one, and then his heart somersaulted with joy as she allowed him to press his lips to hers. . . .

A Heart's Treasure

Teresa DesJardien

ZEBRA BOOKS
KENSINGTON PUBLISHING CORP.

ZEBRA BOOKS are published by

Kensington Publishing Corp.
475 Park Avenue South
New York, NY 10016

Copyright © 1993 by Teresa DesJardien

Zebra and the Z logo are trademarks of Kensington Publishing Corp.

First Printing: September, 1993

Printed in the United States of America

LaJuan—

For Idaho, Utah, Canada, Honduras, and most especially for our glorious adventure through England: thanks for being my traveling buddy, and my best friend.

ACKNOWLEDGMENTS

In addition to research done during my own travels, portions of the county tales contained herein were inspired by and adapted from the wonderful book *The Real Counties of Britain* by Russell Grant, Lennard Publishing, a division of Lennard Books Ltd., Oxford, England.

My heartfelt thanks to Dr. Linda J. Clark of the Wallingford Family Practice in Seattle, Washington, for her research into the nature of eye injuries and the medical care thereof during the 19th century.

Also, I am eternally grateful to my gracious and astute editor at Zebra Books, Jennifer Sawyer, who knows how to suggest improvements to plot points without wounding this author's all-too-delicate ego.

And, to Barbara Bennett, in Zebra's financial department, for not sighing audibly when I call, and for being such a firm supporter of my work.

Chapter 1

*Where your treasure is, there will
your heart be also.*
                    —St. Matthew

The summer heat was oppressive, causing the five
occupants of the room to languish less for effect and far
more for cause. Only Penelope moved at all, plying her
needle with a steady rhythm. Her brother, Xavier,
looked upon the sight with his one good eye, exhibiting
a mild, piqued curiosity, for something in the simple act
momentarily captured his attention. However his interest dissipated only a moment later under the weight of
the great heat, fading as quickly as ice on a day such as
this.

As he leaned listlessly against the mantelpiece, Xavier,
known to the world by the courtesy title of Lord Warfield, went on to contemplate the fact that he had been
a part of such similar gatherings for years. The setting
was much as it had frequently been: a private home
whose sitting room contained himself, the three other

gentlemen of his close acquaintance, and his sister, Penelope. There was the Marquess of Galton's eldest son, Lord Michael, whose pockets were well and truly lined with gold, which purchased for him the liberty of a sometimes barbed tongue; there was Kenneth Mannington, Sir Roger's son, who justifiably avoided his bluff father's company, in hopes of limiting the number of already regular occurrences when his father chose to restrict his allowance. Too, there was Haddy, a nickname that fellow insisted upon, detesting as he did his given name of Hadrian Aubrey Dillonsby—he did not stand upon ceremony with any but the most remote of acquaintances, again preferring the nickname to the more weighty appellation of Lord Moreland. He was the shortest of the four men, with the solid build of a bull, powerful and at times intimidating despite his lesser inches.

The lone female at present among them was Penelope, exercising once again her lifelong habit of remaining wherever the "boys" were. She had known them all since the days of their short coats, and would not now make any silly objection to the fact that they had all doffed their jackets due to the heat. She remained with them, instead of joining the two other ladies in attendance as they languished in the limited shade of the townhouse's small backyard. The gentlemen were so used to the presence of her proportioned face and sensible nature, no one even thought to encourage her to join the two ladies outside.

One of the four gathered gentlemen, Kenneth, disturbed the silence with speech. "I believe the weather means to go on this way."

Listless eyes were lifted, and there were murmurs of discouraged agreement.

"But I have had me a thought," Kenneth went on.

Xavier looked from Kenneth to Penelope, but when she did not look up, he returned his attention to the man speaking.

"Go on, old fellow," Michael said, lifting a languid hand, a fall of lace at his wrist, which appeared noticeably limp in the stifling heat.

"It seems to me there cannot be a more miserable place than a hot and close London, so I thought me: why not leave her? I mean to say, travel north. To cooler climes."

"You mean to abandon us?" Michael said, his eyebrows lifting.

"I mean to take all of you with me. I propose a kind of treasure hunt, culminating at m'family's estate, Brockmore, in Cumberland," Kenneth explained.

"The devil!" Michael cried with signs of real horror, causing Penelope to give him a scolding glance for his language. "You can't be serious? Cumberland?"

Xavier raised an eyebrow, the motion causing his eyepatch to rub slightly over the puckered skin of the scar that showed both above and below the black fabric. He said, "I must say, I cannot help but wonder as much myself. I cannot imagine a more uncomfortable experience than tearing north over dusty roads, only to have nothing but sheep for company."

"Come now, it is not the middle of nowhere."

"Perhaps not, but nowhere may be seen from there."

Kenneth gave a smile, though it was faintly strained. His chin sank into his cravat as the smile faded, and he

9

mumbled rather poutishly, "I was just trying to make some sport."

"You touch me, lad. Your pleas do not fall on deaf ears," Michael said, a hand to his heart. He turned to the stolid Haddy at his elbow, who had stirred only so much as to silently pivot his vision from one speaker to the next, to ask, "What say you, Haddy? Surely Kenneth is right to think it will be cooler in our northern counties. Who knew the summer's heat would arrive so unfashionably early? I say: abandon the season, and let us hie ourselves to some relief, eh what?"

"There's hunting up north," Haddy finally spoke, even as he cast an eye toward Xavier, a long-standing friend of the field, a wicked shot despite the handicap of only one eye.

"Some bird hunting to be had," Xavier shrugged, though he did uncross one foot to stand upright away from the empty grate in something very like approval of the idea.

His sister's head, with her light brown hair pulled up in a knot that vainly sought to outwit the heat, rose up from her needlework. She cast him a glance, one he did not miss as she was sitting to his right, and sighed aloud with something very near to relief in the sound. "You must bring me and the other ladies along, of course."

Xavier crossed his leg over the other again and sank back against the mantelpiece, crossing his arms as well. "What makes you think the other sisters will wish to go? Or that any of their parents would allow such a journey, or Mother allow you to go, for that matter."

Penelope waved a dismissive hand. "Mother shall not mind, and Father shall not say nay if she does not. As for

Lord Galton, he has allowed Genevieve to travel with me before. Recall our journey to Kent last fall when Aunt Ophelia took ill. They shall not object, I feel certain. And you must own that not even they attempt to tell Michael what he may or may not do, nor where he may go."

Instead of appearing insulted at the revelation that Penelope thought his parents incapable of controlling his behavior, Michael merely nodded his agreement with a slight smile.

"Haddy is the head of his household, and if he wishes to travel and Summer wishes to accompany him, there is none to stand in their way."

"But what of Kenneth and Laura? Will Sir Roger approve such a scheme?"

At this, all eyes turned back to Kenneth, whose ears colored a bright red, for there was no escaping the fact that his father was reknowned as a tyrant in his household.

"Do not concern yourself with what my father shall say," Kenneth said at once. "After all, we only mean to travel to one of our own estates. There is nothing shocking or particularly unusual in that." He hesitated, then continued, "I shall find a way to see that my plans go forward—that is, if everyone agrees we desire to make this journey?"

Xavier gave his friend a level look, but he refrained from asking if Kenneth merely meant to leave without obtaining any form of permission at all. If that was the case, it was Kenneth's decision and not his to make. Instead he turned back to Penelope. "Dusty, hot, miserable travel is all you'll get for your trouble," he warned.

"As if I would get anything else here in London," she replied crisply, tossing her needlework aside with a firmness that said her mind was already decided. She proved this by standing and announcing, "In fact, it is a splendid thought. I shall inform the other ladies."

Xavier watched her go, that faint niggling of curiosity striking again, even as he noted the unavoidable line of perspiration that had left a trail exactly down the center of the back of her bodice, to match the one that caused his own fine lawn shirt to stick to his back. It was very like her to make such an instantaneous decision, of course, and who could blame her for wishing to take any chance to escape this heat, but still he found himself frowning. He moved to position himself to see out the leaded glass panes of the garden door, now propped open against the dim hopes of a breeze. He watched as she approached the shade of a leafy birch tree that was surrounded by a circular bench, where the two other ladies sat, their faces and pastel gowns dabbled by errant bits of light that had slipped past the tree's leafshade. He saw that they had abandoned their slippers and stockings, their delicate white feet peeping shamelessly from beneath the hems of their gowns. There was Laura, with her light brown hair that tended toward red in the sunlight, even as it did now. And Genevieve, her hair, lashes, and brows a rich, deep brunette that made one think of wood nymphs, though hers was no slender, willowy form; she had the peachy skin and ample hips and bosom of a particularly pretty tavern wench. He allowed himself to watch the spectacle a moment longer, but then moved away to dissuade any others from joining him at such an ungentlemanly endeavor. However, he did not turn away before he saw the two ladies nod their approval at Penelope's proposal.

"It seems we are committed, lads," he said to the room, turning so that he could see each man's reaction to the news.

There, sprawled across a settee, was Michael, as languorous today as ever he was, temperature or no; in the overstuffed chair to his right was Haddy, a decidedly confirmed bachelor who had a practical nature that brooked nonsense only when it was clear it was strictly in the name of fun, deploring it at all other times; and Kenneth, a likeable, bendable fellow who sometimes did not know his own mind, and little wonder with a father such as Sir Roger. Xavier had known them all for ages, and Haddy since before that fateful seventh summer when he, Xavier, had lost his eye. He knew their sisters as well: Kenneth's sister Laura, and Lady Genevieve, the sister of Michael, those two who reclined even now with bared feet beneath the tree in his backyard. And of course Haddy's fair and delicate sister, Lady Summer, who had not ventured forth today. Her Christian name was actually Rose, but Summer Rose was the phrase that stuck—because it fit her dainty beauty and described the exact color of her lips as no other phrase could—until she was simply Summer, no matter what her family Bible's record might read. Once she was told of the scheme, she would agree to come along, of course, for that was Summer's nature, and because Michael would expect it of her, and she would do anything Michael asked of her.

It was as clear as the delicate nose beneath Summer's sky blue eyes that she was madly in love with the non-

13

chalant fellow, and just as clear to everyone else that he was not half so much in love with her. Oh, it was obvious he knew he had contracted a fair bargain, but their yearlong betrothal had created no particular heat of impatience to marry that Xavier could see. A pity, that. Hers was the kind of personality that created a desire—even in the stoniest heart—to build her a castle turret that she might live within, beyond the reach of the various ogres and dragons and insults the world invariably threw into any life. Such delicate, sweet-natured creatures as Summer had been the cause of the origins of chivalry, he had no doubt.

Xavier had no passion for the girl at all—she was too much a piece of eiderdown for such a one as he—but he sighed to think that Michael had no such passion either. He tried to suggest as much once, and was firmly rebuffed by Michael for his efforts, and so matters stood.

"What is to be our plan then, Kenneth?" he asked, calling himself back to the moment. Just as he spoke the three ladies entered, returned from the garden, bubbling with enthusiasm for the proposal Penelope had carried to them.

"It's rather simple, actually. You know of my studies—"

Haddy and Michael groaned.

"Please," Kenneth said coolly, reaching up to straighten his drooping cravat with a lecturer's intolerant silence, until it had bought theirs. He went on, *"You know of my studies* concerning the folklore of the many counties of England. Mind you, I have taken clues from those tales, and made up a treasure hunt, of sorts. At first I thought it should also be a race, but in truth, what

14

pleasure is there in that? A brother and his sister, tearing across the countryside, with no one to share their tales of an evening? No, I propose that we travel as a group, and it is the placing of the clues that will make the challenge. We will all need to pair off, and then locate the clue that sends us in our next direction."

"Each group gets a clue?" Haddy asked, frowning.

"No, no, not so complicated as that. We'll take turns, but if the first team cannot supply the answer, then they must pay a forfeit, you see? That's how we may all be part of a hunt without having to separate. Of course, the team that avoids the most penalties and collects the most tokens, wins."

"And what do they get for winning?" Laura asked, earning a nod of approval from Haddy for her sensible question.

"I thought perhaps the losing teams must sport the blunt for an exquisite new fan for the winning lady and an equally desirable new snuffbox for the lucky gentleman."

The ladies nodded, well pleased, quite aware they would not be truly expected to extend anything from their pin money, for their brothers would settle any portion of the wager that could be called theirs.

"But you will know all the answers," Michael pointed out, bestirring himself enough to sit up, thereby betraying interest.

Kenneth put his hand to his chin, and murmured, "That's true. I thought about that a while, and I think the solution is simple enough, if you should agree to it: my partner shall be the only one to guess, and if there is to be a forfeit it must be mine alone, not hers."

15

"Hers?" Xavier asked.

"Or his," Kenneth said quickly.

"And how are our partners to be determined?"

"By drawing names."

"I see."

"Exceptional. Splendid. Magnificent," Michael drawled as he slowly pulled himself to his feet. "You lads arrange it all, and send me round a note to tell me where and when to meet you. As for today, I am done. I am going home and languishing in a bath of cool water, from which I will not arise until the sun sets. Do not expect me to be ready to go anywhere until at least four in the afternoon tomorrow."

Kenneth looked mildly startled at that, then nodded. "It might be nice to start off with the relative cool of the evening for our first day, though we won't get very far before we must put up for the night. In fact, I know where we might find a bed for the evening. . . ."

"As you please."

"Do not go just yet, good fellow. You must draw a name from a hat to see who your partner will be."

Michael insisted they should put only the ladies' names in the hat, that each gentleman could draw out a female partner. At Haddy's quizzical look, he explained lightheartedly, "I certainly do not care to have any of *you* simpletons as my partners, so I must insist."

It was quick work to have each gentlemen write his own sister's name upon a piece of paper. "We shall do this alphabetically, I think," Kenneth declared as he gathered the names, tossing the slips of paper in the hat he held forth by flicking his wrist several times.

"Last again!" Xavier gave a mock sigh.

Haddy was first to draw, and it was seen his partner was to be Kenneth's sister, Laura. Kenneth was paired with Penelope, Xavier with the absent Summer, and Michael was paired with his sister, Genevieve. He protested this result vehemently, against a sea of infuriating grins. "I ought to be allowed to have an alternate," he claimed. "Your older sister perhaps, Haddy? She's clever enough, and not half so cutting as my sister."

"She's increasing," was Haddy's dampening reply.

"Then my own brother."

"He's too young, and besides it would make for too many males; awkward for seating at meals," Xavier grinned. "No, dear sir, the drawing stands."

As they were retrieving their jackets, hats, and canes, and urging their sisters to find their shawls, Haddy said to no one in particular, " 'Tis a fine plan."

"Do you find it so?" Kenneth beamed.

"Oh, aye, any excuse to leave London and to run the fields is a fine plan by me."

"Well, there won't be much hunting to be had at first, old boy. That first night we'll only be able to go so far as Wycombe Marsh. Perhaps you know the place, it used to be known as Haveringdon?"

"I know it. *Only*, you say? That's twenty or thirty miles from here, Kenneth! I'll tell you here and now that Summer's not up to long, fast days of travel."

"No, of course not, nor any of the ladies."

"We could make off without 'em . . . ?" Haddy suggested hopefully.

"No, no," the other man said at once, flushing dark in the neck and lower face. He cleared his throat and added, "It would be churlish to disappoint them."

17

"Suppose so," Haddy agreed reluctantly.

Xavier looked on the exchange, but said nothing until Kenneth turned to him with a bit of bluster to say, "I must be off, if I'm to send my man on his way before us, to set our clues."

"Of course. We should hate to overtake him before he can complete his task." Xavier leaned forward to whisper quickly, "Should you care to trade partners . . . ?"

"No, no, it's quite all right," Kenneth said, shaking his head quickly and pressing his lips together. "A kind of mending time, you see."

"Quite," Xavier said, stepping back even as his one eye purveyed the man for any signs of discomfort, which indeed he found. It was not to be wondered at, for although it was not largely known, not four months earlier Kenneth had asked for Penelope's hand. Asked, and been refused, though that was not a great surprise to him, surely. Kenneth, only the son of a mere knight; she, an earl's daughter. Granted, Kenneth had sufficient—though far from exorbitant—funds, but that was near all he had, and Penelope's father looked to the higher social strata for his daughter, as any good father ought, of course.

Give the man his due, though, for Kenneth had taken the denial with aplomb and refused to break up their long-standing circle, as most men would have done. If it had been awkward for several months after that refusal, most of the others had missed the fact, with the exception of Michael, of course, who had a nose for just such hidden waters. But even Michael had kept his own counsel on the matter, a fact Xavier found almost as disturbing as if he had bellowed the matter to the rooftops.

But now it seemed Kenneth wished to mend fences even further, even going so far as to accept Penelope as his partner. Perhaps he regretted the loss of her friendship, since it was clear he could not have either her hand or her heart. And perhaps that was the truth of what had disturbed Xavier briefly earlier today, a renewed sense of his sister's . . . well . . . heartlessness, that she could sit and stitch and never pine for a man that he, Xavier, had once thought might become his brother-in-law.

Xavier only knew that his relief was immense when he had seen that Penelope and Kenneth meant to maintain cordial relations after the betrothal had been refused. He had so few he truly trusted, the thought of disassembling this, his tiny inner circle of friends, was nearly terrifying. Although their elder by a handful of years, he had been drawn to the younger group after his accident, for little children could be so immediately accepting, even of the maimed. He might have only one good eye, but he had never been blind to the curiosity, and sometimes even the repulsion his scarred face inspired. The scar was ancient but uneven and scarlet still, and short of wearing a patch that would cover nearly all the left side of his face—which was awkward at best, idiotic at worst—it was quite noticeable as it trailed under the patch from his forehead to well down on his cheek.

He had never been attracted yet to a lady who, upon closer acquaintance, had not requested to see beneath the patch—and that was ever the end of the relationship. He knew it was idle curiosity, and knew that to satisfy it would even perhaps put an end to it, but he could not help the resentment that surged into his breast whenever those fateful words were whispered: "Might I see it for myself?" And so he never accommodated them, and never thought to marry, for the intimacies of such a connection seemed insurmountable. To have the patch slip in the midst of a caress or a kiss was the death of passion. He knew. He had seen the look on more than one doxy's face when it had happened.

Penelope told him it was not so terrible as he saw it; she told him that others were far worse scarred from the war. He knew these things, too, but much as he knew and silently grieved for the pain of his countrymen's various disfigurements, he also knew it was the rare man who could face the world with a ruined countenance. Some men were missing a hand, or an arm. Other men could no longer dance, their legs taken, but their faces still comely enough to invite a caress. And that was all the difference, of course, for if as Shakespeare said "the apparel oft proclaims the man," then surely, too, did the face, the seat of all expression.

It was not that he was craven, nor even that he had not grown to some degree used to the inevitable staring, for he certainly did not hide at home. He went his own way, belonged to his club, hunted the field, and sometimes pursued the release a body needed, but as to romance—he had no place in his world for it. He was not unaware of the need for it, could not cease his own restless dreams at night, could not completely smother the flights of fancy that his mind sometimes took in the company of a beautiful or charming woman, but in practice made no effort to find whether such a face as his could be somehow found dear—or not—to one special lady.

He had Penelope, Mother, and Father, and this, his

circle of intimates, and that was enough, and he was grateful for such bounty, which was more than many another man had in this world. That was only the truth, and well he knew it, and therefore he cherished it.

The gentlemen made their bows, the ladies their curtsies, and the group as a whole their exits. Haddy promised to speak with Summer, but no one was in any doubt that she would accept the idea.

As their carriages rolled away, Xavier turned to Penelope, who froze when she felt his gaze upon her. She was silent a moment, and it seemed as if she might suddenly dart away, as was her wont of late, but then she turned to him with something very like tears in her eyes. He had not seen tears since the day after Father's refusal, when he had come upon her in the garden. He had put his arm around her, allowing her to ruin his new waistcoat with her copious tears as she gasped out her threats that she would elope with Kenneth, that she didn't care a fig what Father thought, that she would throw herself in the Thames, or she would refuse to ever come out of her room.

He had only smiled, unable not to, even though he felt her heartache in every sob, for every word was Nelly all over again. He was careful not to let her see it as he soothed, "There, there. You'll do none of those things."

At that, she had reached up to dash away her tears, straightened her spine, and stalked away from him, never to shed another tear.

But now her mouth worked for a moment, as though to mark the fact that she was a lady of few words. Finally she said on an unsteady sigh, "I am glad to go. Glad for the excuse. London, now . . . "

He reached up a finger, stroking her cheek in a gesture that said she might cry again now, if she chose. How glad he was to see that brimming moisture in her eyes, the first sign he had seen in four months that her heart had not been completely locked away. Since his own was firmly encased in an iron box, he was glad to see she did not completely share that fate with him, as he knew how much a duty it was to guard such a heavy treasure by day and night. "Perhaps it would be easier to stay behind, Nelly. I could make an excuse for you—"

"No," she reached up and grasped his hand with her own. "No. It's time."

He nodded, and sighed, chagrined by his own renewed relief that she would not undo his small, private, safe world.

Chapter 2

The huntsman winds his horn:
And a-hunting we will go.
        —Henry Fielding

"Tally ho!" Michael cried with a flick of the driving whip, a sign of enthusiasm such as was infrequent with the man. It caused Haddy to frown at him, and murmur that hunt phrases were sacrosanct and ought to be used only for such, but the cry was echoed by the other passengers who were not such sticklers.

The first of the two carriages rolled forward, Kenneth having insisted upon the Oxford & Cheltenham mail road to start their journey, with a crisp clip ordered once they were free of London's traffic and tollgates. No one asked how his interview with Sir Roger concerning this journey had gone, and certainly no one asked if any such interview had ever taken place. Xavier did not drive, his blind side being a possible threat to his passengers' well-being, but he sat beside Michael, to offer his unneeded but comradely advice, and because—by his estimation, quite rightly—it was far too close an afternoon to sit within a crowded carriage. His horse was tied to the back of the vehicle, and Kenneth rode his own steed behind the second coach, to act as a kind of outrider.

The second carriage, filled with baggage, was driven by Haddy, who had firmly declined any need for a groom, and squelched any protests that the ladies needed either maids or chaperones.

"Act as maid to one another, and of course you are all safe enough with brothers coming out of every seam!" he chided. "As to the road, we've fists and guns aplenty to keep us safe from footpads. I tell you, I'll not have my sport dragged down any further with unnecessary baggage."

This command was not complied with literally, of course, for the ladies had brought a plethora of cases with them, complaining that if they were not to have maids, then they must at least have access to their accoutrements. After a great deal of fuss, the coaches had been readied, and now they were rolling forward, to everyone's undeniable excitement, and not some little relief.

The relief dissipated very soon, of course, for the evening was heavy with the heat, the open windows of the ladies' coach only allowed dust to filter in, and the conversation melted away by steady degrees. Summer leaned back against the squabs, a lacy handkerchief pressed to her nose and mouth, her face growing a little paler as they traveled onward down each mile.

"Whose idea was this?" Genevieve murmured into the growing gloom as evening approached.

"Kenneth's," Laura and Penelope answered together, the one with a sour note, the other with resignation.

Summer merely coughed, her bonnet bobbing forward and falling over her face until she reached up, untied the strings, and discarded it altogether. Her white-blond hair was stuck to the sides of her pale face, causing Genevieve to sit forward and take her hand. "Just a little farther, I think," she smiled, and Summer smiled back, however unsteadily.

"I'm fine," she said, and everyone knew it was not quite true, for Summer was the kind who could not dance two dances together without respite, and did not wish to but still fainted at the sight of blood. Her health was not infirm, but delicate, easily disturbed, as though to match the light, lilting voice that she never raised.

Genevieve looked at her, longing, as usual, for something of that delicacy, that irresistible softness. She herself was as hearty as the cattle on her father's estate, and just about as subtle. It was unfair to compare herself with Summer, of course, who was slender as a reed, and walked as though on water, but Genevieve did feel as though her five feet and three inches was something quite monstrous next to this tiny, sweet-faced creature. Her own dark brown hair seemed mousy when next to that ethereal blond head, her dark brows and long lashes coarse beside those airy arches, and her curves almost obscene when seated near that slender form. It amused even as it chagrined her to know, despite all of that, that she loved the dainty creature she called friend, because one simply must love Summer, and because Summer loved her back so unconditionally. Genevieve's own inadequacies—which seemed less so anywhere else—

were worth the knowing, because she also knew that she had a lifelong friend in this other girl. Penelope must be described as "coolish," Laura a little cynical, but Summer was always charming and sweet, endearing qualities even if it made Genevieve purse her lips to keep from laughing with mingled exasperated dismay and gratitude whenever she was in her friend's presence.

She was not dismayed to find that her brother, Michael, with his quick tongue and his slightly too long hair, was to be her partner. She knew him well, and from the standpoint of the game, knew they could be clever when they put their wits together. From a totally different standpoint—that at least he was not to be Summer's partner—she felt momentarily befuddled, and chewed on her lower lip. He was entirely too unhurried about this marriage. She failed to see how he could have escaped falling in love with his fiancée, but it seemed to be the case. Of course, he was young, only three-and-twenty, and that was an uncertain age for a man, so Papa had explained repeatedly, but still it was unsettling. She herself was only nineteen, and a little concerned that she had not "taken" yet, and this her second season. Marriage was very much on her mind . . . but not so her brother's. It was different for men, of course, but four years of age seemed a very large one to her, and she could not help but wonder if Michael ever *would* realize what he had in Summer if he did not recognize it by now. She could not bear the thought of the betrothal dissolving—oh, but surely it would not, that kind of thing just was not done!—but, too, the thought of a loveless marriage for her dear, dear friend, even with her own brother, was just as terrible a thought. Worse, almost.

Well, perhaps this unplanned jaunt into the country would help. They would all be together a great deal, in a new setting. Sometimes romance flowered under such circumstances. It was a possibility, not without hope. Perhaps she could arrange for them to be alone sometimes. Perhaps Michael just needed to stop and think, and be with Summer a little, to see her in a fresh light. One could get too comfortable in a relationship, so Papa said. Yes, yes, she would have to be sure to see that the couple had some special time alone in the next few weeks.

Her reverie was broken when Laura sighed "Here at last!" as they pulled through the gates of a posting house into the large courtyard behind the opened gates. Ostlers sprang forward to assist with the horses, and a moment later the coach steps were lowered. Genevieve was handed down after urging Summer to go before her, and it was quite some fifteen minutes of confusion and bustle as the ladies' cases were ordered to various rooms.

"You will share a room with me, will you not?" Summer asked, smiling with obvious relief to be free of the coach.

"Of course," Genevieve answered.

Penelope and Laura exchanged nods that acknowledged they would be sharing a room with one another. The innkeeper stepped forward to assure the ladies that he had sixteen rooms free, should any of them desire one of her own.

"They can certainly share," Haddy jumped in, approving his sister's nod toward economy, "as will we gentlemen."

Xavier grinned, catching Genevieve's eye for a moment as they both smiled around that fellow's head at his penny-pinching. He came from a great deal of wealth, yet still jealously guarded that part of it that came to him by way of his quarterly stipend, even though none of them had ever known him to live a single day without sufficient funds. His suggestion, however amusing, was also entirely reasonable and therefore quickly agreed to, much to the innkeeper's disappointment.

"I'm with Haddy," Xavier said.

Haddy nodded at once, his thick neck disturbing his cravat as he did so, though he needn't have bothered to assent, for whenever they traveled together, it was their arrangement. Only Penelope knew the real reason for this—that cursed scar—but it was such a long-standing settlement that no one else thought to dispute it. Michael only grumbled, "Kenneth snores," but quietly, so that the ladies should not hear such a personal comment, and without any real malice.

Before he would let the ladies follow the host up the stairs to their chambers, Kenneth called, "I really think we ought to begin our treasure hunt. May I expect you ladies to return to the courtyard in no more than twenty minutes?"

"Twenty minutes?" Laura protested, but Summer sweetly said, "Of course," thereby answering for all the ladies, will-they, nil-they, for none would gainsay her. If she could be ready in twenty, it behooved them to do so as well.

It was not quite twenty minutes before they were

returned, to find the men pacing, a fact that made Laura roll her eyes. "It is nearly full dark," she complained as she stepped next to her brother, craning her neck to see what was darkly shadowed in his hand.

" 'Tis a ring of keys," he explained at her unspoken question. "My servant, Opperman, kindly went ahead and procured them for us from the lord's man at the great house, and had them awaiting us here with the innkeeper. I have a treat, I believe, for you ladies. We are going past the locked gates, into the Wycombe Caves."

"Good gad!" Xavier said, exchanging a glance with Michael. "Kenneth——!"

"Not to worry, good fellow. There are no more . . . er . . . of Dashwood's Apostles about. It's been years since any of that has gone on. I asked, you see."

"Dashwood's Apostles?" Summer asked, her brow wrinkling slightly.

"The Monks of Medmenham," Genevieve supplied, surprising a glance from the gentlemen. At Summer's continued perplexity, she explained, "The members of the Hell-Fire Club. Devil worshipers."

"Well, now, Genevieve, that was never proved, I daresay," Kenneth coughed into his hand as though to cover her knowledge of the vulgar. He rushed on, "But, truly, it is a wonderfully special place to begin our adventure, I think, but if you ladies would rather not——"

"Oh, Kenneth. Just tell us what we are to do! I vow I am too wearied to much care what manner of caves they are," his sister, Laura, commanded. "And I hold out some hope they shall be cooler."

"Quite," Kenneth agreed, pleased. "Here it is then:

we are to enter the gates and walk down into the chalk mines. They are wide enough for approximately three across, and tall enough to walk freely upright, at least in most of the corridors, though you ladies may care to mind your bonnets. It is three hundred feet down and in, and when we reach what was once known as . . . er . . . the 'Inner Temple,' there we shall draw to see which team shall have the attempt at our first clue. It *is* a little unsettling down within, so if any of you ladies do not care to go . . . ?"

Everyone looked to Summer, who looked to Michael, who only yawned. Summer said, "I am sure it will be quite interesting," causing the other ladies to nod whether they felt agreeable to the plan or not.

Lanterns were obtained from the innkeeper, and Kenneth pointed up the hill. "You see that church up there? The caves are in the hill below it. 'Tis a little bit of a climb, but not far, and the caves themselves are not so very steep. Find your partners, if you please," he said, offering his arm to Penelope.

The stifling heat was somewhat relieved as the night deepened, and so worked some restorative magic on the travelers as they walked sedately upward. By the time they reached the grillwork gate, set in stone and mortar, the conversation had turned lighthearted.

"Was it necessary to crawl into a hole to begin this?" Xavier asked good-naturedly as they all leaned forward to see the dark and gaping entrance beyond the gate.

Kenneth pulled the key away and swung the gate open. "Of course not. I just wanted to do something memorable."

"You have managed to do so," Laura said, eyeing the

30

dark and narrow portal before them. The lantern's light reflected back eerily from the chalky white walls, accentuating the murky tunnel beyond.

"Oh, my," said Summer faintly. Xavier automatically covered her gloved hand with his own and offered, "We may wait without, if you so desire."

"No, no, of course not," Summer replied, stepping forward, following Michael, who had already moved ahead, leaving his sister, Genevieve, to trail behind him unescorted as he lifted his lantern near his head to light their way.

"I say, what a place!" he cried, leading the way forward and downward, his voice echoing up to the stragglers still at the gate.

"I pray this does not indicate how the rest of this so-called 'treasure hunt' is to be enacted," Laura said crisply, delicately holding her skirt to one side to try and avoid too much of a dusting from the uneven floor as she came forward on Haddy's arm.

"Three hundred feet down!" was Haddy's only reply.

"It branches here," Michael called back, adding, " 'Stay to the right,' that's the rule. Stay to the right, and you will never be lost."

"Is it so confusing then?" Genevieve asked as she turned down the corridor behind him.

"No, in fact I do not believe it is," Kenneth answered.

"Still, it is the rule," Michael cautioned as he disappeared from sight.

Xavier did not hurry, for he did not expect Summer to do so. They had their own lamp, after all, and she was not the kind of lady that one whisked about. If one waltzed with Summer, one did so slowly, with temper-

31

ance and grace. Now he matched his stride to hers, and noted, even in the dim light, that some of the color had returned to her cheeks now that they were free of the coach. Haddy and Nelly were not far in front of them, and he followed Haddy's lead by removing his curly beaver and stopping a moment to set it on the floor where all the other gentlemen had cast their tall hats, thereby leaving his hands free and his head clear of the low roof.

Penelope reached out a hand, touching the white wall at her side, and pulled her fingers away with a grimace. "Moist and slick!" she cried.

"But it is cooler, is it not?" Summer sighed.

"Quite," Penelope agreed, a note of contentment in her tone.

Further ahead they heard a "boo!," followed by a small female cry, and came around the bend in time to see Laura scolding Michael as he hurried outside of her reach. "Really, Michael, do not try to be any more of a nodcock than you naturally are!" she called after his dancing figure.

"I'm glad it was she and not I," Summer said, smiling up at Xavier. "I should so hate to look the goose by fainting or arriving at the hiccups, but I declare these caves unnerve me somewhat."

"A natural response."

"Come along!" they heard from quite a bit further ahead Michael's voice echoing. "You must see this!"

The others were oohing when Xavier and Summer belatedly joined them, for before them was a smallish cavern of whitish brown, misshapen stalactites reaching down toward their brother stalagmites below, a narrow stream of water running at their footings. Summer clutched her hand upon Xavier's arm, which he covered with his own hand reassuringly.

Michael was holding his lantern aloft, his face reflecting disappointment. "Is this as far as we go then?" he asked of Kenneth.

"The 'monks' would not let a little thing such as this puddle stop them, surely," Haddy said.

"No, indeed," Kenneth said. "They called this the River Styx, but it is hardly so formidable as its name implies. There should be a boat . . . why yes, see there, and all nicely tied to this side as well."

"Let me help you," Xavier said to Kenneth, taking Summer's hand and pulling her forward, only to settle her hand on Michael's arm. Michael turned at the touch as he lowered his lantern a little that the small boat might be better illuminated now that it had been located.

"How wide your eyes are," he said to his fiancée, smiling at her a little.

"Do we go on?" she said in a small voice.

"Of course. We must not spoil Kenneth's sport."

She smiled back, somewhat tremulously, but her other hand came up to snake around his free arm, thereby pulling herself closer to his side.

The boat was pulled to a little ledge before them, and Kenneth leaped into it, making it rock dangerously for a moment until it steadied. Xavier held the short rope that had secured it. "Only room for three at a time," he cautioned, reaching up a hand toward the nearest lady, Genevieve.

She put out her hand and one foot, and her elbow was

steadied by Xavier as Kenneth helped her down into the dinghy. She was followed by Laura, who rolled her eyes anew at her brother, but made no comment.

"There are no oars," Kenneth belatedly noted.

Michael leaned forward with his lamp, and it was seen that a short pole lay in the bottom of the boat.

"So I am to play gondolier," Kenneth said, and proceeded to serenade the ladies with a snatch of Italian opera, which earned him a Here here! from Michael. The crossing was the work of a moment, cutting short his performance, but getting out on the other side took longer, as he had to awkwardly scramble past his sister to obtain the bank, to assist the ladies up and out. This accomplished, in a trice he had slipped back across the stream—little wider than the boat's length—ferried Summer and Michael across, then Penelope and Xavier, and lastly Haddy, who brought the remaining lanterns.

Summer reattached herself to Michael's arm. Unable to hurry her anymore than Xavier had, he matched her pace, so that this time it was the one-eyed man who moved ahead of the group.

"Are you quite sure these caves ever end?" Xavier called back to the party.

Michael gave a peal of ghostly laughter as answer, grinning to see some of the others jump.

"Michael!" Laura scolded, as Summer clutched his arm all the more tightly.

He continued to grin, making no apology as Xavier slipped around a bend, only the slight residual bobbing light from the lantern suggesting to those behind him that he had passed that way. "This is it then," he said when the others had followed his lead and joined him.

Before them was a "room" with a vaulted ceiling carved from the chalk. There was a table and a few empty and discarded bottles. Short of the signs of drinking, whatever debaucheries had been practiced here were not visible, yet Genevieve crossed her arms in front of herself, as though to ward off a chill. "How do we go about finding this clue of yours, Kenneth?" she asked.

Kenneth kicked a bottle, stared at another, then bent to pick it up. Out of its neck stuck a curled piece of pale blue paper. He gave a pleased sigh and said, "Here it is. Now, who is to be our first clue-solvers?"

"Age before beauty?" Xavier suggested.

"No, old man," Michael cried, emphasizing the words "old man." "Papers in a hat!"

"I have neither papers nor a hat," Kenneth replied, reaching into his pocket. "But I do have a deck of cards."

The gentlemen relented at once to the obviously planned logic of this approach, and after Kenneth shuffled the deck quickly, each reached for the card of his choice.

"A deuce," Michael groaned.

"Lads, I give you an ace!" Haddy crowed.

The others stated they had received an eight and a seven, which they handed back to Kenneth. He restored the deck to his coat pocket and presented the neck of the bottle toward Haddy.

Haddy pulled the paper free, turned to Laura, and offered it to her as he asked, "Will you do the honors, my dear?"

"Pleased," she replied, folding the curls back and adjusting her position until one of the lanterns' light fell

35

upon it. She read, " 'From the deck your fate was read, now you must look above your head.' "

At once they all raised their faces toward the ceiling, which was largely lost to shadows.

"I could stand atop this table, and hold up a lantern," Haddy offered to Laura.

"Er . . . no, it was not meant to be taken quite so literally," Kenneth supplied.

"Oh, I see!" Laura cried. "You do not necessarily mean this cave, do you? But explain the rules to me: how many guesses do we get?"

"Only one, and then it passes on to the next team."

"Can we look about before we announce our decision?"

"Well . . . a little, I suppose. That seems fair enough."

"You have a ten-minute limit," Michael announced, extracting his watch from his fob pocket. "Beginning now."

"Come along!" Laura cried, snatching up Haddy's arm. "It is clear we are to look up outside somewhere. Hurry!"

Penelope, Michael, and Kenneth hurried after them, leaving the other three to trail behind, which was just as well, as they would have to wait their turn for the boat anyway. When they reached the bank of the tiny river, Michael threw the pole into the boat and pushed it across to Xavier, who caught it easily. "All right then, fellow?" he called.

"Quite all right," Xavier answered.

Michael then hurried after the others.

"I never thought to see Michael move in anything like

haste," Genevieve commented as Xavier handed her into the boat.

"He is a different man when he is free of London," Summer agreed, and even in the dim lighting of their single lantern, it could be seen how her eyes glowed. Genevieve and Xavier exchanged a glance over her head. She looked away at once, as though to acknowledge his glance was to somehow betray her friend, but then she recalled that he, too, was a friend of longstanding and realized that the speaking look was not mocking, but equally as unsettled as her own. She looked again, but he was busy poling the boat, his tight-fitting coat quickly unbuttoned to allow his arms the freedom required. His waistcoat sparkled with metallic thread, its light blue color turned to lavender in the reflected light of the cavern. His was a long, lean frame, and she had a sudden impression—as one does at the oddest moments—that for all his wiry length, his was also a body of some considerable strength.

It suddenly occurred to her that hers and Summer's brothers, Michael and Haddy, were nowhere in sight. She pushed the thought away—they had all known each other an age, after all!—and instead concentrated on trying to steady the boat against the bank into which it repeatedly nudged, so that Xavier might climb out past her. His coattails swept across her face as he did so, but he did not seem to notice, and a flick of her wrist restored the misplaced lock of hair that peeped around her bonnet.

They followed the others up the winding tunnels, staying to the right as Michael had cautioned. The gentlemen retrieved their hats as they came near the mouth of the cave.

They emerged into the darkness of the night, giving a group sound of disappointment to find how heavy and thick with heat the evening air still was as they stepped out into it. After only the merest moment wherein the warmth seemed refreshing after the cool dampness of the caves, Genevieve found herself longing to be back underground.

Penelope and Kenneth were standing a little off to the right, staring up the hill that rose beyond the entrance to the caves. A quick glance showed that Michael was partway up the hill with one of the lanterns, though he had stopped there, gazing up through the dark toward where another lantern bobbed against the hillside. "Where is she going?" he cried to the others below him, indicating the climbing Laura above him with a lift of his arm. Beside him, Haddy shrugged, perplexed.

Laura responded to the question, her words echoing down to their ears, "The church!"

"The clue said 'From the deck your fate was read, now you must look over your head,'" Summer reminded them all.

"Well, that is most assuredly over our heads," Xavier replied, wry amusement in his tone.

"Come on then," Michael called, now with a wave of his arm to summon them upward. "If *I* find I am willing to climb this hill in this dreadful warmth, then surely the rest of you must as well."

"Ladies?" Xavier turned to include them all.

Penelope shrugged her shoulders, "Oh, very well. It would be unsporting to miss the first guess."

"Michael?" Summer called, but he must not have heard her light voice, for he climbed on ahead without hesitating. She turned to Xavier and murmured as she took his arm, "If you would not mind . . . ?"

"Certainly not. However, Nelly, make sure we are awaited at the top before anyone proceeds. I do not care to make this excursion merely for the exercise."

Penelope nodded, lifting the front of her skirt to keep it out of her way as she stepped upward.

They were all breathing heavily when they reached the steep top, and Summer hung just a little more than before on Xavier's arm, a handkerchief from her reticule fluttering about her face as though to create a breeze.

"Is *that* the church?" Genevieve asked, indicating the stone walls before them.

"Hardly. Look, 'tis some kind of . . . I don't know what you would call it . . . a pavilion, I guess. It has got statuary inside, see? I think 'tis supposed to appear Roman," Haddy supplied with a look of obvious scorn. "Though 'tis no older than I am, by my guess."

"Dashwood obviously had it built. He was a strange old bird, was he not?" Michael echoed the sentiment.

"I am not interested in this," Laura declared, backtracking at once to say, "Or at least, I do not believe I am. No, I believe the church holds our clue. Have you a key to it, Kenneth?"

They all moved as a group toward the heavy doors as Kenneth brandished the key ring to prove it was still on him.

Suddenly Michael stopped short and called out, "The devil!"

"Michael, we are on holy ground here, or very nearly.

39

Your language, please!" Genevieve scolded her brother.

"Look there," he said as a reply, pointing where the church's spire ought to be. They all stopped to ogle the strange, large golden ball that seemed to float above their heads.

"Strange bird indeed!" Haddy said.

Kenneth motioned his teammate, Penelope, to step forward and hold the lantern, and then it was the work of only a moment to unlock the door. Xavier wondered if he was the only one who noted that she was careful not to stand too near her one-time would-be suitor.

They stepped through the double doors as a group, revealing the church's smallish interior with the uncertain light from their lanterns.

"What a pretty little place!" Summer cried. " 'Tis Italianate, is it not?"

"Quite. I say, I rather fancy the way they have painted the walls. It is called St. Lawrence's," Kenneth said.

Laura interrupted this observation to say, "I believe our clue must be even further above us, in that strange gold ball that makes up a part of the spire."

"Too easy, eh?" Kenneth said with obvious disappointment.

"Hush, do not give anything away," Laura responded, softening the chide to her brother by adding, "The first clues have to be easier, so the players do not get frustrated too early on."

"That's just as I thought," Kenneth said, mollified.

"Then we must go up," Michael said, moving toward the steep steps.

"It is too crowded," Xavier observed. "Perhaps we should send just Laura and Haddy?"

This was agreed to, and they were gone up the stairs with the aid of a lantern, and almost as swiftly down once more.

"It is a card room!" Laura cried as she came off the last step. "It could sit six."

"It never looked so large from outside," Genevieve said.

"Charles Churchill said it was 'built aloft in air, that serves for show if not for prayer,'" Kenneth said, his eyes glittering at the chance to show off the knowledge his studies had brought him.

"But, to the point, what clue was left?" Xavier asked.

Laura put out her hand, revealing a playing card that was laid across her palm—a knave of clubs. Haddy lifted a piece of pale blue paper and handed it Xavier. "This was attached to the playing card. I believe," he said, "that you drew the eight, and therefore are the next to solve a clue?"

Xavier in turn handed it to Summer. She put it near a lantern, caught some of the light, and read their clue in her soft, clear voice:

> " *If you've knowledge to gain,*
> *Then to knowledge should ye go.*
> *Take a Heavenly Walk,*
> *And the truth thy heart will know.*' "

She looked up, "Why, whatever could that mean?"

" 'Tis decidedly a more difficult clue than Laura and Haddy received," Michael said as they all exchanged

41

puzzled glances, with the exception of Kenneth, who shifted from one foot to the other, as though the motion would keep him from blurting out the solution.

"It matters not tonight," Xavier said. " 'Tis late, 'tis far too warm, and we are all wearied, I have no doubt. Let us retire—"

"Ho no!" Haddy cried. "You've ten minutes, the same as Laura and I, to solve the riddle, or else it goes on to the next couple!"

"Ah, quite right," Xavier conceded. "In that case, Summer, if you please, a moment of your time?" He put out his arm, which she accepted that he might pull her a little aside.

The others watched as they exchanged whispered conferences, the top of Summer's fair head coming no higher than Xavier's shoulder, so that he had to bend at both the knees and the waist to whisper in her ear. Michael and Haddy debated briefly and quietly on what they thought the clue meant, but no consensus was reached.

"Why, how clever you are!" they heard Summer say as she laid her hand once again upon Xavier's arm, this time to be led back to the group.

"We have a solution, I believe," Xavier announced.

"And it is?" Kenneth asked eagerly.

"Summer, if you would be so good as to read the clue one last time?"

" 'One last time,' says he," Haddy said in a loud aside to Michael, plainly scoffing.

" 'If you've knowledge to gain, then to knowledge should ye go. Take a Heavenly Walk, and the truth thy heart will know,' " Summer read.

42

" 'Tis clear, of course," Xavier said.

"Not to me," Penelope said. "What does it mean?"

"Not what, dear Sister, but where. Divinity Walk at Oxford, I should think."

"Bravo!" Genevieve cried, seeing the logic of it at once, even as she half turned to see Kenneth's assenting nod.

"Not such a difficult clue then," Xavier said in Michael's direction.

"Not exactly sphinxlike, no," Michael drawled.

"Ah-ah! None of that, Michael, my dearest sibling," Genevieve warned. "You are setting us up to fail miserably, and be the subject of everyone's sport! As to that, Kenneth, what if a team should guess wrong? Surely you shall not allow us to go racing about the countryside in the wrong direction, shall you?"

"I shall not. But as to that, we all know we wish to end up at Brockmore in Cumberland, so you may safely assume we will be traveling in a primarily northerly direction. But, Xavier, how did you solve it so easily?"

"It was the card—a knave. Representing a younger man, of course. Let us think, perhaps, of a schoolboy? And we *are* on the road to Oxford, I might point out. A 'heavenly walk' made me think first of a church, but then it struck me—'Divinity Walk,' of course."

"Well, I hope I am half so clever when it comes to the clue that is given to Michael and me," Genevieve approved, smiling brightly up at him.

Xavier looked down at her, momentarily caught up in that glowing regard, smiling without thought or effort in return—until some little part of his mind rebelled, panicked, and acknowledged that her smile was having a

43

physical effect on him. His mouth flickered downward, then up again. His eyebrows drew together, and then he turned his face away, hiding the scarred side of his face in a long-standing habit, as he always did when he was shaken or unsure.

Even as he turned away, he was all at once annoyed, then dismayed, by his own behavior, by this sudden uncertainty he felt. He had known Genevieve for years . . . ! Why, of a sudden, was he experiencing that awful awkwardness that one sometimes feels in the presence of the opposite gender? That terrible, gaping indecision and reservation that unexpectedly binds one's tongue where it had never been bound before? Why did the blood that coursed his veins take a sudden leap, taking his breath away merely because a longtime friend smiled so warmly and kindly up at him?

Though . . . he knew well enough, knew and called himself a fool for it; like a priest who had sworn never to taste the joys of the flesh, he doubly knew the sting of denial when such longings reared. Knew them, called them by name, and cursed them. What a sorry oaf he was to allow any flicker of his own relentless and point-less desires to surface at all with this woman, this friend, no matter that she offered him what seemed a heartfelt compliment, that she praised him and thought him clever. To let any idle, mindless reaction enter the har-mony of this small group . . . it was nothing less than wrong. Hopelessly, even vilely, wrong. He formed the harsh thought, even as he struggled to keep that ruthless reflection from entering his features.

Belatedly he realized that Genevieve was staring up at him, her smile fading, a flicker of misgiving settling in her deep, dark brown eyes, proving he had not been entirely successful at repressing his self-loathing.

"It is very warm," he croaked out an excuse, stepping away from her.

She stared after him for a moment, shocked by his sudden coolness. She had seen that tight, pinched look on his face before, always the result of a cruel comment, thoughtless and even sometimes deliberate. But what had she done to merit such a look herself? Or had she been entirely mistaken? Could it be he was in some kind of physical pain?

She might have gone after him to seek an answer to her questions, but Kenneth stepped forward, coming between her and Xavier. The moment faded, the opportunity to speak lost to doubts that sprang up even as she had a moment to ponder. Maybe his shoes were pinching his feet . . . or maybe he was merely weary and out of sorts . . . ? She was uncertain enough that she could not pursue him, could not demand that he explain his sudden abruptness, even though she saw that he could not stand still, pacing slowly in a semicircle around his friends, careful to avoid coming near where she stood.

"You must keep the playing card, Laura. It is your token for guessing correctly about the church. It will become more difficult to collect the tokens as we go along. I assure you all, the clues *do* become more complex," Kenneth warned.

Laura placed the card within her drawstring reticule, patting it briefly in a sign of satisfaction.

"Then we need our rest, that our minds should be sharp for the morrow," Xavier spoke suddenly, ceasing his restless movement abruptly before Summer. He offered his arm once again to her. He added firmly, not looking in Genevieve's direction, "I suggest we retire for the evening."

Penelope walked by him, now on her partner, Kenneth's, arm. "The ladies will retire, you mean, while you gentlemen find the common room and a cup or two of ale," she said in a crisp—though not truly disapproving—tone of voice.

"One must be pleasant to the locals, sampling their wares and all," Xavier replied. He struggled for a moment until he was able to rearrange his face, supplying them with a smile that falsely crinkled the skin at the corner of his visible eye. Genevieve watched the exercise, then glanced around, only to find that no one else seemed to have noted that the smile was a performance.

"And one must make an opportunity to provide our good host with some extra coinage for his trouble, of course," Xavier went on.

"Of course," Penelope replied tartly to her brother, shaking her head even as she smiled.

Genevieve followed in silence, speculating to herself that if Xavier had not planned earlier to sit belowstairs and drink a series of rounds tonight, there was that in the set of his shoulders that now said he planned to do exactly that. She knew that something had suddenly gone wrong—though she could not imagine what. Was it physical pain? Surely not from his eye, for it was such an old scar. From some other ailment then? Or had she—or someone else—after all said something to offend? Her brow puckered as she walked toward the inn, unable to think what had caused that awkward moment, and wondering why no one else had noted it at all.

Chapter 3

So may the outward shows be least themselves:
The world is still deceived with ornament.
— Shakespeare,
The Merchant of Venice

The gentlemen took the corner table in the common room, taking off their well-fitted coats and loosening their cravats now that the ladies were no longer among them. When it was seen that they were merry despite the evening's warmth, and that they were neither haughty nor tight-fisted, several of the locals turned on their stools to trade comments with the urbane group.

"See 'ere," one man said, standing and reaching over the waist-high counter. He produced a stretch of delicate fabric, which he carried over before the foursome. "This be some of our lace what we makes 'ereabouts."

"Very fine," Xavier deemed it, after examining the stretch he had taken between his fingers. "You challenge the lacemakers of Holland." He looked around the table and added, "Let us buy an ell or two for our sisters, eh?"

This was greeted by a round of nods and cheers from the locals, which in the end resulted in having encouraged the gentlemen into purchasing the entire bolt, to be divided among the ladies later.

Before long a group was gathered around them, and a game of dice was introduced, a farthing a point. Haddy scooped up the dice, inspected them, and declared them acceptable.

An awkward silence fell. Xavier looked to Haddy and lifted one eyebrow in amused censure.

"Er . . . and of course you must allow me to purchase a round for everyone," Haddy announced as he reached for his coin purse.

This cheered the crowd considerably, and the game began. Once or twice the landlord begged the gentlemen to remember the ladies abovestairs, and the group would fall to murmurs for a short while, but then ale and good spirits soon had them again shouting at their good or ill fortune.

Xavier had thought he longed for the numbness that the quarts of ale could bring him, but as the evening progressed he found the brew and its promise of oblivion held no real appeal for him. Better to laugh and talk and game, for this was his world, the world of bachelors, of nights away from womenfolk. Let its familiar nature soothe his beastly heart, for then at least tomorrow he would have a clear head, and could think how to avoid those situations that aroused his own base nature.

One fellow, who was clothed in the suit and the manners of a farmer, knew no such restraint, laughing frequently between deep draws from his mug. Late into the evening, he leaned forward on his three-legged stool toward Xavier, surprising that gentleman when he managed to not tilt off his seat. "M'lord," he slurred, "how comes it that yers wears that patch on yer eye?"

Xavier sat up stiffly, and slowly the conversation around him died as all became aware that an offense had been offered. Michael and Kenneth exchanged glances, for even they did not know how the injury had been obtained. Xavier had never said, despite hints or even outright requests.

Haddy belatedly cried, "Enough of that! Now, as to this wager, I will——"

"No, Haddy. This fellow asked me a question," Xavier said in a cool and quiet voice. "He deserves an answer."

He sat back in his chair, knitting his hands together over his trim stomach, the look on his face steady and cold. After a sizable pause the cool mask was cast aside, replaced with a faint smile, and he began to speak slowly, in a storyteller's voice. "It was during a terrible storm at sea, my laddies. My father thought I ought to gain a little knowledge of the world, so he sent me to work as the bosun on a ship sailing for the Far East."

Kenneth turned to Haddy, an expression of disbelief written across his face.

Haddy made a discreet shake with his head, then lowered his eyes to the tabletop, pressed a finger to his upper lip, and did not stir as Xavier finished his tale. Michael leaned forward, not bothering to hide his interested grin.

"You should have seen it, my boys! A creature, the like of which I have never seen, nor even heard of before. An octopus, they call it, with tentacles twenty feet long, and a great bulbous head the size of a bull."

Some began to realize they were being roasted, stirring on their seats with either scowls or grins, but one man called out, "Aye, Oi've heard of them, what-yer-say, them there occupuses!"

Xavier pointed at him, speaking gravely. "Then you will have heard it said they can reach right up to the deck of a great ship and snatch a man down to his watery death. It wraps its mighty tentacles about the man, squeezing the life from him, making him gasp for breath even as its terrible jaws come down and tear his head from right off his body."

"Is that right, Harve? Them occupuses got great, big jaws, do they?" Harve's neighbor asked anxiously.

Harve looked uncertain, but then he nodded. "Right then, that's what Oi've heard."

"So an octopus attempted to tear off your head?" Michael grinningly supplied the question for Xavier, that the tall tale might be finished, while he began to play with the now neglected dice. Xavier acknowledged the favor with an inclination of his head.

"Oh no, 'twas the captain that had his head torn off. But, as he was being dragged across the deck, screaming and thrashing as a man would, his hand—which was a hook now, due to another unfortunate encounter with just such a terrible beast—raked across my face," he cried loudly with a gesture to accent the story, as his voice dropped gradually, becoming more and more quiet until the final word was almost whispered, "taking my eye and leaving me with this terrible reminder of that poor soul's final moments."

A silence filled the room for a moment, broken only by the ticking of a clock above the empty grate.

"Go on wit' yer!" a voice suddenly called from the back of the crowd.

Xavier now smiled broadly. "But 'tis true. Every word."

Harve looked about, realizing the truth a little too late when he saw the open doubt on the faces around him. The severely drunken man turned to him and bawled, "You booby!"

"Booby, am I? *Yer* the drunken sot—!"

"Gentlemen, may I suggest you assist one another in returning home?" Xavier said. His smile had evaporated in a moment, and his gray eye stared out at them in sudden steely command.

Harve and the drunken man fell still, until Harve sheepishly said, "Right-o, m'lord," even as the landlord reached for his arm to "help" him make just such a decision.

As the two men were escorted from the premises, Kenneth took advantage of the resulting commotion to lean toward Michael. He whispered, "How *did* he lose that eye? I have never known."

"Nor I. I asked once and received a sock that gave me a bruised arm for a week for my trouble."

" 'Tis odd, that we should not know. Well, one of the ladies will know how it happened, surely. Penelope, if no one else."

"I leave it to you to ask her," Michael replied in a low voice, his tone suggesting he doubted it would be a successful interview, and certainly not one he would undertake. Everyone knew how close Penelope and her

51

brother were. He spoke up, in a normal tone, "I wonder if the ladies will speak with us at all tomorrow, for I suspect we have disturbed their rest this evening. . . ." He checked his watch as he moved toward the stairs, "Make that, this morning."

Chapter 4

Even if strength fail, boldness
at least will deserve praise:
in great endeavours even to have
had the will is enough.
　　　　　—Propertius,
　　　　　　　"Elegies"

"There are a great many trees growing very near this inn," Genevieve said, following Summer's lead by sitting up in bed. "And they house a great many birds. Singing, chirping, twittering birds."

"I heard them, too." Summer rubbed the sleep from her eyes, the morning light that streamed through the gauzy curtain at the open window making her light hair seem almost pure white.

"I have listened to them since five o'clock this morning," Genevieve replied, pointing at the clock on the dresser that now showed the hour as a quarter past eight. "I never knew I could detest birds, but now I find I really most particularly do." She gave a smile to show she was not deadly serious. "Of course, this was after being kept awake until two in the morning by the raucous noises from the common room."

"You've been awake all that time? Oh, my dear, you've scarcely had a bit of sleep! I finally managed to fall asleep beneath my pillow, despite the sounds from belowstairs. But did you hear the host knocking on all the other doors at six?"

"Indeed. I wanted to go into the hall and tell him it was not necessary to bellow, but apparently it was. Our immediate neighbor needed to be summoned three times before she finally made her departure. I heard him tell her that she had missed any chance at a breakfast and was only five minutes away from missing the morning mail coach."

"I hope they allow a later breakfast for those traveling by private coach," Summer said as she pushed aside the single sheet they had shared and swung her feet over the side of the bed.

"I am sure they will. Our brothers will see to it."

" 'Tis heating up already. It is scarcely even cool this morning. It will be another terribly warm day."

"Thank goodness Oxford is not so very far from here. With any luck it will not be more than a two- or three-hour carriage ride."

"Do you think we will go on from there, or remain in Oxford for the rest of the day then?" Summer asked, her delicate hands coming together in a clasp before the waist of her nightrail, as though in supplication against the thought of too much travel.

Genevieve shook her head reassuringly at her. "We will go as far as we wish, of course. We shall stop there for a nuncheon, if nothing else, and go no farther if we do not care to do so, as long as there is an inn to be had."

"Haddy will wish to travel on. I am convinced he agreed to come just so he could have the opportunity to do some hunting up north. The sooner we get there, the better, that's what Haddy will think."

"Then Haddy will just have to be disappointed, will he not?" Genevieve's smile broadened. "Leave it to me. I would have no trouble persuading Haddy, or Michael for that matter."

"No," Summer said as she stared through the flimsy curtain that fluttered in the light morning breeze. "You will have no trouble with that." She sighed. "I wish I could say as much."

Genevieve lowered her eyes, not knowing what to say. For all that Summer's delicate femininity could be envied, it also had its drawbacks, for nothing was more difficult for the girl than speaking up in anything like a forward manner. She would gladly suffer a fifty-mile carriage ride than dare to suggest it was too long. She sometimes had to decline to dance with a gentleman, but then she devoted herself to entertaining him for the next hour, whether she cared for his company or not. She never openly disagreed with her hostess, merely falling into silence when she was not in accord. Yet, for all that her behavior was faultless, it was also quite plainly a burden at times.

"But, my dear, your civility does you credit," Genevieve said to show that a difficulty could also be a virtue, leaping off the tall bed as she spoke. "My father approves heartily of our friendship, as he hopes that someday I might learn some deportment from you."

Summer smiled in return, blushed a little, and said, "Stuff!

"No, 'tis true! I am forever giving my opinions, or pronouncing my likes and dislikes. Father says that since I do not have a mother to guide me, I ought to have at least had several older sisters to teach me the way a lady comports herself. Since I do not, you must stand in that stead. He says I am forever in danger of seeming a harridan, for I must add my view to every discourse. Or, perhaps worse yet, a bluestocking, as I cannot confine my table conversation to the weather or my latest frock, but must discuss the latest issue before the House of Lords, or the last battle on the Peninsula."

"He might have remarried if he felt you were lacking for a mother-figure . . . ?" Summer suggested gently.

"Oh, he tried. You know how atrocious I was to the ladies of his preference, and I quite frightened them all away, I fear," Genevieve replied not quite blithely, for now she saw her childish acts had been just that. Denying her father a bit of future happiness because she was so very lost and hurting at her mother's passing. She picked up the hairbrush she had set out last night on the armoire, and turned away from the glimpse of self-blame she saw reflected in the mirror. As she plied the brush, she sighed for real, and dared to reveal as much to her good friend. "Had I to do it over again, I should have been a far more pleasant young lady, I do believe."

Summer crossed and took the brush from her hand, signaling Genevieve to sit on the stool before the armoire, that she might brush the long wavy dark brown hair for her. "Even if you had had a stepmama in the house," she said quietly, "it does not mean you or your father would have been happier."

"No, but perhaps Michael might have been," Genevieve replied with a hint of bitterness in her tone. "When Mother passed away, I am afraid Father paid far too much attention to him. They were more like companions than parent and child." She suddenly remembered to whom she spoke, and pressed her lips firmly together. She would not add her thought that Michael was a little spoiled because of the doting attention he had received, combined with a lack of parental discipline—not to Summer. After all, Summer had known Michael since babyhood, and had chosen to become betrothed to him. Whatever his faults, Summer must know and accept them, surely.

Now the fairer girl said nothing, only going back to the subject of the weather when it was her turn to have her long radiant hair brushed out. They chatted amiably as they sponged and dressed, complimenting each other on their choices for travel gowns when they were at last ready to exit their room.

They made their way to an upstairs sitting room, the windows already open against the growing heat of the day. The innkeeper's wife greeted them, and announced what was available for their breakfasts. Soon they were joined by the other ladies, and belatedly the men entered as a group. Upon seeing the eight tables all laid out apart from one another, they promptly seized some of the furniture and pressed the tables edge to edge, making one long "table" at which they all could sit. The innkeeper's wife, Mrs. Hummock, was startled when she returned with a rack of toast to find them thus arranged, but only for a moment before she assured the others that their breakfasts would be forthcoming shortly. Haddy was disappointed to learn there were no kippers to be had, and mumbled something about ham having to do instead.

Xavier saw at once that there was nothing for it. There was only one seat left by the time he moved around the table; he had to sit in the chair to Genevieve's right. He pulled out the chair, checking the impulse to make an excuse about not being hungry. That was not how he would go on, and so he had decided just this morning.

He had stared at his own face in the mirror as he shaved, the patch pushed up somewhat out of the way but not completely removed. After all, Haddy had still been in the room; he did not subject others to the sight of his injured eye. As he had vaguely ignored Haddy's mild curses at the unaccustomed task of shaving himself, he had become aware of his own reflected visage. Not so terrible, at least not with the patch in place. His chin was strong, his mouth even, his nose straight. His hair was thick and dark, with a bit of wave that others tried to emulate with the use of pomade but which haloed his own head quite naturally. Even the good eye was an acceptable gray, with long dark lashes complimenting it. Perhaps if his skin had not been quite such a smooth, even texture his scar might have stood out less, but at least most of it was hidden from sight by the eyepatch. If it was not for the scar, he knew he might have turned a head or two.

His birth did that for him anyway; there was always a young miss on the hunt for a title or a fortune. He was

Viscount Warfield, a courtesy title he would use until he took his father's place as the Earl of Ackerley, and there were only a few eligible females who would turn up their noses at the chance to be a viscountess and eventually a countess. If the title wasn't enough, he had enough of the ready to satisfy all but the most avaricious seeker. And certainly no one could fault his standing as a most acceptable social *parti*. He was welcome anywhere—he had worked to make it so. How better to hide from the truth than in a crowd? How better to learn to ignore a lady's too-long stare than to encounter it everyday?

So he had remembered who and what he was as he gazed at himself in the mirror. He was Lord Warfield the Pleasant, the partygoer, the ever-gallant, the sociable fellow . . . who was at heart always alone. And that was his secret, the price he paid for his ability to go forth of a morning, to dance with a lady and make conversation with her: that he was alone in his bed at night, unable to inflict anything but his public persona on a woman. It was his way of facing the world despite his marred appearance, and had been so for a very long time. And must continue to be so.

Especially with Genevieve, a friend too dear, too long a part of his world, to lose over mindless selfishness.

Now he turned so that he could see her, forcing his chin up, with a polite smile formed on his mouth. "Good morning," he said, finding her gaze was indeed readied to meet his own.

"Good morning," she replied with a little nod. "I trust you rested well?"

"Indeed. And yourself?"

"It was cooler near morning," she said, making that

an excuse for her loss of sleep. She was not about to chide him for the noise that had surely kept all guests awake until well into the early morning hours, especially not now that he was looking at her with his usual steady gaze once more.

She returned his look, until the slightest smile touched his mouth and he said rather wistfully, as though in some private jest, "Yesterday was far too warm, I'm afraid."

"It was," she agreed, finding herself staring at him, searching his face, trying to determine from whence came the humor, softly colored as it was with something she could not quite define. She parted her lips to speak, to say something, though she did not know quite what, only instead Michael spoke, drawing Xavier's attention away from her.

"Tell us, Kenneth," Michael said, one arm hooked over the back of his chair in one of his familiar nonchalant poses, "what does the day hold for us? What manner of wonder have you prepared for our delectation?"

"You shall not know the answer to the clue set forth yesterday, of course, until we have obtained Oxford, but I *do* have another small surprise for the day."

"Do tell," Laura instructed her brother as she applied marmalade to her toast.

He reached into his coat pocket and drew out a slip of folded white paper. "I believe I shall call them Little Riddles. Small tests as to my companions' knowledge of their own fair land, which—I say with quite some confidence—I expect to be most limited."

There were some good-natured noises of denial and false offense.

"You mean those of us who get our noses out of a

60

book now and again," Haddy challenged. "But you are mistaken, my dear bookworm! Just because I prefer hunting to reading does not mean I do not know the lay of the land."

"A hunter, indeed, must know the lay of the land," Michael pointed out. Summer smiled at his humor, winning a nod in return.

"But what point these Little Riddles?" Kenneth's sister asked. "What is to be gained?"

"The joy of knowledge is not enough, Laura?" he replied archly.

The loud series of boos forced a grin from him. He waved down their protests, crying, "Very well, very well! Some sort of forfeit perhaps?"

"Tokens!" Laura cried.

"No, tokens are for the treasure hunt."

"A kiss!" Summer said, her soft voice managing to override everyone else's, as usual. They all turned to her as she breathlessly rushed on. "A kiss from one's partner."

"I am not kissing my sister," Michael declared flatly.

"Then from whichever lady you choose," Summer went on, blushing bright pink under their collective stares. Her eyes flickered to Michael, then dropped demurely to her lap.

The partners Haddy and Laura eyed each other doubtfully, then their eyes traveled speculatively on to others in the party.

Genevieve felt the tension that suddenly sprang up beside her, and saw one of Xavier's hands knot into a fist where it lay on the tabletop. He obviously found no merit in the thought. She started to speak, "I do not think—"

"Come! One would think we are not all friends!" Penelope spoke. Genevieve turned to face her, faintly startled to find that the cool and reserved Penelope was advancing Summer's proposal. "I have had a kiss from each of you at every Wassail and at each New Year's Eve since I can recall. What makes our little adventure all so very different from those occasions, I ask you? I find it a perfectly appropriate gesture: 'the Kiss Triumphant for the Conquering Pair.' " She looked about, nodding her head firmly. "There, 'tis decided. Kenneth, go on. Let us hear this first Little Riddle."

He blinked at the awkwardness that still filled the room, but he did not put himself forward to argue with her any more than anyone else did. Genevieve glanced at Xavier, but he was looking at Penelope, his unpatched eye slightly narrowed. She saw then, too, that Summer leaned forward a little; it was obvious her hand squeezed Penelope's under the table.

Kenneth handed the folded paper to Laura, who was on his right. " 'Tis just a little thing. I have compiled a question or two regarding each county through which we will travel, one for the breakfast meal, and perhaps another at luncheon. Merely to help us enjoy our travels. There is no time limit. They are not meant to be especially difficult. In truth, I expect one of these fellows to know this first one right away."

Laura unfolded the paper, and read, " 'What is the motto of Oxfordshire?' "

"The motto?" Haddy echoed, a disbelieving look on

his face. "What manner of question is that? Who knows mottos and things like that?"

"Not huntsmen obviously," Michael laughed. "Come on, Xavier, you've a taste for that sort of detail. Seems to me I've heard you mumble a motto or two in your time. What do you think?"

Xavier sat very still until he shook his head once, denying he knew.

" 'Tis surely something Latin," Genevieve said at his side, to cover for the lack of response that was so unlike him. She could not think what was wrong with him, but he radiated distress. She could only respond by attempting to turn attention away from him and asking Kenneth, "Perhaps you have another question?"

Kenneth parted his lips to reply, but he was interrupted.

"No," Xavier said, his voice perhaps a little thick, almost a croak. Genevieve spun in her seat to face him anew. He was looking right at her, his mouth grimly arranged. He spoke, "It is 'Sapere Aude.' It means 'Dare to be Wise.' "

The perfect advice for me, he thought. It was, after all, a game. Only a game, no matter that it involved a kiss. What was a kiss anyway? And he could take one from his own sister, or even Summer if he chose—he need not ask it of Genevieve.

Though he would, of course, to prove to himself that he could, that he knew exactly how such games were played.

"Exactly right!" Kenneth said. "You see? 'Tis merely a simple riddle or two a day, to keep our ennui at bay," he chanted, smiling at his own poetic wit.

"The reward," Summer prompted Xavier, smiling sweetly even though she blushed again at her forwardness. "You must claim your reward."

"Ah, yes," Xavier heard himself mumble. He dare not think. He dare not wait. He leaned forward, pressing his mouth quickly, dryly against the smoothness of Genevieve's cheek.

A round of applause filled the room, and whether it was for the kiss, or for the platters of breakfast that came through the doorway just then, he could not say. He sank back into his chair, flooded with the relief that it was done, and that he apparently had not made a fool of himself.

He was so busy concentrating on eating with the exquisite manners of a preoccupied man, he was unaware that, despite her occasional smile or nod, Genevieve was unusually silent for the remainder of the meal.

Chapter 5

*One more such victory and
we are lost.*
                            —Pyrrhus

Genevieve remained occupied with her thoughts as the carriage rumbled toward Oxford. Even though she'd had most of the morning to contemplate the strange shifts in Xavier's moods, and had come to no sure conclusions why a sudden awkwardness had sprung up between them, it was her own reactions to the same that bewildered her. She could understand her desire to shield him from that which he resisted—though she was unclear exactly why such resistance had come into being—and she could understand her desire to be once again on easy terms with him; what she did not understand was her reaction to that very brief kiss. It had tingled her skin, actually made it shimmer with sensation. Of course, she had not really been expecting to be kissed so suddenly, had thought it would be more of the formal cheek to cheek exchange such as they had known in the past, but even so her own physical reaction to the brief caress seemed most peculiar.

Her thoughts wound around her brain, circling and achieving no resolution despite the three hours of travel. She could not really concentrate on the other ladies's desultory comments about the brown-faced Oxford sheep they passed, finding she really could not care when Laura noted that they were raised as mutton, which product was superior to their short wool. It was difficult to admire countryside that seemed remarkably repetitive after so long a drive through it, and the weather was a subject that was long since exhausted. She gave up trying to be part of the limited conversation, only to find that, given plenty of time to think, she still obtained no understanding.

The carriage came to a halt, and the door was opened by Haddy, who was seated upon Kenneth's horse. As he leaned down on the horse's neck to peer in at them, he jovially cried, "Why, what a lot of wilted wonders."

If any of the ladies had pondered why Haddy remained a bachelor, they no longer did so, and as a group they cast him dark looks.

Becoming belatedly aware that his comment may have had an edge to it, Haddy hurried on to say, "Our last hostess provided a midday repast for us, which even now is being readied for your pleasure." He swung down from the horse, quickly securing the beast to the carriage, and offered his hand to the occupants.

It was none too soon for any of them, and so they told him as they descended one by one. Some of their annoyance dissipated however, when they saw their brothers had already laid a cloth out before them on the bank of a river, upon which resided a repast of cold fried chicken, pickled cauliflower and carrot slices, fresh bread with sweet cream butter, and an apple tart, along with an opened bottle of white wine to slake their collective thirsts.

"You needn't ask me twice," Penelope said, crossing at once to settle on the cloth, directly next to where the fried chicken lay exposed atop its wrapper of paper.

The others followed suit, arranging themselves around the offerings.

"What river is this?" Genevieve asked, the last to turn from the sight of the gracefully flowing waters to look about for a spot to seat herself.

" 'Tis the Thames, though locally it is known as the Isis," Kenneth said.

"You were last to come to table," Michael joked, pointing at his sister with a chicken leg. "Therefore you must pour out the wine for the rest of us ere you sit down."

"Are there now penalties for other than the treasure hunt?" Genevieve protested mildly, even as she crossed to where the bottle—already opened by one of the gentlemen—was propped against the hamper.

"We've no servants, so that seems a fair manner by which to divide up the duties we must perform," Michael countered.

"Fair if *you* are determining the rules, you mean."

"Exactly so."

Genevieve made a face at him, then said, "For that, you shall be served last." She reached into the hamper, felt around, then leaned over it to glance inside. "There are no glasses," she announced.

"Pass the bottle 'round then," Haddy said in his practical fashion.

Genevieve tilted the bottle to her lips delicately, and as she pulled it away from her mouth, nodded at the sweet flavor. Xavier watched her for a moment, then he lowered his vision to fix upon the buttered bread in his hand. It was only with an effort that he managed to force himself to look up again, his face stoically arranged.

"There is no silverware either, other than Xavier's penknife," Penelope added, holding her piece of chicken gingerly as she bit into it.

"But there are, thankfully, serviettes," Xavier spoke hastily, as though the words were suddenly squeezed from his throat, for Genevieve was holding the bottle toward him. He accepted the bottle with suddenly clumsy hands, and for a moment thought he would drop it.

"Thank heaven for small favors," Genevieve said as she settled onto the cloth, searching the offerings before her for the most tempting bits.

Xavier steadied the bottle and raised it to his lips, finding it sweet as she had done, though there was a hint of bitterness in his mouth as well, due to his acute awareness that hers were the last lips to touch the bottle before his. He took another swallow of the wine, hoping to drown the flicker of flame that sat somewhere, unwanted, in his belly. He passed the bottle on, happy to let it pass out of his hands.

"This food, this place . . . these are more than small pleasures," Laura said with feeling as she looked about the scenic spot. Although her face was still flushed, she appeared far more comfortable than she had but minutes before, a faint breeze stirring the damp reddish brown curls at her forehead.

"And let us not forget to praise the shade," Summer added, her eyes closing for a moment as though to relish that of which she spoke.

"To the shade!" Michael cried as the bottle was at last passed to him. He tilted back his head and took a long draw, then passed it on to Haddy.

Genevieve also cried, "To the shade!," as did Haddy and then each member as the bottle passed into their hands and began its journey around again. If Xavier's salute was lacking in enthusiasm, no one noticed.

When the bottle came back to Michael, that gentleman upended it, showing that only a drop more resided there. "I do not suppose there is another bottle in that hamper?" he asked with a patently mournful sniff of regret.

Genevieve shook her head and smiled at him, understanding for a moment why Summer loved her brother. He could be light and sweet and amusing when he wanted to, as he did now. It was difficult to remember, sometimes, that he ever made one wish to throttle him for his insensitivity and that marked air of callousness that reared its unwieldy head at the most awkward of moments. No, when he put himself forward, he was really the most charming of men. . . . Genevieve only wished charm was not such a fleeting attribute for him.

It need not be, of course. Only look at Xavier: he was nearly always entirely charming, in a quiet manner that seemed somehow more trustworthy than the bright smile and smooth compliments that most men exercised in the name of charm. Of course, there were those odd times when she had seen him white about the mouth, looking almost pained, abruptly excusing himself from a party or gathering. Stung as he was by some errant comment about his appearance, some thoughtless question or barbed remark, she had never labeled his inevitable exodus as a lack of charm. If anything, it was his silent refusal to sting in return that proved his worth. He possessed an innate graciousness which Michael ofttimes seemed to lack. Even now, she thought as she idly watched Xavier, obviously lost to his own thoughts, his was a quiet withdrawal, one that did not reflect on the company. If someone told a joke, or asked him a question, he would rally in a moment's time, pleasant as ever.

Even as she thought this, his eyes raised to meet hers. She suddenly stilled, the hand that was brushing back a lock of her own errant hair frozen for a moment, and the sound of conversation dimmed in her ears. His gray eye sparked, becoming the color of smoke just as he blinked, slowly, then shifted his gaze away from her.

Her hand completed the task, settling in her lap gently, as though to contrast the rapid beating of her heart. There had been something there, some interchange that she could not quite define, but which made her suddenly feel exposed. She shivered, unable to stop herself, crossed her arms before herself, and refused to meet anyone else's eye.

Haddy did not allow them to linger over the meal, loudly fretting about the horses who had been left to stand. He furthered his point by announcing that they must find new horses for the next stage of the day's journey, and also be on their way if they were to solve the "Oxford" clue and find lodging for the night. The ladies made faces at one another, but otherwise did not refuse the return to the stuffy carriage.

Where before Genevieve had enjoyed the relative quiet of her carriage mates, now she wished they would chatter. Then she had wished to think, now she was unable to do so. She had no shape or form to give her jumbled impressions, and could not like the uncertainty that they caused to flicker through her mind.

She was most grateful for the arrival of their carriage into the heart of Oxford University. Summer was pointing out some of the buildings, reading the names of those that were posted, and guessing at others, creating a welcome distraction. "I do say," she said, smiling at Genevieve, "I almost feel as though I have been here before, for Michael has described these very scenes, these very streets, to me."

Genevieve nodded as the door was opened, and they stepped down, exchanging the stifling oppression of the carriage only to stand under the merciless sun.

" 'Tis your clue, Xavier, Summer," Kenneth prompted, lifting a hand to make a circle in the air, a movement that incorporated the many streets that ran through the institute. "Where to?"

It was a listless party that followed Xavier's lead, stepping slowly and with only a limited amount of pretense at interest. No one responded when he explained that Divinity Walk used to be next to an apple orchard.

At last he came to a halt, hands on hips, to turn to Kenneth and say, "Here, then, are some apple trees that I deem to be in the right location, but how are we to go on from here?"

"Have a seat, everyone, if you please," Kenneth re-

71

plied, removing his hat to reveal that his usually light brown hair had darkened and flattened with perspiration. "You have the great honor of receiving a two-part clue, the second part of which is a story from which you must garner the essential fact. That fact will tell you where to look for your token." He lowered himself to sit beneath the shade of the nearest apple tree. "Come along, then, and make use of the shade. I have a tale to tell."

"And I have a nap to take," Michael said, lying out full length upon the grass at their feet, and promptly tilting his hat over his eyes.

Summer moved to settle beside him, her skirts tucked daintily about her feet, as the others stepped forward to choose their places in the sun-dappled shadows.

"And I have horses to tend," Haddy said, at once making a dismissive motion at Xavier, who had turned to offer his assistance. "Stay and hear your clue, man," Haddy said, gladly enough pulling his coat off against the heat in preparation of working with the animals. Xavier nodded his acquiescence, finding a seat in the inadequate shade with the others.

" 'Tis a sad and shocking tale," Kenneth began. "You see, once there lived a simple maiden, a local brewer's daughter. She fell in love with a university student, and I am sad to say that the cad left her in a family way, without the good grace to offer her a wedding ring."

Laura gave her brother a level look, mutely disapproving of the subject matter, but Kenneth went on, ignoring her. "Whenever they met, she begged him to wed her and give her child a name, but he always refused. Weary at last of her piteous entreaties, he agreed to meet her one night, here at Divinity Walk, in the moonlight. The girl was so happy, thinking that the lad's heart had been touched at long last, and that a romantic offer was to be made in the moonlit night, so that she arrived at their destination early. In order to wait in the dark and still remain safe, she decided to climb an apple tree to await her beloved. She found a level branch that stretched out straight and laid along it, to watch for her sweetheart.

"Eventually the fellow arrived, and just as she was about to call out to him she saw that he, oddly enough, carried a spade over his shoulder. She kept her peace as he walked up to the very tree in which she laid hidden, and proceeded to dig a large, narrow hole."

Summer made a little noise of distress, and Genevieve looked toward her, just in time to see the girl reach to gather up one of Michael's hands. He did not bestir himself.

"The poor creature was no fool, and knew that the student was digging a grave, and that it was intended for her. She waited silently in the tree, for a long time, until the student at length gave up waiting for her to make her appearance. As soon as he was gone, she ran home to her father's house.

"The next day, the student saw her on the street and greeted her in a loving fashion, indicating he wished to make a new assignation with her. But the girl said:

> 'One moonshiny night, as I sat high,
> Waiting for one to come by,
> The boughs did bend; my heart did break,
> To see what hole the fox did make,' "

Kenneth said, allowing his voice to rise to a spooky falsetto.

Laura nodded, apparently commending the girl's accusation, if not her brother's story.

Grinning, realizing he had caught his audience's fancy, Kenneth went on, his voice growing as he spoke. "Hearing that his secret guilt was out, the student drew a knife and *plunged* it into the poor girl's heart! Others in the lane tried to restrain the student, but then a battle of confusion began, between the Town and the Gowns, one set accusing the other, so that in the end the gutters ran with blood. You will be content to know that the evil student was killed in the fray, but—alas!—naught could bring back the poor brewer's daughter. To this day, they say she is buried in the very grave that her false lover had dug for her."

"How terrible," Summer said.

"What piffle," Michael drawled from beneath his hat with no particular rancor, only a yawn to show his sleepy nature.

Looking toward Xavier, his glance encompassing Summer, Kenneth explained, "I have a poem that may assist you should you care to read it?" At Xavier's nod, he reached into his coat pocket, extracting a folded blue note. He checked the writing that resided on one side, then handed it to Xavier, who also read the message: "Oxfordshire, No. 1." Obviously Kenneth had more than one clue in his pocket this day, and was verifying that he was handing out the proper one. Xavier leaned forward, stretching out his arm to hand the folded note to Summer.

74

She released Michael's hand to receive the paper, unfolding it to read:

> " 'A grave, a grave my lover dug for me.
> He wanted no love—nor child—did he.
> On an apple bough that sad night I saw,
> He would no' be a groom nor a papa.' "

Laura scolded mildly, "Kenneth, what a sordid tale! Not to mention atrocious poetry."

"I was attempting to be helpful, not write great poetry," he replied.

"I believe I have taken your point," Xavier said decisively, rising to his feet. "Twice you've told us that the lady was 'laid along an apple bough.' I presume that means we must locate an apple tree that has a low, flattish branch wide enough to support a woman's weight."

"Lead on, good fellow," Kenneth said expansively, unable to resist a small nod of confirmation, also coming to his feet.

Michael stirred himself enough to pull his watch from his waistcoat pocket, cocking a glance at its surface from under the hat. "Ten minutes," he warned, settling back.

Summer looked down at Michael, obviously longing to remain at his side, but then she pulled her eyes away and offered her hand up to Xavier, who was quick to take it, though he did not at once assist her to her feet.

" 'Tis very warm," he offered her an excuse. "I do not mind trudging about alone. I shall return the token here, shall I?"

"I must be at my partner's side." Summer shook her head, blushing a little that he had read her so easily.

He pulled her to her feet, hiding the awkward moment with action.

Laura declined the "pleasure," remaining with Michael in the shade, while the rest of them wove a pattern between the sun-spotted trees, trailing behind the partners. Genevieve actually saw the playing card wedged into the bark of a certain tree before Xavier or Summer saw it, but she managed to refrain from pointing it out, allowing them to win their token. The tree certainly met the description, for the branch was low enough for a person to grasp on tiptoe, and a bend in the trunk provided a place to put a foot and assist one's ascent. The branch itself grew out from the trunk in a decidedly horizontal pattern, and was thick enough to support even a grown man's weight.

"He would've had to have been very caught up in his digging to not note that someone—particularly someone in skirts—was lying atop this bough," Xavier commented, "for his head would have touched the branch should he have chosen to stand directly beneath it." Summer stood on tiptoe, extending her arm for the card, her fingers reaching. However, it was placed a bit high, just out of her reach. Xavier leaned over her, causing her to fit, for a moment, into the curve of his body as he grasped the card and pulled it free.

Genevieve watched, her smile all of a sudden fading just a little, as a strange prickle tingled behind her ears. She saw as Summer shyly smiled her thanks up at Xavier, watched their fingers touch as the card transferred from one hand to the other, saw them exchange a few murmured words, words she could not quite hear for the prickling that had become a buzzing in her ears. *Oh no!* she heard a voice, an inner voice, call out, astonished and dismayed. What was happening between these two? Had Xavier recognized Summer's worth; had he discovered the treasure that Michael could not see? The thought made her stomach ache, even as it made a host of impressions slide into a reasonable order, made sense of what had not made sense before.

Suddenly she was aware that someone was speaking to her. She shook off her shock, and turned to find Haddy looking at her, as though expecting a response. "I am sorry! I . . . I was woolgathering. What did you say?"

"The card," he pointed at the playing card that Summer grasped. "I said, 'tis the ace of spades. An ominous card, eh?"

"Quite," Genevieve replied, her brow puckering for a moment, as though at some brief internal pain. She murmured, "The death card."

"Well, that is appropriate, is it not? Given that the girl's grave is presumably under this tree, or one very like it."

She nodded, unable to find anything to say. She certainly did not wish to reveal the confusion that filled her. The death card? Could the card be eerily accurate, pronouncing the beginning of the end of Michael's betrothal to Summer? Had what she feared already begun?

Chapter 6

*You may drive out nature with
a pitchfork, yet she'll be
constantly running back.*

> —Horace,
> *"Epistles"*

"I believe the next clue goes to Penelope and myself," Kenneth announced. A brief, warm breeze stirred the leaves of the apple trees over their heads, casting uneven light to dapple the familiar blue paper he produced. He checked the writing to be sure it was the proper one. Satisfied, he moved to Penelope's side, looking down at her. "What say you, since you are in the unhappy position of being my partner and having to solve the riddle by yourself? Will you see through one of my clues as easily as Xavier has?"

Xavier watched as his sister scarcely looked at Kenneth, giving only a minute nod of acknowledgment. Really, it was quite bad of her, he thought. But then she looked up and asked, "So I am to solve this by myself?"

"I'm afraid so, as I already know the answer. But, remember, if you are wrong, only *I* shall pay the forfeit. And I assure you, starting with this clue, there will now be forfeits to pay in addition to not receiving the token."

"Ahh!" Laura said, "how are we to know what makes up the forfeit then? Do we get to choose what they shall be?"

Kenneth reached into an inside pocket on his jacket and produced a small velvet bag with a drawstring. He hefted it, presenting it to them. "The penalties are within. Nelly . . . Penelope will draw for me, should I be so unfortunate as to have to pay a forfeit." He turned back to her. "What say you?"

"That seems a fair compensation for my handicap." She glanced up at Kenneth briefly, and indicated the blue paper in her hand by waving it back and forth once. "Are you prepared for me to read my clue?"

"Please. We must know our destination, that we might travel on."

Penelope made a brief face, disapproving of the thought of returning to the carriage, but opened the note to read:

> " *In 1519 we were burned.*
> *Because of the prayer our children learned.*
> *'Twas not in Latin, but our tongue*
> *We wished it taught to them, our young.*' "

Penelope looked up, a faint frown settling between her brows as she silently read the clue to herself a second time.

"Oh dear," Kenneth said, his hand going to his breast

as his eyes danced with mock alarm. "Your expression does not bode well for me. Have you no guess at all?"

Penelope looked up, her expression warming to a kind of amused dismay to match Kenneth's, causing Xavier to nod in approval to see some of her more natural spirit come to the fore.

"I must admit I cannot fathom what this could mean," she said. "I know we must be traveling north, so . . . I may as well guess what town might do . . . Banbury?" When he shook his head, she offered a second guess, "Warwick?"

"Ah-ah! That's two guesses!" Laura cried, shaking a finger forbiddingly.

"Forfeit!" Haddy cried.

"Forfeit!" Laura echoed, obviously delighted by her brother's misfortune. They were joined by the others in the entourage for a third cry of "Forfeit!"

"Foiled by my own cleverness it seems," Kenneth cried dramatically, pulling the sides of the drawstring purse so that the top gaped open. "If you will, please," he said to Penelope, offering the bag to her, balanced on his palm. Her fingers fumbled in the small opening for a moment as she murmured, "I have gotten more than one," but finally she produced one small piece of folded paper.

"Oh, do read it aloud!" Laura urged.

" 'Forfeit,' " Penelope read formally, giving Kenneth a quick apologetic glance. " 'As the parties are required to walk or ride, they shall do so backward, for the following hour, commencing at once.' "

"Oh, I do like that one, Kenneth!" Laura crowed.

"You must be most annoyed to find you have put your-self in such a situation."

"Not at all. In point of fact, I feel enormous relief to know that I have managed to obtain this particular forfeit and not some of the others."

The possible nature of other such forfeits made for lively conversation despite the heat as they retreated from among the trees, but not so lively that the group forgot to insist that Kenneth walk backward, much to their amusement.

"You are a cruel lot," he informed them after tripping over a root, an action that almost sent him to the ground. Only Xavier's quickly outstretched hand saved him from a dusting. "I shudder to think how loud the gales of laughter would be, should I happen to take a real tumble and break my neck."

"I recommend you stay clear of the riverbank," Laura said with an evil gleam in her eye.

The parties grinned at each other, and Genevieve saw from the corner of her eye that Summer shared a laugh with Xavier as she strolled along on his arm. Her own amusement ceased at the sight. Things were not looking well, not looking well at all in that direction, Genevieve thought as her fingers absently worried the hem of the lacy summer glove on her left hand.

As they neared the carriages, Haddy moved forward of the group, obviously intent on reharnessing the horses. Xavier murmured to Summer, who removed her hand from his arm, so he was free to join his friend at the bothersome task. For a moment Genevieve watched him walk away, his legs taking long strides with an easy grace, but then she turned to observe Summer. She knew a sense of relief and a reassuring doubt of her previous conclusions, for Summer crossed at once to where Michael still rested beneath his hat. The blond beauty nearly collided with a backward-stepping Kenneth, reaching out a hand to touch his arm in warning as she cried out, "Do not tread on Michael."

Michael sat up at once, his hat tumbling to the grass, even as Kenneth came to an abrupt halt, looking over his shoulder to see that he had been about to do just that.

"I say!" Michael scolded, lifting the hem of his jacket to see if any footprints now resided there. He dusted at the fabric with the back of his hand, scowling.

" 'Tis not really Kenneth's fault," Summer soothed. "He is paying his forfeit, you see. He must proceed backward for the next hour."

"And must watch and see that he does not trample people, I should say," Michael replied.

Kenneth merely grinned, offering no apology on his own behalf. "Time to wake up anyway, old boy. It is now your team's turn to make a correct guess, or else—as I myself have done—suffer a forfeit."

"Ah, at last a chance to show true genius at work," Michael said, coming to his feet. He bent to retrieve his hat, which he placed on his head as he announced, "Very well! I am ready for the clue."

"It has already been read."

"Kenneth, you dog! You are making up new rules on us—" Michael began to argue.

"I made the game, I can make the rules—"

"Bad form! Bad form, I say," Michael interrupted.

"Bad form! Well, as to that, so is napping when others are willing to play along," Kenneth said with a hint of warmth as two spots of color appeared high on his cheekbones.

"Oh, dear," Summer said in a light voice. "Please do not argue. . . "

"Do not interrupt a gentlemen's discussion," Michael said sharply to her.

"Michael!" Genevieve cried, stepping forward to come between the two men before Michael could go on.

"What?" he asked, for all the world as though he hadn't a clue as to why his sister had raised her voice to him.

She gave him her most exasperated expression and said in a tight voice, "You are being rude, both to Summer and to Kenneth. I think you owe them both an apology."

" 'Tis the heat. It makes us all cross . . . ," Summer murmured, her small hand touching Michael's sleeve.

The two men exchanged speaking glances, but then Kenneth said, "No, 'twas nothing. A mere quibble. Perhaps Michael has a point; a rule about the number of times a clue may be read was never established. Too late to enforce a one-time rule now, I rather suppose. Here then, Summer, you still have the last clue? Please give it to Genevieve, and she can explain it to her partner." The twin spots of color faded from his face.

Genevieve did as she was bid, taking the opportunity to get past the awkwardness. She made a point, however, of insisting that Michael ready his watch, so that the moment she had read the prepared clue again, their ten-minute allowance for a guess would begin at once.

" 'In 1519 we were burned. Because of the prayer our children learned. 'Twas not in Latin, but our tongue we wished it taught to them, our young,' " she read it through again, then crooked her neck to mark the time on her brother's watch. She looked up at him then. "Where do you suppose this occurred? I declare I have no notion myself."

"I am about to prove that I was not asleep during every Antiquities class I was forced to endure: seems to me we must be speaking of the Lollards here."

"The Lollards?" Haddy asked, approaching the group. "Carriages are ready," he interjected, making a motion with his thumb over his shoulder, but then returned to the former subject without a pause. "Were they not a group of religious types who wanted everyone to cut off their hands and poke out their offending eyes, and what all?"

"Bible literalists, yes," Kenneth nodded. "In the fifteenth and sixteenth centuries."

"I can see by the light in Kenneth's eyes that we are on the proper track here," Genevieve pointed out. "But what city?"

Michael put his hand to his chin. "That is a puzzler. I remember something about . . . I think it was that some townsfolk did not wish to make their children learn the Lord's Prayer in Latin, and so the church up and burned 'em all."

"Also the Ten Commandments. And it was seven craftsmen," Kenneth supplied. "But in what *town* did this take place?"

Genevieve and Michael stared at each other. "I do not know. Have you a guess?" She turned to Kenneth. "Guesses count, if they are right, do they not? Penelope was guessing, even though she was incorrect."

"They better count, or we will be at this the rest of our lives," Haddy grumbled.

"Very well," Kenneth conceded.

"We know from Penelope's missed guesses that Banbury and Warwick are incorrect," Genevieve explained to her brother.

"Ah, is that so? Well then, let us figure this logically," Michael said, rubbing his chin. "We know we are to go in a primarily northern direction. We further know that Banbury and Warwick are incorrect."

"I never said Warwick was incorrect," Kenneth put in.

"Well, is it or is it not?"

"Is that your guess?"

"Kenneth!" Haddy growled, pointing at Michael's watch to emphasize the passing of time.

Kenneth sighed. "In the interest of saving daylight traveling time, I will concede the information this one time. Warwick is *not* correct."

"Very well then. We know we are heading up into Warwickshire. What cities or towns do you know of in that county?" Michael asked his sister.

"Stratford," she answered.

"Possible," he murmured. "Oh, and there's that other place . . . it starts with a K. Kenilton? Kenilsby?"

"Kenilworth?"

"Yes, that's the one . . . though, I know for a fact it is not on the larger road. I think we would all be happier if we stayed on the better roads, and I am going to assume Kenneth, clever fellow that he is, has thought of that as well. Ahh, there's that one city . . . its name is right on the tip of my tongue . . . ! Oh, you know it,

Genevieve; you spent a summer there one year, with that little redheaded friend of yours—"

"Hetta?"

"That is the one."

"Well then, you must mean Coventry."

"Exactly!" Michael cried. "I think that would be our best bet." He turned to Kenneth. "We guess Coventry."

Kenneth inclined his head. "Quite right. Though I must say it is a good thing for you that guesses are allowed."

"Oh, who would know anything from that clue?" Laura said, waving her hand in the air as though to fan away the dispute.

"A scholar?" Kenneth suggested archly, handing a playing card—an ace of diamonds—to Michael. Michael turned to Genevieve, giving her possession of the token.

"Or perhaps only those who must walk backward," Laura responded, and was rewarded by a dark look from her brother and a chortle from Haddy. That fellow then said, "Enough! We've our destination, so let us away before the horses get too restless."

The ladies piled back inside the carriage, uttering various remonstrations against the heat of the day. It was only the matter of a few minutes before they talked each other into disposing of their gloves, shoes, and stockings for the time being, and silently envied the gentlemen who could ride either atop the carriages or on one or the other of the saddle horses Kenneth and Xavier had brought with them, where one had the hope of catching an errant breeze.

Haddy drove the ladies' carriage, leaving poor Michael to swallow his dust as that gentleman maneuvered the second carriage. Kenneth and Xavier chose to ride, with Kenneth backward in the saddle, much to his chagrin. He marked the time on his watch, noting he only had thirty-seven more minutes to endure his forfeit. He made a point of being on the right so that Xavier could see him as they talked back and forth.

"Comfortable?" Xavier asked with a straight face.

"No," Kenneth answered dryly. "But all I ask is that we keep forward of that carriage. You know the ladies would not spare me."

"True. Then, lad, put your heels to your steed, if you do not think it will overly confuse the poor creature, and we will ride ahead a bit."

They complained for a while about the unusual weather. They speculated on what Kenneth's estate in Cumberland would be like this time of year, and tried to recall if they knew of any posting houses on the road they presently traveled. At precisely thirty-seven minutes later, Kenneth reined to a halt, and remounted properly.

They rode on, discussing the fact that they only expected to travel half the distance to Coventry this afternoon, and that only if the quality of the roads remained such that negotiating them was not especially difficult. They would need to find a place for the night fairly soon.

They dismounted again to stretch their legs in Cottenham, and to supply Haddy with some of the ready for he was the best of them all at negotiating a fair price for a new team of horses. Waiting for the dickering to be done, and the new horses harnessed, they exchanged desultory comments with the ladies, who were also taking the opportunity to stretch their legs.

"I believe I am very grateful Haddy has such a well-sprung carriage," Genevieve sighed, wanting to but not rubbing the part of her anatomy that was grown quite weary with the day's travels.

Kenneth made no comment about discomfort.

" 'Tis not much longer until we put up for the night," Xavier assured Genevieve, even as he allowed his good eye to take in her appearance. She was obviously too warm. Her face was flushed. There was a bit of hair on the top of her head that was sticking straight up. Her gown had long ago gone limp, clinging in places she probably didn't realize it was clinging, and her gloves were missing entirely. None of the ladies bothered any longer with a bonnet, and a quick glimpse when she had stepped down from the carriage had made him think that although she wore her slippers she might not be wearing her stockings. There was a sprinkle of perspiration across her forehead, and her lips were reddened as though she had been wetting them all day. In short, she looked an absolute ragamuffin, a sight that made him smile secretly even as it filled him with a strange warm glow.

He could not help himself; he reached out and smoothed down the stray hair at the top of her head.

"Oh dear," she murmured as soon as she realized what he was doing. "I must look a fright."

"Not at all," he said, his voice constricting in his throat. If anything, she looked entirely kissable. That thought brought him up short, and his hand fell away as though leaden.

"We are hitched," Haddy cried.

Xavier turned gratefully at the interruption, abandoning his manners by not handing the ladies up into the carriage. Avoidance was the key, even if it meant occasionally appearing thoughtless.

Kenneth chose to ride beside him again, though now a quiet period fell between them. Kenneth appeared lost to thoughts that might have had a lot to do with the great discomfort of wearing a jacket in the hot afternoon sun, or perhaps some weightier matter. Xavier did not notice Kenneth's distraction, for he was busy silently berating himself for a fool.

Kenneth at length broke the silence, recalling last night's stay in Wycombe. "That was quite a tale you told," he said, grinning at Xavier. "About your eye."

Xavier raised a handkerchief to his forehead, blotting at the moisture there. At least he did not feel constrained to wear his hat, having left it in the second carriage with all the luggage. "Tale? Do you say you do not think it was true?" he smiled back.

"No. But it was well told," Kenneth replied. Then he shifted in the saddle, half twisting in Xavier's direction. "But, I say, I have been wondering: I do not think I have ever heard how you really lost that eye. I have known you so long, it never occurred to me to ask——"

"It was an accident," Xavier stated flatly.

"Yes, of course. But"——Kenneth hesitated, hearing the coolness in Xavier's voice—— "But . . . what sort of accident?"

"A painful one."

"Yes. Quite. But what *happened?*"

Xavier sighed, but then his voice became oddly animated, his free hand moving to emphasize various points as he spoke. "My parents were hosting a party. I was only seven, as you know, and therefore most unwelcome at the event. I sneaked down the darkened stairs and hid in the shadows, watching the dancing and the partygoers from behind the rails. A military man, a sergeant I believe, was asked to demonstrate his prowess with his sword, and I am afraid he made a thrust directly at me. I must say, he was most upset, and he did apologize quite prettily."

Xavier turned to Kenneth, his expression frankly daring. Kenneth blinked, confused, until suddenly he cried, "You are gammoning me!"

"Am I?"

"You are."

"It could be so."

Kenneth stared at him a moment longer, but Xavier only stared back, until he put his heels to his mount and rode ahead, leaving a puzzled Kenneth behind him.

Kenneth rode in silence, not spurring his horse forward to catch up with the man, lost to the puzzle of why a man went out of his way to avoid telling a true tale to even his closest companions.

As the sun sat low on the horizon, Haddy called out that Banbury was just ahead, and that they would be finding rooms for the night there, to everyone's relief.

The first inn they came to had no rooms for the night, but the innkeeper recommended his sister inn, which was "only a mile further, not the first ye see, but the second, t'one with far newer chimneys." They found the place after only twenty minutes, although Kenneth announced he could not see that the chimneys looked any the better than those of the inn they had bypassed, and he thought the rest of it showed signs of better days.

There was no need to worry about smoking chimneys anyway, for no grates would be lighted in this heat, as Laura informed Kenneth. She went on to let the gentlemen know that their sisters were beyond weary with traveling, becoming brazen enough to forget her breeding and call as much out the carriage windows, making it clear she had no desire to travel on and search out a different inn.

Haddy, as was his wont, argued for a moment with the innkeeper about the price requested, but then a mutually satisfactory cost was settled upon when the man agreed to supply three bottles of wine with their dinner. Genevieve saw that Laura noted when Kenneth pulled forth his purse. He frowned as he counted the funds remaining to him, and Laura averted her eyes, no doubt not wishing to draw attention to the fact. Genevieve followed Laura's lead, pretending not to have seen the man's concern. It was not Kenneth's fault that he was not set up to run with a fast set, not with his father, Sir Roger, controlling his purse strings so tightly. And, as to that, what would Sir Roger make of this sudden journey to Brockmore? Genevieve did not know, but she did know that if that gentleman came upon them at this moment, Kenneth would quite probably turn quite white in the face to find himself in his father's presence. Laura had once confessed that Kenneth was forever on the verge of being cut off entirely, and it was easy to believe a pleasure trip such as this would not sit well with such a parent.

As Michael descended from the second carriage, it was seen his clothing was coated with dust, and his face was streaked from a combination of dirt and perspiration. "I shan't be second man tomorrow!" he declared. He gave Haddy a quick glare, " 'No grooms,' he says. Ha! Then *he* can chew the road dust."

"You would not have to eat so much earth if you did not drive so close on my wheels," Haddy replied.

"I would not have to drive close on your wheels if you ever let out your strings. Devil take it, man, we have had nothing but fine roads! You might as well put them to use."

Haddy replied, "We are not in London, lad. We are covering distance these days. Got to spare the horses."

The debate might have gone on, except that the ostlers came forward to remove the luggage, and the grooms moved to take care of the horses and the carriages. The ladies took advantage of the pause in the discussion to declare they wished to sit down to a meal as soon as they'd had the chance to freshen up.

"No one requires a freshening more than myself," Michael said, agreeing with the pronouncement, as he futilely tried to brush some of the dust from his sleeves.

"Trays in our rooms?" Laura asked.

"No, we have hired a sitting room. Let us eat as a group. Then Kenneth can produce another of his Little Riddles for our edification," Michael said, still dusting his coat with little apparent result. "It has been a dull day—"

"Oh, surely not while we were finding the card among the apple trees," Genevieve said.

"Granted," Michael said, though his tone implied he had his own opinion as to the matter. "As I was saying:

92

I see no reason to sit alone in our rooms, when we can enjoy an evening together. Whist, perhaps?"

Everyone agreed. Even Xavier nodded, though he was careful to see that no one heard him offer a strained sigh to go along with his nod.

Chapter 7

Alas, all the castles I have,
are built with air, thou know'st
—Ben Jonson,
"Eastward Ho"

"No!" Haddy winced, putting one hand to his forehead in disgust. "Whyever would you play *that* card? Ought to have played that one," he said, pointing at Michael's hand.

"You may now stop looking over my shoulder," Michael said dryly, turning so that his cards were out of Haddy's view, "for you play whist far more poorly than I do. If you doubt this, you have only to look to the fact that you are no longer in play, and I am. Your advice is not only unwanted but incorrect."

"I ran out of coinage, that is why I am no longer playing," Haddy replied.

"And could not conspire to find more? I think not. I think you had grown tired of losing your blunt."

"More fun to watch you squirm than to play myself."

"I am not squirming. I never squirm. And although I will admit that Genevieve was fleecing me royally for a while there, you will note that I have recovered nicely. In fact, I believe I may beat her on points at the end of this hand. Summer, I do hope you are paying attention to the play," he warned his partner.

"I am trying," she replied with a little frown of concentration. She selected a card and played it on top of the others that lay before her on the table.

Michael made a disappointed noise and gave her a level look, even as the others, who had left off the play at their own table to watch the match at this one, gave a collection of sounds that proved the card played had been an unfortunate choice. "Really, Summer!" Michael scolded. "You obviously did not think that all the way through."

"You know I have no card sense," she said quietly, biting her lower lip as she lowered her eyes to the tabletop.

"Makes no never mind, I suppose. Just for sport," Michael conceded as the last round of cards was played, and he leaned back in his chair to pull his purse from his pocket.

Summer's eyes came up, plainly relieved by the brevity of his censure. Her brother fished in his own pocket, then leaned forward, dealing out coins with his fingers as he counted them off, his lips silently moving. He matched the pile that Michael made, thereby paying his sister's debt for her, as was only proper.

Genevieve scooped up the coins, slipping them into her discarded glove since her reticule had been left upstairs in the room she shared with Summer. "Whist was an excellent idea," she grinned at Michael.

"I quite agree," Kenneth said, pocketing the other pile, for he had been her partner this night.

"How pleased I am to have entertained you," Michael said in a sour tone, although he was half smiling at his own ill luck.

"Are we for bed then?" Laura asked, standing and stretching.

" 'Tis early yet!" Michael cried. "Does anyone care for another game of chance?"

"No, let us have one of Kenneth's Little Riddles," Xavier said, leaning back in the settee he had drawn near the table to watch the others at their gaming. Genevieve looked at him as she nodded agreement, glad to see him join in. He had been rather quiet all evening, which may have had something to do with the early abandonment of the card play at his table, as her own table had been exchanging pointed, amusing comments all evening, as long-standing friends will. Still, she was surprised he had chosen to promote the riddles, for she had seen for herself that he was not eager for the opportunity to exchange kisses, however innocuous. But then, he need not offer an answer, if that was the way he felt.

Xavier had no idea why he had suggested the riddle, wanting to kick himself even as Kenneth reached into his pocket to find a marked note. Was it to prove to himself he was in command of his own feelings, his reactions? To prove it to someone else? Or had it something to do with wanting to think of something other than the way the lamplight flattered Genevieve, especially when she smiled?

Kenneth read, "In the fifteenth century, fourteen of *these* were sent to the Duke of Bedford while he was in France. What were sent?"

"Wives?" Laura asked.

"This was the Duke of Bedford, Laura, not some Turkish sheik or other," Kenneth chided her.

"Well, you never know. Perhaps some sheik or other sent them to him."

"No," he said firmly.

"What could it be?" Summer asked, her forefinger touching her chin. "His cats, perhaps. Some people are so very fond of their cats. No, better yet, his dogs."

"I can see an Englishman wanting his dogs with him, but no," Kenneth said.

"Horses?" "Sons?" "Carriages?" came the guesses from around the room, at each of which Kenneth shook his head.

"Think, gentlepeople, think! Where are we?"

"Oxfordshire."

Kenneth rolled his eyes.

"Banbury!" Michael and Summer cried together, and she laughed.

Kenneth exaggerated a nod, his hand making a rolling motion to encourage them onward in their thinking.

"What is Banbury famous for?" Xavier asked. "Cakes, of course."

"One of my favorites," Laura crooned, thinking of the little sponge cakes that were made with currants, spices, and honey, and wrapped in a puff pastry. "So then, is that the answer, Kenneth? Did the duke receive Banbury cakes?"

"No, but you are right to be thinking of foods."

"Cheeses!" Summer declared with a little hiccup of sudden inspiration. "It has to be cheeses. We had some Banbury cheese with our fruit just this past meal."

"Just so!" Kenneth declared with an affirming nod in her direction. "I cannot tell you why, but one has to suppose the good duke missed our good old English cheese and sent for it to be brought all the way to France."

"Well done!" Michael said to Summer as he rose to his feet.

She flushed, and Genevieve thought how pretty she looked under the effect. Perhaps Michael thought so, too, for he lowered his mouth to hers, quickly taking the kiss she had earned by solving the Little Riddle, and she made no move at all to protest that perhaps he was not the one she had wished to bestow that honor upon. Michael then raised his head, grinned, and turned to Haddy to ask, "Have you that piccolo of yours with you?"

"I have," Haddy said, patting his coat pocket.

"Then play us a tune if you will, for I've a mind to dance with my lady."

"Happy to," Haddy agreed, pulling the piccolo from his inside pocket. He blew a few discordant notes on it, then broke into a simple jig tune, proving once again that, although he was usually abrupt and serious in his nature, he understood there was a place and a time for frivolity.

Summer accepted Michael's hand, her face remaining flushed as she gave him a wide smile, and he pulled her at once into a lively dance that matched the tune.

Laura turned to Xavier and with mock offense said

down to him, "You have not yet asked me if I would care to join you in a set."

"Would you care to join me in a set?" Xavier unfolded himself from the settee at once, smiling slightly.

"Why, it would be my pleasure," she said with a grin.

He took both her hands and they joined Michael and Summer in the center of the room, trying to match Michael's rather vigorous steps.

Haddy broke off playing just long enough to say in his practical fashion, "Better move the furniture!" and then began the same tune again, only now a little faster. Summer gave a cry that was mostly a laugh, and lifted her feet, striving to match Michael's enthusiastic response.

Genevieve moved to help Kenneth by holding the various lighted lamps and bibelots while he pushed the selected pieces of furniture against the walls. Satisfied that they had done what they could, Genevieve stood back and clapped her hands to the music, aware of Kenneth at her elbow. She also became aware that for a moment his eyes strayed to Penelope, who was watching the dancers with a steadfast gaze, her posture rather rigid.

Two heartbeats passed, then Kenneth turned, perhaps reluctantly, to Genevieve and said, "May I have this dance?"

Genevieve hesitated, unsure what to do. Once she had thought Kenneth and Penelope were developing a *tendre* for one another, but for four or five months relations had been sometimes noticeably strained between them. She had thought they had come to some kind of accord, some mutual understanding, but Kenneth's lingering gaze of a moment ago had placed a shred of doubt in her mind. If the two shared a dance would it help or hinder whatever the situation was between them? Hard to say, especially as she did not know what that situation was. Well, there was surely one way to find out: that was to let it happen.

"Oh, thank you, but no, Kenneth," she said, smiling as she shook her head. "Too quick a step for me."

"Oh?" he said, obviously surprised by her refusal. "Are you sure?"

"Yes. Perhaps the next . . ."

She did not need to make any further excuse, for already his head had pivoted away, his eyes already settled again on Penelope. Genevieve watched as he crossed to the other lady's side to ask the same of her, and offered up the quick little hope that she had not tampered with something that was better left alone. At least Michael was paying attention to Summer, she thought, reminding herself that, if nothing else, one thing had gone right this evening.

Penelope accepted the offer, and she and Kenneth joined the dancers. However, they did not step in so high and lively a fashion as the others, and Penelope seemed to have very little to say.

Haddy ended the tune and cried, "Change partners!" He then began to play again, this time a pretty country tune.

Michael escorted Summer to the settee, made her a bow and excused himself, leaving her to rest for the space of the next dance as her frail nature required. He turned to the nearest couple. "Surrender the gel," he said to Kenneth, stepping up and removing Penelope's hand from that fellow's arm.

"Kenneth, you are with me now," Laura cried to her brother, taking up his hands and moving at once away from Xavier into a new dance.

That left both Xavier and Genevieve without a partner. A long, awkward pause ensued, but then he turned to her, perhaps rather stiffly. However, his voice was normal as he asked, "Might I have the pleasure?"

She hesitated, remembering she had just turned down Kenneth . . . and half afraid that Xavier made the offer out of a sense of obligation. "I—," she began, unsure what she was going to say.

"Come along then!" Michael cried at them as he danced by.

"Yes, of course," she breathed, and her hand was caught up, and they joined the others.

She stared for a solid ten seconds at their hands where they touched, pretending to concentrate on the dance, but then she raised her eyes, ducking her head for a moment more when she found him looking down at her.

"So. We are off to Coventry tomorrow," he said, just to make conversation.

"We were lucky to have guessed that correctly," she said, adding unnecessarily, "Michael and I."

"Yes."

"Michael is usually very clever about riddles and puzzles and such."

"Yes, I think so, too."

For a moment she could not think what more to say, for the only thought running through her mind was to wonder how and why this estrangement had come between them. They had never been especially close, but also they had never been awkward with one another as they were now. Was it something to do with Summer then? Did he think he had revealed a growing affection in that quarter? Was this why he was now so uncomfortable in the company of Michael's sister?

She needed to say something, anything. "You were awfully clever, too. About the tree bough, and the motto, and all."

His hands slackened on hers for a moment. "No, I am not awfully clever," he said in a low voice.

"I think you are," she assured him.

Now the pressure on her hands returned. "You flatter me."

"And you refuse to take a compliment," she said in a quiet voice that bordered on accusation. She did not stop to think her question might be rude, but uttered it at once, wanting to understand, "Why is that?"

He flushed scarlet above his cravat, and his mouth quirked once before he answered. "Maybe I do not deserve compliments."

"Nonsense—" she began warmly, but got no further, for Michael interrupted.

"I've a thought for a new dance, everyone! We need more people, usually, but we will make our own way out of what we have, eh?"

He organized them into a fractured version of a line dance. They formed twin lines, males on one side, females on the other. Genevieve found herself separated from Xavier, so that there was no opportunity to pursue their perplexing conversation. Her agitated attention settled on Kenneth, who stood across from her, but he seemed lost to his own thoughts, brooding almost. A quick glance at Penelope showed that the woman stood far too still, as does someone who wishes nothing so much as to turn and run, but may not. Summer, on the settee, was looking cast down, no doubt due to the fact she must cater to her own frail nature. Genevieve forced her attention toward Michael, listening closely to his explanation, trying to fill her mind with something other than the undercurrents of emotion that seemed to fill the room.

He showed them that sometimes one couple stepped out of the line to do a kind of sideward sliding step between the rows as the others did their designated steps, and that at other times the entire line did quarter turns to face various partners. Laura, carefree and apparently unaware of the atmosphere of general dissatisfaction, started to laugh at the mistakes they made as they attempted to learn the steps. Michael seized up Summer's hand and returned her to the dance as part of the women's line, causing her face to brighten as though by sudden magic. With the extra female added, there then was always one woman who was forced to pretend to be dancing with a partner. When it became her turn to curtsy to and promenade with an invisible partner, Genevieve could only put aside her confusion and join Laura in laughing over the illogical dance. Michael pretended to protest their amusement, which caused Summer to start giggling, and then Penelope, and finally everyone joined in, down to Haddy, whose laughter put a discordant end to his playing.

The music having stopped, so, too, did the dancers, as they collapsed onto various seats, still chortling. Michael began recounting the various absurdities the dance had created, which led to contributions from each of them for the next quarter of an hour more, until it was decided they should all find their beds.

It made for a pleasant note on which to end the evening, Genevieve reflected as she headed toward her room. Summer was on her arm, bubbling with gaiety still, her dancing brown eyes glowing with satisfaction. It was not fair, Genevieve thought in a wistful humor, that Summer's dark eyes—a charm not so very unlike her own—were somehow of a decidedly more enviable nature, due to the contrast this made with her white-blond hair, no doubt. But that was an old truth, and did not stand in the way of her smiles as she listened to her friend recount the night's events. Though, as they readied for bed, the smiles became increasingly infrequent. She ought to have been just as caught up in the mood, but a different tone surfaced again in her thoughts. Poor Xavier. He was obviously unhappy to be included in this journey. Ought she suggest that he return to London? Tell him to take one of the horses and go, or else leave their company by way of the mail coach at the next posting house? And just how could she do that? No, it was not possible without appearing utterly rude. So what could she do?

There were only two choices remaining, and she hated to think of them both. She could either help him to come between Summer and Michael—she paled to think of it—or else keep him as far from Summer himself as she could. Physically separate the two, come between them, allow no time for anything more to grow or flourish. Was that possible? What kind of friend was she to even think it? And to which of them did she owe the most allegiance? Her brother? Her friend, the ofttimes neglected fiancée? Or the friend with the secret yearnings?

She did not know. It made her head spin to think of it. Well, she had no doubt she would have to do something, so she would do what seemed best.

Of course, the difficult part came in not knowing what was "best," not for any of the three. Or even herself.

Chapter 8

Xavier faced his mirrored image once again, scraping the day's growth of beard from his own chin, shifting a little to one side so that the bright morning light beaming through the window did not reflect quite so blindingly into his eye.

"Do you know what I most dislike?" Haddy asked from where he sat on his bed, scowling at the boot that rested along his forearm. Next to him sat a tray filled with dirty dishes and the remnants of a meal.

"What is that?"

"Polishing my own boots. I had quite forgotten how time-consuming it is. I brush and I rub, and I'll be hanged if I can get the things to shine the way my man Warton does."

"What, old Warthog never told you his secret?" Xavier asked, smiling slightly.

"Secret? What secret? If there is a secret, he would have told me."

"He spits on them."

"No he does not!" Haddy said in something very like horror.

"He does. Told me so himself. Thinks about mince pies and roasted pheasants, and after five minutes of thought, has enough spittle to polish two sets of boots."

"Gods! I thought only schoolboys ever did that," Haddy growled. He then promptly spit on his boot and began vigorously rubbing the leather with a soft cloth. He held it up before him, looking with a critical eye. "I do not see that it makes any difference."

Xavier looked over his shoulder for a moment, then shrugged, resuming his morning's shave. "Perhaps it needs be an old man's spittle."

"Gad! I always thought he used champagne, or some oiled cologne or other. I wonder if I shall be able to bear wearing the things, now that I know they have an octogenarian's antique spittle on them . . . ?" Haddy mused, holding both up for further inspection. "I have only got my pumps with me otherwise, and they would never do for racing across the countryside, so I guess it makes no never mind." He pulled the boots on, only grunting a little, for his muscular arms had the strength to pull the calf-tight boots on without assistance. For himself, Xavier had brought his old, soft hunting boots, knowing he would be forced to dress himself.

Haddy stood, assured himself from a distance (in the half mirror that Xavier was using to shave by) that he was adequately put together this morning. He touched a finger to his brow in a salute. "I am off to see about horses. I think we might be in need of a new right leader, as I was not pleased with the fellow's hoof last night. Bruised, I think. I shall tell anyone I see of our party that we are leaving in twenty minutes, if you would be so kind as to do the same."

"That means you are leaving me to rap on the ladies' doors, does it not?" Xavier accused good-naturedly, lifting a cloth to wipe the blade of his razor.

"They are in the first two rooms to the left up the stairs," was Haddy's brief reply as he slipped out of the room.

Xavier shook his head, smiling, as he finished shaving his neck. He looked into the mirror then and uttered a small oath; he had gotten shaving soap on his eyepatch.

He reached up and pulled the black patch from his eye, taking the cloth and wiping at the soapy marking. That only made the problem worse, so he opted to drop the eyepatch in the bowl of still lukewarm water that he had filled from a ewer a footman had brought up with their breakfast trays. He swished the fabric in the water for a moment, then decided it was adequately cleaned. He pressed it flat between his two hands, wringing whatever water he could from it. At home he would have hung it on a peg on his mirror to dry, but he did not have that option in a posting inn. Instead he crossed the room and slipped it into his coat pocket, making a mental note to hang it up tonight when they were at whatever inn they found. He then crossed back to the stand with the mirror, retrieving his razor. He thought about throwing the used water out the window, but then opted to leave it for the servants to clean up. He half stepped back, reviewing the stand to be sure he had not left his watch or monies or any such items behind, and then looked up, seeing his reflection in the mirror.

He winced, as he always did when he saw himself without the patch. It was not a pretty sight. The scar, rough and red, was bad enough, but the eye itself was no congenial sight. The lid permanently drooped, more than half closed all the time. He could force it open with his fingers if he chose to, which he seldom did. He seldom even touched it. He could not like the way the lid hung limp, flat, almost concave, reminding him that the ball underneath had lost half its size, its viscous contents lost as a result of the injury. He could not like its cloudy color, the way what remained there looked like an old man's eye that had become overgrown with cataracts. It ruined the symmetry of his face, this drooping, sightless, atrophied organ.

He reached into his vestpocket, pulling out the spare patch he always carried with him. He had been caught out before without a spare, once. When he was just getting used to the bedamned thing, the thong that wrapped around his head had snapped unexpectedly, there in church, in front of God and everyone. A little girl down the pew from him had actually screamed and pointed. His mother had walked him home, not staying for the end of the service, and he had walked the whole way with his head hanging and his hand covering the left side of his face.

More than once the patch had been wrestled off of him and lost in the midst of either a game or fisticuffs, sometimes by design, sometimes by accident. His mates had either reacted to those unplanned revealings by sometimes finding the sight of his injury engrossing, or, more often, they reacted with cries of disgust that reflected how startling the sight of it was. After being evicted from school for fighting three times, and taking three hard paddlings accompanied by three long lectures from his father on how the Earl of Ackerley's son was expected to hold up his head regardless, eventually he had learned to be aware of the patch always. It was ever in his mind, even if only dimly, this awareness of the black velvet cover, and he would reach to feel the patch a dozen times a day, or move his cheek so that he might feel the comforting rub of the fabric on the left side of his face.

When it did slip, he knew it at once, his mind attuned to the ever-present need to remain hidden. He would dash a hand to his face to cover it before anyone could see his fault laid bare. If his arms were not available—when he must hang on to the ball during a game, or when he was pinned to the ground—he learned to turn his face into the dirt until his hands were free to come up and hide his difference from prying eyes. After that time in church, he always had a spare with him, even on the playing field. It would be in his stocking or in his shoe, if there were no pockets to be had. Always. And the spare would be affixed on his head before he would allow his face to be raised out of the dust. Not even an instructor's shrill demands could move him until he was sure he had spared the others—and himself—the offense of such a sight unshielded.

Now he crossed to his traveling case, removing another patch, which went at once into his vestpocket. The one that dangled still from his fingers was lifted and slid over his head, fixed in place with the smoothness of long practice where it needed to lie to hide his disparity from the world. He moved back to the mirror and looked at his altered reflection, leaning for a moment on his knuckles before the image, still and silent as a bird who suspects it has become some other creature's prey. He stared into the singular gray eye, but saw only a reflection, not a magnification of the soul or a clarifier of muddled dreams, and so he turned away from his own too-familiar visage, no lighter in spirit.

As he rolled down his sleeves in preparation of donning his jacket, he smiled then, just a little to himself, thinking prosaically that the time spent before the mirror had only served to see that he was no longer burdened with beard stubble, and that his twenty-five years on this earth ought to have taught him by now that all the looking and hoping to see any other kind of change would not make it so.

"Ladies?" Xavier said, the sound of his knock echoing faintly in the narrow hallway. Speaking loudly, so that his voice might carry through the door, he added, "Haddy has ordered the horses ready for"—he pulled his watch from his pocket, lifted the lid with his thumb, and read the time—"half past the hour. Will you be ready?"

The door cracked open; Summer stood there, her hair pulled back but not yet pinned up. "Half past?" she echoed.

He nodded.

She turned back into the room, making a soft inquiry. He heard Genevieve's voice responding, though the words were unclear. Then Summer smiled out at him. "Yes, very good."

"I shall send the servants up for the baggage, shall I?"

She gave a small frown, glancing back into the room. "Mmmm . . . yes, please." Her mouth slanted into an apologetic little smile. "I *think* I shall be packed very shortly. Haddy does so always wish to do things in a timely manner . . . so we shall make haste."

A muffled commentary came from inside.

"What was that?"

Summer shook her head, saying, "She said *festina lente,*' whatever that means."

"Ah. It means 'make haste slowly,' actually," Xavier supplied, grinning. "Sage advice."

"If you say so. *I* still do not know what it means," Summer said as she gave him a quick smile, a nod, and closed the door.

He proceeded down the hallway to the next door, and repeated the procedure. Penelope agreed to the suggestion at once, accepting for an absently nodding Laura, who he saw was sitting at the room's vanity, making an entry in a small journal.

Xavier knew that the other gentlemen of his party had already descended, so, after waiting for a rather stout squire with three equally stout bags to precede him down the narrow hallway, he went below to summon someone to retrieve the ladies' bags.

That was a problem. It seemed they were not the only guests who had chosen to leave at the relatively late hour of half past nine. There were at least six carriages waiting in the drive, and each of those was aswarm with ostlers, grooms, and various other servants who had been pressed into service for the morning's exodus. Someone's pet, a small dog of uncertain breeding, harried a large flock of chickens that had wandered into the bedlam, until its owner—an elderly woman who deigned to call the creature "lovey"—scooped it up and carried it like a baby into one of the waiting carriages. Haddy was standing, arms akimbo and face slightly red with ire, arguing some point or other of horsemanship with a groom; perhaps there was no extra horse for hire to replace the one with the possible bruised foot.

Xavier turned, his head pivoting as he reentered the inn, but he only came across one servant, a kitchen maid of diminutive size. She would hardly do to carry out baggage, especially the two rather awkward trunks some of the ladies had esteemed absolutely necessary for this stop. He mounted the stairs, knocking again at the first room.

This time Genevieve opened the door, her rich brown hair unbound, flowing past her shoulders. In one hand she held a pair of pale blue ribbons of a color that matched her gown, in the other a silver-backed brush.

She obviously had not expected a familiar face, and it was equally obvious she was not sure how to react to this one after last night.

She settled on a brisk friendliness as she cried, "Xavier! I thought you were a servant."

"And so I am," he replied, shrugging his left shoulder to begin the removal of his jacket. If she was unsure how to behave, he was doubly so; he chose for a light tone, one that always worked well in social settings. "Or so I

113

am today at any rate. You have none but myself to do the taxing task at hand. Would you be so kind as to hold my coat?"

"Of course," she said, stepping back to open the door more fully and allow him to enter. Summer was seated at a vanity, just placing the last few pins in her hair. She caught his eye in the mirror, and stood at once, blushing a little to have a man in her room, even one of such old acquaintance. She murmured in mild anxiety, "Oh, I am not quite done with packing."

"Not to worry. I shall take these two larger bags for now, and fetch the rest on a second trip, shall I?"

"Not at all," Genevieve said firmly. "I shall take this small one now, and you may take those two, and then we'll be done with it, for Summer can certainly contrive to bring down the last bag herself."

"Of course I can," Summer agreed at once.

" 'Tis settled then," Genevieve said with a quick nod.

"Very well, though I should complain, for although I still must act the part of servant, now I have lost my chance to receive a gratuity," Xavier pretended to grouse.

Genevieve reached for the other bag, and looked up at him, smiling in amusement, her deep brown eyes filled with laughter, any reservation she had felt wiped away by his attempts at lightness. This was the way it had been for years, the manner she had missed in past days.

Xavier's ability for banter slipped, not wholly unexpectedly, as his heart did a breath-stealing jig in his chest in response to that smile. He recalled how it felt to touch her hair, now long and loose and cascading past her shoulders, how it had been to move that stray piece yesterday back into place; how it had felt to hold her small hands in his while they danced; how she had struck sparks off his steely heart when she filled his ears with impossibly kind words.

He didn't know what ailment filled him, but he knew he was consumed by it, and he knew further that the cure was painful beyond imagining.

No. There could be no cure. To separate himself entirely from her—or, even less acceptably, cause her to be the one who was chased away from all her friends— was impossible. So if not a cure, then what?

Careful monitoring. Doses of pain relief. Vinaigrettes for the soul, if not the body. He would take what he could of her, little things: smiles, laughter, dances, kind words. And if the medicine was bittersweet, was she to blame for the disease? Of course not. He had only himself to blame. Only look at her now, smiling, doing all she could to be charming, helpful, and generous with her affection, however idle that affection might be.

He had raised his hand a hundred times to hide his face from the world. Now he would raise whatever powers he had within to hide his heart from one young woman. She would never know. Could never know.

He picked up the two larger bags, putting on a crooked smile, for it was all he could manage. "Your lack of haste was beneficent for me," he told Summer, just to say something. "Now I need only carry two bags from this room, whereas before 'twould have been four." He turned to Genevieve, trying to make the motion as smooth as it ought to be. "Ready?"

"Lead the way."

He gave a shuddering sigh inwardly, relieved to see she knew nothing of the turmoil she had caused in his chest. He might have offered to come back in a minute, after she'd had a chance to put her hair up, so that she need not accompany him now with her hair as loose and unfettered as the girl she no longer was, but he was not sure he was strong enough for too many new beginnings a day. Better to seize the moment, better not to think, not to have to contemplate what their encounter would be like anew.

"There is good news today, I think. I believe it will not be so very warm," he babbled as he led the way to the stairs.

"That is very welcome news. I fear it has been somewhat trying for Summer," she said, then wished she could bite back the comment. She had to make an effort to avoid giving him conversational opportunities if she meant to go on with her plan to segregate the two of them.

To her relief he did not seize on the opening, instead saying nothing as he led the way down the narrow stairs.

He waited at the bottom, for she was slower, needing to step carefully to avoid catching her slipper in the hem of her skirt, which was pressed against her legs by the traveling case she held before her. He did not put down the bags and offer his hand to help her down the last few steps as he might have done, but he positioned himself so that if she should stumble she would fall into his length. She did not miss the fact, and nodded a thank you, which was also an acknowledgment that she was ready to proceed. He led the way to the front doors, where he did put down one of the bags to open the door, signaling with a movement of the other bag that she ought to precede him.

As they moved out into the bright morning, it was not an entirely comfortable silence Genevieve sensed as she sighed inwardly, wondering if it had been hers or Summer's presence in the room above that had caused this renewed awkwardness.

Xavier arranged the bags in the carriage while chickens ignored the bedlam around them, pecking for their breakfast in the dirt under the very carriages whose restless teams threatened their immediate existence.

Genevieve broke the silence, striving to speak lightly. "I was a bit sorry to have a tray brought up this morning. I rather enjoyed eating breakfast *en masse* yesterday."

He turned his head to glance down at her out of the corner of his right eye, still arranging the bags to his satisfaction. Then he stepped back, dusting his hands and reaching for his coat, which she had carried along, thrown over her arm. As she passed it to him, he thought how to answer, and decided that here was his first dose of medication. Better, he knew, to take it quickly, without resistance, and so he suggested, "This evening we should inform the innkeeper if that is our wish for the morning."

"I would like that," she smiled, and he turned away again, finding a place inside the carriage to lay his jacket. He astonished himself when he turned back to her and answered honestly, "So would I."

She tilted her head just a little on one side, aware the mood had once again shifted. Yet, for all that she stared into his gaze for a five full seconds, she could not put a name to the tangible thing that hung in the air between them. Not enthusiasm, but also not regret. Amusement, mixed with chagrin, perhaps. His steady regard in return did not waver, but she saw his shoulders tense, just as she saw that he struggled to keep them from doing so. A part of her longed to cry out, "What? What is it?," but a more rational part knew she would never get an answer and would probably engender resentment with such an outcry. There was nothing for it then but to take him at his spoken word, however little it told to the heart of the matter . . . especially as she was not sure she truly wished to know the depths of his feelings for Summer.

"You will need help with Laura's trunk, although I believe you could contrive to carry Penelope's . . . ," she said uncertainly, casting a glance toward the inn as though mentally reevaluating the stairs, although in truth she could really just no longer meet his gaze.

"I shall drag them down, literally," he said, and then he smiled, for a smile could cover many things, such as tension, fear, and the taste of bitter medicine. "Maybe they will break a seam and be henceforth unusable." He surprised himself again as his own smile grew, became real, spreading with mirth as her eyes returned to his with an expression of mild shock.

It was only a moment more before she saw the humor resting there, and realized he was teasing. "Then do not drag them, push them," she advised.

The awkward strain that had begun to grow again between them suddenly broke, shattered by their laughter. Startled hens scattered from the morning's pecking at the sound, and more than a few heads turned to see the source of such humor in the morning.

"You are full of sage advice this morning," Xavier said, also glancing toward the inn, rubbing his hands together as though in anticipatory glee. He then sketched her an exaggerated bow, elegant for all that he did not wear a coat, and said, "I thank you for the scheme you propose, and go now to put it into practice."

She gave him an equally exaggerated curtsy as he stepped past her, and called after him, "How pleased I am to assist you, my lord, although you must know that I shall deny any knowledge of any such scheme should I be questioned."

She was rewarded by another round of his warm, deep laughter, and the unmistakable sense that whatever grievance he had held against her had somehow been resolved.

She liked it when she made Xavier laugh. In fact, alone and without anyone of her party around to see or make it happen, still she blushed to find how very much indeed she liked it.

Chapter 9

*This is the monstrosity in love, lady,
that the will is infinite, and the
execution confined; that the desire is
boundless, and the act a slave to limit.*
                              —Shakespeare,
                              Troilus and Cresida

"Let us have a little Riddle!" Laura said to her
brother.

"Yes, give us a Little Riddle," Michael echoed with a
yawn, stretching out on the nuncheon cloth, as though
prepared to nap for the second day in a row. He had
been riding with the ladies for the last half hour and had
grown somnolent with watching them ply their needles
in and out of the lace that had been purchased in High
Wycombe, not to mention the swaying of the coach.
Only their stop for the midday meal had kept him from
nodding off.

It was a testimony to the day's lesser temperature that
the ladies had brought forth needles, thread, and scis-

sors, and conspired to work with the lace to make a set of four shawls, one for each of them. There was even a light breeze that suggested perhaps such shawls might actually be necessary of an evening. Their work was now set aside, awaiting them within the carriage for when they returned to the day's travels.

"Why are you such a sleepyhead?" Laura nudged Michael with her foot. " 'Twas Kenneth and Haddy who did all the driving."

"I said I would eat no more dust, and I shall not. I refuse to be made to feel guilty that Kenneth must lie in the bed he made by suggesting this journey. But as to your question, it is exhausting work watching ladies sew. In and out, with very little change to be noted. How you manage to stay awake yourselves is beyond me."

"Perhaps we have something rattling around inside our heads to keep us awake."

" 'Rattling' being the appropriate word."

"Is that so? Well, let us have my brother's Little Riddle and we shall see who has more between their ears," Laura huffed, nudging him again with her foot, this time none too gently. She turned to Kenneth, giving a militant nod that said he was to proceed.

He obliged, this time from memory, not bothering with a clue from his pocket, if he had even bothered to put one there. "Since we are now in Warwickshire, our question should relate. What is Alcester famous for?"

"Famous for? The better question might be: what, or where, is Alcester?" Haddy asked, rolling his eyes. "Kenneth, one day you shall have to ask a question I know *something* about."

"If I slip and knock my head and lose half my mind,

121

then I might be able to manage it," Kenneth said with a teasing grin.

Haddy scooped up a handful of dry grass and tossed it in Kenneth's direction. The grasses danced in the light breeze, settling largely on the remains of the meal. The group groaned as Laura scolded, "Haddy!"

Genevieve moved forward on her knees, picking pieces out of the meat pie and off the thin slices of bread that had been generously smeared with strawberry preserves. Xavier watched her, almost moving to help, but thinking better of it. To move among the collection of foodstuffs and sprawled bodies, displacing a goodly portion thereof with his size, would only draw attention to the fact that he had offered. He had vowed not to show any signs of his preoccupation with the lady. His altruism would be suspect where his laziness would not, so he had to resist his impulse.

"Alcester. What can it be famous for?" Laura reminded them, reaching out a negligent hand to sweep bits of grass off the cloth.

"Cheeses," Summer said, smiling from where she was, as usual, settled next to Michael.

"Yes, cheeses," Michael said, rolling on to one side to grin up at his fiancée's joke.

Kenneth did not deign to respond, though one side of his mouth slanted upward.

"Lollards," Haddy supplied.

This time Kenneth threw a handful of grass at *him*, more of it floating into the food than hitting its target, again.

"Boys!" Penelope scolded, moving forward to assist

Genevieve, who had stopped to put her hands on her hips in disapproval.

Xavier lowered his head, hiding a grin. He had seen her do the same any number of times, and had not realized how endearing the mannerism was—at least, if someone else was the recipient.

"Could it be wine?" he ventured, to join the discussion.

Kenneth shook his head.

"Coal?"

"We are nowhere near Newcastle."

"I do not know about Alcester, but I do know that Coventry is known for its silk. Could it be silk, Kenneth?" Laura asked.

"You are growing nearer the target," he conceded.

"Nearer the target?" Michael echoed, meeting Summer's gaze where it looked down upon him. "Satin? Brocade?" he asked as Kenneth shook his head at each question.

"Perhaps they make thread?" Summer asked, looking at Michael, not at Kenneth.

Kenneth did not say no, but shook his head briefly.

"Closer and closer to the answer grow we," Michael chanted in a singsongy voice.

Genevieve sat back, her skirt caught beneath her, revealing the form of her thigh underneath the fabric. Xavier noted the fact, if no one else did, letting his vision stray in that direction every so often. " 'Tis to do with sewing," she announced as she began to wrap the remains of their luncheon.

"Velvet?" Michael asked, but Kenneth shook his

head at once. "Not a cloth then. Not cloth. Not thread. What else has to do with sewing?"

"Thimbles?" Laura asked.

"No."

Summer folded her hands before her breast, a gesture of inspiration as she cried, "Needles?"

"Summer has it again," Kenneth nodded.

"Thou art a genius!" Michael cried, sitting up and coming to his feet. He lowered both hands to Summer's, and pulled her to her feet, once again claiming her kiss before she could offer it.

"Michael!" she spoke breathlessly, unable to make it sound like a scold.

He turned to the group and announced, "Do you see, lads? I am to wed the brightest in the group."

Summer glowed, her smile up at him as bright as the halo her hair made around her face in the afternoon sunlight.

"And when is that wedding to be?" Haddy asked as he brushed some crumbs off his shirtfront. Belatedly he looked up, and then his eyes darted around the group as he realized that several pairs of barbed looks were being cast his way.

Summer, if she was aware of the sudden lapse in conversation, seemed to ignore it. "Yes," she echoed softly, "when is that wedding to be?"

"Someday, my dear," Michael said, slipping her hand over his arm. "Someday when we cannot think of something other to do. As for the moment, shall we stroll ere we travel on?"

Some of the light faded from Summer's features,

though not disappearing completely as she suggested, "Perhaps we can talk as we stroll?"

Michael's answer was a nonchalant nod as he pulled her forward.

"Not too long," Haddy called after them, though they did not appear to hear. "What?" he cried as more dark glances came his way.

"Honestly, Haddy, have you no romance in your soul at all?" Penelope asked, sounding rather cross.

"Romance? I do not take your meaning——"

"Exactly. That is your sister," Laura chimed in, pointing in the direction of the couple that strolled away, "trying her best to get her fiancé to set a wedding date. And what do you do to help? You tell them not to take too long. Bah!"

"Bah yourself!" Haddy bristled. "I am the one brought up the subject of weddings in the first place."

"And fortunately for Summer it may not be an utter disaster. Haddy, *everyone* knows that Michael has refused to set a date. How is it that you appear to be the only one who does not know it, or else are so gauche that you lay it out like a raw wound, as you just did!"

"They cannot very well discuss it if it never comes up——"

"Oh men!" Laura cried, throwing up her hands and receiving a commiserating nod from Penelope.

"They are strolling happily enough," Xavier noted, to smooth over the moment.

Genevieve turned to him, wondering if she heard a wistful sound in his voice.

"They have the correct idea, I believe," Penelope said, rising to her feet. "I think we should all take a stroll

125

before we travel on. I am for the shade myself." She did not wait for an endorsement of this thought by anyone else, stepping off toward a small wood.

"And I am for those wildflowers," Laura said as everyone came to their feet. She indicated with a sweep of her eyes a variety of flowers that were scattered through the tall grasses of their luncheon site. "I like to press the tiny ones, then affix them to the wax when I seal my letters."

"Oh yes, I have noted that! I find it most charming," Genevieve said. "I will help. Haddy? Xavier? Kenneth? Would any of you care to join us?"

"Certainly. May surprise you to know that I have quite an eye for the flora," Haddy responded.

"Not at all. A huntsman would know that sort of thing, would he not?" Genevieve said. "Different animals live in different environs."

"Exactly so!" Haddy said approvingly.

Xavier joined them silently, spending at least as much time watching the way Genevieve moved among the tall grasses as he did ostensibly looking for miniature wildflowers. He liked the way she had commended Haddy's interest, how she had not scoffed at his declaration of interest in botany. It was easy to make fun, much more difficult to know when not to—and that was a gift that Genevieve possessed, he thought to himself. Then he forced his vision away, watching the irregular flight pattern of a gnat, even as his jaw tightened while he wondered why he could not merely turn off such thoughts. But they came anyway, remembrances of fleeting moments, errant touches, gentle words, and all the times he had ever made her laugh, or she him. Old memories, some of them, mingled with new, making a montage of impressions that left him feeling slightly breathless as he wandered aimlessly through some farmer's field.

At length it became a kind of torture, this watching her while pretending not to, then forcing himself to look away, to clear his head of the silly notions that floated so easily into it. No one seemed in any hurry to be off, not even Haddy for a change. He felt a need to hide, from himself as much as anyone, and so Xavier lowered his length to the earth, pressing down the long grass stalks with his weight, to stretch out, his hands behind his head. As he stared up, his eye saw only the yellows and greens of the tall plants that reached up around him and the faded blue of the heavens above.

He drowsed a bit, now that he was hidden, letting his thoughts wander where they would. Imaginary scenes flitted through his mind, scenes wherein he rescued a particular dark-headed damsel from a castle turret, or lay down his many-caped coat that she might tread across a puddle safely, or how it came to be that they found themselves quite alone in a snowbound hunting cabin. Nonsensical, impossible thoughts, the sort that stirred the soul even as they strangely enough soothed the body, which was not so foolish as to hope such dream-wishes might come true. They were not thoughts of possession or definition, but idle ones of longing so secret and infeasible that he could find a kind of contentment in just the yearning itself. They were daydreams, not even hopes.

A shadow crossed over the sun, and Xavier found his eye had closed and that he had been more than half-asleep. The absence of the sun's warmth roused him, though, and his eye opened to find a dark-haired figure standing over him.

"We were wondering where you had gotten to," Genevieve said, her dark hair haloed by the sun behind her, her face lost inside that brilliance. The bright light behind her, the murky loss of her features, made her for a moment seem a part of one of his daydreams. He stared, nearly reaching to catch her hand, to pull her down to his side just as his dream-self would do, but then she shifted, the sunlight now no longer behind her, able to light the familiar face, to remind him how very real she was.

He struggled to sit up, even as she bent down, settling in the tall grass next to him, her pale green skirt billowing around her softly as though to chide the grasses for turning brown and dry.

"Is it time to go?" he asked at once, blinking back the drowsiness that had filled him until a moment ago, preparing to stand.

She put a hand on his arm, which served at once to keep him where he was, and shook her head. "Penelope has not returned. Haddy went to find her. There is time yet."

"You do not think anything has gone amiss——?"

"Not at all," she soothed at once. "Or, at least, nothing unfortunate . . . I hope."

He looked at her, the way her head was canted to one side, the uncertainty in her voice, and then he leaned back, his arms extending behind him, supporting his weight. He crossed one leg over the other before he said "Ah." He paused again, but her serious expression spoke volumes, urging him to say what her features declared. "Am I correct to think that perhaps Kenneth is missing also?"

She nodded, slowly, not happily.

"I do not know how it lies in that direction," he said, returning her steady gaze, answering her unspoken question. "We all thought, once, that something was occurring there. Father was right to put an end to it, as unkind as it may seem, for Kenneth is but the son of a knight, with very little in his pockets, and Nelly the daughter of an earl, but still . . . one wonders. . . ."

"One wonders," she repeated.

"I had thought perhaps this journey would clear the air between them, but sometimes it seems to be working the other way."

"And at other times, it seems perhaps a spark remains among the coals?" she questioned.

He nodded, reluctantly admitting the bald truth of that.

She drew up her knees, her skirt forming a circle around her, and hugged them to her chest in a manner that only long acquaintance would allow, putting back her head to gaze at the sky. "Things are changing," she said carefully. "On this journey, I mean. Between us all."

He did not mean to speak, but suddenly the words were out, softly spoken, "I feel it, too."

"Does it frighten you? Does it make you want to stop time and return home, and give up the whole idea?"

He laughed then, but not from humor, and watched himself as he dug the heel of one boot into the earth, as though to turn up some comfort there.

"You laugh," she said, sounding puzzled, and he felt her gaze settle on him once again.

"Not at the question. But at the answer."

"The answer?"

He looked at her steadily then, having learned earlier today how to do so. "My answer. For you force me to admit that, yes, it frightens me."

"How is that so?" she asked, her face reflecting the honesty of the question. But then she seemed to think better of her blunt words, rushing on at once with a small dismissive wave of her hand. "You need not answer such an odd question. I do not know what it is today . . . something about this field. It is warm and large and peaceful, but somehow it has set all my faculties aflame with a kind of edgy, tingling feeling. I feel as though any moment a cannonball will smash among us, and scatter us all to the winds. . . ." She ducked her head into her arms for a moment, blushing a little. "I am being silly. Forgive me."

"There is nothing to forgive. I feel it, too. Are we just a little bored, and imagining things?" he asked, wondering if it was true. If he was in London right now, would the sight of this woman still stir him? Did the novelty of the attraction stem from the novelty of the setting?

"I am *not* bored," she said firmly. "No, 'tis nothing so commonplace as ennui. Do you know what I think it is?"

"What?" he asked, really wanting to know, wanting to put a title to this hum of energy that flowed between them.

"I think we have become something other than we have been all these years. I think we are all, of a sudden, grown up. No longer children. I always wondered what 'grown up' would feel like." She laughed at herself a little, picking up a tiny twig to trace around the grasses and find the earth below. She added, "I do not think I care for it much."

He said nothing, only nodding once, not really needing to confirm her observation, for it was only the truth.

Of course things were changed. They could not encounter one another without seeing those changes with their own eyes. And they would continue to change, for the girls had put up their hair and become women, had had their come-outs, been presented to and acknowledged by their Queen at court. Once they returned to London, the Season would be fully under way, and some of them would no doubt find husbands, and then have children. Their families would move on to winter estates, and they would enter new circles of acquaintances as they moved through the lives before them.

With just such certainty—and although perhaps their journey together as man and woman had galvanized his thoughts—Xavier knew that it was not, nor ever had been, merely the locale that had awakened his slumbering emotions. It was rather the bright-eyed—and yes, now grown up—woman beside him herself who battered away so devastatingly at the lock on his heart.

"I am a bit old for it, but, yes, it does have that feeling. The decided sense that this is the last summer of our youth," he murmured, finding a twig himself and tracing a pattern next to hers.

"Xavier," she said, turning a stunned face to his, her brown eyes wide. "I believe it is! Our last summer. How extraordinary!"

"Extraordinary to realize it."

"That is exactly what I mean." She tossed aside the twig, and rose to her feet, now excited, her hands on her hips, her face glowing. Her voice grew as she spoke. "We do not really have any say-so, do we? I mean, we cannot help becoming what we will be as adults, can we? That quite explains to me why everyone seems so on edge. Do you know, you have quite chased away that odd feeling I was having. We have put a name to it, and so banished it! Now I feel entirely differently. Now I wish to complete this journey, to enjoy every moment of it! It will never be the same as it will this year, will it? No, we must cherish this summer. That seems so clear now. Do you feel it, too? Do you feel this need to be as gay as we possibly may be?"

He stood more slowly than she had, and the admission was wrung from him by the clarity of her gaze upon him, forcing him to speak no half-truths. "Yes," he answered her.

For a moment her enthusiasm waned, as she noted the somber way he spoke. He was thinking of Summer, of course. He had been aware, it seemed, on some level of his own that he was as much a part of this "change" that surrounded them as anyone. If he was falling in love with Summer, was it his fault, or an occurrence beyond his control? How was she to judge him, to stand in his way, if it was something beyond them all? No, she had no right, no right at all. Things must happen as they would.

She felt an enormous weight lift from her shoulders, knowing now that it was not her place to control the lives of those closest to her. Life would unfold as it would, and it was not her role to work against it, but to be there, to be a friend, when it did, no matter how it did.

"Come along then! Let us go on, let us be on our way to the rest of our adventure," she cried, her eagerness returning. She spun in the direction of the carriages, parting the grasses with the purposefulness of a ship's masthead as she moved away from him.

He followed in her wake, his steps leaden. "Our last summer together, forever," he said very quietly to himself, following behind her with a heaviness in his chest that grew from the knowledge that the words were all too true.

Chapter 10

*For man plans, but God
arranges.*
—Thomas A' Kempis

"Hell and damn!" Haddy swore, kicking at the broken wheel before him.

Michael stood up from where he had been bent at the waist with his hands on his knees, peering under the leaning carriage for himself and said unnecessarily, " 'Tis most decidedly broken. We'll have to have a new one."

"Why did we let Kenneth go ahead with the other carriage and the two saddle horses?" Haddy groused.

"It seemed logical at the time, instead of making him drive in the dust," Xavier said. "He'll be sitting and sipping ale at whatever inn he has found, thinking us a number of slow nellies."

"All right, lads, put out your fists," Haddy said. " 'Tis time to pick our rescuers."

The men moved into a tight circle, one fist held before

each of them. Haddy laid out the rules matter-of-factly. "Count of three, show me one, two, or three fingers. If two are of the same number, they are to ride the carriage horses to the next town and fetch us help. More or less than that, and we try it again." The heads around him nodded understanding. "One. Two. Three."

Their fingers uncurled to display their selections: Xavier held out three fingers, and Michael and Haddy both held out two.

"I am beginning to regret this expedition. I have had the worst luck on it," Michael growled.

"Of the two of you, Summer is the one with good luck," Haddy agreed.

"Perhaps that is why I'm marrying her."

"*Planning* to marry her," Haddy said, beginning to frown.

"Quite," Michael answered distractedly as he glanced down the road as though to gauge the distance he would be forced to ride without benefit of a saddle and only a leading rein.

"Have you a pistol?" Xavier broke in before Haddy could go any farther than to open his mouth to say something in return. Xavier glanced at the sky, hurrying on, silencing Haddy's retort by doing so. "It will be nightfall ere long, and full dark before you can ever get back to us. You will need to have a care and watch for footpads."

"I've had my pistol in the panel pocket in the carriage," Michael answered, moving in that direction to retrieve the weapon.

"Mine's in m'pocket already. You can never be too prepared," Haddy said, patting his hip to show where the pistol resided. He reached into the opposite pocket and drew forth a more than slightly tattered map drawn on oiled paper, and muttered, "We should have stopped at Southam, blast it all." He unfolded and surveyed the map critically, not overly satisfied with what he saw. "Damn thing's harder to read than a Latin text. But, see here"—he indicated the map with a nod of his head— "at least we cannot be more than a few miles from either Stockton or Long . . . ? Does that say 'Itchington'?" he asked of Xavier, balancing the parchment in one hand, as he pointed with the forefinger of his other. The dark head nodded, and Haddy went on, "Long Itchington. It appears here that as long as we keep to the main road, it will branch, bringing us to one or the other, whatso-ever their names may be." He folded the map, sliding it back into his pocket.

"Let us be on our way then," Michael said, the pistol now a noticeable bulge in his right coat pocket.

"Arm yourselves as well," Haddy cautioned.

"Ourselves?" Xavier questioned, since he would be the sole remaining male.

Haddy lifted his chin, indicating his sister, sitting ten yards away with the other ladies. "Summer knows how to fire a pistol. Father and I figured a frail, pretty thing such as her ought to know how to give a bit of a sting if needed."

Xavier's eyebrow lifted in amused agreement. "Wise choice."

"We thought so."

"I have a rifled long gun, and she may have my pistol."

"Give me a hand up, will you, Xavier? This fellow,"

Michael said, indicating the horse, "is seventeen hands, I have no doubt."

Xavier cupped his hands to provide a stirrup up for both Michael and Haddy, who mounted the matching horse. They had neither saddles nor proper bridles by which to guide the animals.

"You may care to take a more leisurely pace than you normally would," Xavier grinned up at Haddy.

"Damned if I will!" Haddy cried, offended. "I can sit me any horse I care to sit, saddle or no. Now, Michael, on the other hand . . ."

Xavier laughed as Michael put his heels to his horse, springing away without notice. Haddy gave a cry, then answered the challenge by urging his horse forward in the next moment, and was off down the road, easily displaying he knew how to sit his steed and that Michael would be sore pressed to outride him.

Xavier watched them until they were lost in the growing haze of twilight to the north. He then turned to the carriage, extracting from among his own gear a percussion lock long gun and a small purse that contained the ammunition, and the fulminate of mercury "pills" that created the necessary explosion and that were far superior to the loose powder he had used as a boy. He primed the muzzle-loading weapon, reassured by the hefty weight of it in his hands. This held at his side, muzzle down, he turned toward the ladies, who were sitting in the limited protection of a hedgerow that divided two fields of new, green hay.

"I see Michael and Haddy are off to find us some assistance," Penelope called to her brother.

He nodded as he walked to where they sat among the

as yet short stalks. Its owner would not appreciate their trampling of his crop, but the hedgerow provided a modicum of protection against a slight breeze that had blown up. "I am afraid it may very well be quite some hours until we are settled for the evening."

"Sit with us then," she said, indicating a spot next to her, and he complied, laying the long gun along the length of his outstretched leg.

"How are we to entertain ourselves till then?" Laura asked, her annoyance at the situation plain to see.

"But, Laura," Genevieve said, smiling, "you sound cross."

"I am cross. I am hungry and tired, and did not care at all for the bumping we received when that wheel collapsed."

"I have never been in a carriage accident before," Genevieve said, her eyes shining. "Did you not find it an interesting experience?" She caught Xavier's eye for a moment, and he felt the impulse to smile back at her unbridled enthusiasm.

Instead he said, "Interesting, yes. Safe, no."

"Painful, yes!" Laura cried. "I was sorely wrenched, and at the bottom of the heap, if you happen to recall, when it came time to crawl out."

"Yes, but think what a wonderful tale it will make when we return to London," Genevieve argued, still grinning.

"Whatever has gotten into you?" Summer asked, laughing a little.

Genevieve shrugged with an eloquence that spoke volumes, telling more than her words as she responded, "Summer—the season, that is—is here. We are on an adventure. We are young. We are free. We do not have to go anywhere we do not care to go. Do you not find that exhilarating?"

"I find being free of my chaperone exhilarating, I will own to that. Old Phelps is a positive dragon at times, and I cannot miss her presence," Laura nodded.

"Exactly my point! I find my Miss Wheaton to be quite the dear, but she would have had a fit of the vapors when the carriage slanted over as it did. And I would still be trying to rouse her even now if she had been here," Genevieve agreed, her dark eyes shining like tiger's-eye stones in the intense golden light of the setting sun.

"So are you saying that we ought to arrange to have a carriage accident every day, just to enliven our otherwise dull and uneventful lives?" Laura drawled. Penelope and Summer exchanged amused glances.

"Not at all! All I am saying is that I think it behooves us to enjoy what *does* come our way. No one was hurt, and you have to admit it was momentarily exciting, so why should we not relish the moment?"

Laura turned to Summer and Penelope, encompassing Xavier with the move. "Do you suppose she struck her head?"

Penelope grinned. "No, I just think she is young and full of a sudden love of life. This latter condition is no doubt due to the excessive heat of the past few days having baked away whatever sense was once in her brainbox."

"Cant, my dear?" Genevieve said archly, immediately following this with a wide grin of appreciation.

"If you are going to be allowed to be in love with life and all its messy little details, such as broken carriage wheels, then I must be allowed to speak a word or two of Cant," Penelope defended herself blithely.

" 'And So It Shall Be,' " Genevieve quoted formally in as deep a voice as she could manage, sounding rather like their local Vicar.

"For It Hath Been Spoken," Laura chimed in, catching the spirit of the moment.

They turned expectant eyes to Xavier.

"Until the End of this Journey Doth Us Do Part," he added to their raillery, though he could not completely keep a wistfulness from coming into his tone.

"Why so somber, Brother?" Penelope turned to him in surprise.

"Was I?" he hedged, glad of the failing light, not looking toward Genevieve.

"He is thinking of a conversation we had earlier," she supplied. "We believe this will be our last chance to adventure as a complete party together. Soon we will begin to marry, to have duties elsewhere. Once the children begin to arrive, who of us shall have either the time or the inclination to go on a treasure hunt? No, I am afraid our conclusion is most correct: this is the last 'summer of our content,' to misquote the Bard."

"Why, I believe you have something there," Laura said, nodding in agreement.

"Yes, I believe you do," Penelope said, and this time it was her brother who gazed at her in surprise. He parted his lips to question her tone, in which he had heard a touch of unspoken emotion, but Genevieve stood, interrupting the moment.

"I believe I would care to have a shawl now," she said. "May I bring one for all of you?"

The other ladies nodded as Xavier rose to his feet, offering as a gentleman ought, "I shall assist you."

Shawls and a lap robe were supplied, and were promptly wrapped around shoulders.

"I fancy we rather look like those American savages you see written of in the newspapers," Xavier said.

"I am only glad that it is not so chilly that we have to decide whether to climb back into the carriage or not," Summer said.

"Oh, I suspect it would be safe enough, if highly uncomfortable sitting at an angle like that," Xavier assured her. "The biggest danger lies in the fact that it remains squarely in the center of the road, and that there is always the possibility some fool would not see it there before he ran into it."

"He would have to be a rather great fool," Genevieve said, eyeing the straight, level spot of road before them. "Still, 'tis a risk we ought not take."

The ladies nodded, and Genevieve said, "I believe that would be too much adventure even for me."

Laura chortled, her face etched golden in the last dying rays of the sun, but then announced, "My shawl is not sufficient." She reached for the lap robe that had come from the carriage.

"Hardly surprising, since they are nothing but lace," Penelope noted, gathering up Laura's discarded shawl and wrapping it over her own with a little shiver.

"I thought we had just decided it is not particularly cold," Summer said through gritted teeth as she tried to wrap the edges of her shawl more firmly around her arms.

"The sun is all but down, and it is growing a trifle

brisk," Xavier said, offering at once to Summer as he stood. "Here, take this." He unbuttoned his coat, shrugging out of it and passing it to her. She took it with a little demurring sound, which he waved away, saying he had his waistcoat to help keep him warm.

For a moment he almost smiled to himself, remembering a daydream wherein he had offered his coat to a lady—a lady of utterly different coloring—finding the fantasy far more congenial than the fact, as he wrapped his arms about his body to try and shield himself a little from the bite of the cool wind.

"Come on then, Nelly," Laura said, opening her lap robe and indicating with a movement of her head that she meant to share. Penelope moved at once to her friend's side, and the ladies stretched the lap robe over their shoulders and passed their shawls to the other ladies.

"Genny?" Summer said, indicating they could pile the shawls in a shared fashion over both sets of legs if they sat side by side. Genevieve rose to her feet, helping to arrange the shawls, trying to make it so that Summer got as much coverage as possible.

"Tuck the ends under you. That helps to keep you warm," she instructed Summer, reaching to help with the process.

Xavier looked up at the sky, tsking his tongue. "I think we have clouds gathering up there. Could be we will see some rain ere morning."

"Just so it is not for the next few hours," Penelope said.

He shook his head, but whether that was in doubt that it would rain, or doubt that it would hold off, was unclear. "Well," he decided of a sudden, "this is ridiculous. I could wish to use the carriage, but it seems totally impractical. Not only would you ladies be tilted one on top of the other, but with this breeze I am concerned that I might not hear a runaway carriage in time to alert you to descend. No"—he bent and gathered up the rifle, then crossed to Summer, reaching into his jacket where it hung from her shoulder to extract a small pistol—"I think I must attempt to find us some shelter."

She looked up at him with large, rounded eyes as she accepted the weapon. Genevieve saw concern, and possibly fear, in those eyes, and felt its shadow leap through her own internal systems.

"Please do not be gone long," Summer said in a near-whisper.

"I shall not."

Xavier's absence was swiftly accompanied by the last fading of the sun, plunging the circle of women into the grayness of twilight. If they were warmed by the lap robe and shawls, they were nonetheless chilled by the absence of light. "We should have had him put a flint to the carriage's lantern before he left," Penelope grumbled into the growing gloom.

"I wish there had been a way he could have taken one with him," Summer said, concern etched on every word.

Genevieve turned to look at the girl's expression, but it was obscured by the lack of light and color. The shawls on their legs took on a grayness that spoke of spiderwebs, and Genevieve shuddered where she sat pressed next to her friend. Summer's arm slipped around her waist, and they shivered together.

"We have gotten used to the excessive warmth of

late," Laura said, tugging at her corner of the lap robe as though to make it stretch further somehow. " 'Tis really not so chilly as all that."

"No," Summer agreed through teeth that may have chattered.

Darkness fell, settling on their shoulders, suppressing their words so that they only spoke in short, quiet sentences, and that only occasionally. Some kind of chittering animal call caused them all to jump and cry out, and then sit silently and listen pensively for it yet again. Summer settled the pistol in her lap, then picked it up, only to lay it down again nervously.

A rustling sound, loud in the stillness, reached their ears, and the ladies stumbled to their feet, the pistol back in Summer's hand, although it was wisely pointed at the ground. Laura caught Penelope's hands in her own as they peered through the dark at an approaching figure. It lifted its arm, and Penelope was the first to relax, sighing, " 'Tis Xavier."

The other ladies let out their breath as one, and Summer slipped the pistol back into Xavier's coat pocket where it hung on her shoulders.

"I have found something. 'Tis just a bit of an overhanging dirt bank, but I think it will provide more shelter than these hedges. 'Tis several hundred feet that way," he pointed behind him.

"How will the men find us?" Penelope asked.

"We shall leave them a note. There is paper and graphite pencils in the panel pockets of the carriage."

The note was written and mounted on the carriage by way of lifting one of the glass windows so that the paper's edge was caught, the note then stirring in the night breeze in a rather noticeable fashion. As he did this, Genevieve and Penelope went through the baggage they could easily reach, and extracted two more shawls, one of Indian muslin and one of silk. "None of us saw a need to pack wool or jersey, that's a certainty," Penelope observed wistfully.

"Nor thought to be traveling at night," Genevieve agreed.

Some of the extra paper was shredded, and Xavier put a spark to it by way of his flintbox. Once this tiny flame was aglow, he was able to light a long, dry weed, which he then used to light both of the carriage lamps, burning his fingers in the process. "We cannot remove the lamps," he said after pulling his offended digits from his mouth, "but at least it might save some poor fellow from crashing into our little mess here, and would also show Haddy and Michael where we are exactly, or at least where to find our note." He stood back, shaking the hand with the singed fingers while grimacing. "I shall get a fire going, if possible, near the bank, and we shall all be toasted in a trice."

"I take that as a promise." Summer tried to smile from beneath the extra shawl Genevieve had taken from her own legs and insisted Summer put on her shoulders atop Xavier's jacket.

"Promise it is. But first we need to gather what we may that will burn. We are too far from that wood over there"—he indicated a distant blur on the horizon with his thumb—"so this hedgerow will have to provide what little there is to be burned around here."

The ladies bent toward the earth, trying to see what they could find in the dark, ill-lit as it was by the carriage lamps. When everyone had what they could find—twigs and some branches and dry grasses, hardly more than a handful each—he put out his elbow, which was taken up by his sister.

He led a train of ladies through the dark to what was exactly as he had said: a dirt bank in the middle of a field. Still, it was nearly as tall as his head and did create a windbreak of sorts. The ladies dropped their cargo, and arranged themselves, huddled near the dusty vertical wall, watching with eyes that had adjusted as much as they ever would to the dark, as Xavier worked to gather flammable material to go with the twigs they had carried and the extra paper he had brought. Before too very long he had his spark, and then a small fire, by the light of which he was able to increase his search, finding a few more clumps of dry grass to encourage the small fire into a larger one.

"It will not last long," he warned them. "We've only the little we found, and even if I pull up our unknowing host's green crops, they will not burn well, nor long. If only we were near a wood."

"There is that one. Perhaps it would be worth the walk . . . ?" Penelope remarked, but not hopefully.

"Too far," he asserted again, rubbing his arms to increase the circulation in them. "Your fire would be quite out before I ever returned, and no doubt our rescuers returned by then, as well, making my journey pointless, not to mention unsafe in the dark. No, we shall warm ourselves by what we have until it is gone, and make use of this shelter, however minimal. It should not be too much longer a wait," he said, smiling at them reassuringly in the fire's glow.

A half an hour later the fire was all but dead, only a few dim, tiny red coals remaining. They huddled around the remains, absorbing the residual heat, which was too quickly becoming less of a contrast to the growing chill of the night. Clouds had definitely gathered over their heads now, and there was a suspicious scent on the wind that none of them dared to name.

Summer rocked back and forth under her coverings, denying with words if not actions that she was cold. Just as Genevieve reached for her shawl, meaning to surrender it to the fair-haired girl, Xavier rose and stooped beside Summer.

"Here then," he said gently, reaching for the lap robe, "we must share, else we shall both take an ague before morning." He removed the shawl from Summer's shoulders, handing it to Genevieve, who gratefully piled it over the one she already had. He stooped, settling the lap robe over his own shoulders, then reached to envelope Summer with his blanketed arms. He sat back, pulling her with him, and leaned against the dirt wall, cautioning her as she settled against him to watch that her skirts did not trail into whatever coals might still be alive in the gray powder that had once been a fire. He wrapped the lap robe around them both, the two ends just meeting before them, embracing the woman against his chest. "Button my jacket, it will keep you that much warmer," he told her, and Genevieve watched through the dark as Summer tugged and moved under the lap robe Xavier held around her, presumably working the buttons of his coat. She saw as Summer settled back into his chest, at first shivering more, but soon giving into the warmth their mutual shelter generated. She noted how the blond head fit nicely, as though quite meant to fit there, under his chin.

Genevieve turned her eyes away, for some reason annoyed that the night's dark had not been deep enough for her to miss observing the little scene enacted before her. It seemed far too familiar an action, despite their predicament, far too personal an encounter for witnesses.

Amid the nameless annoyance, she also felt a stirring of admiration, and her face softened for a moment. How gallant Xavier was! He saw to their comforts before he saw to his own. He tried to reassure them all. He had found them this shelter, where others would not have thought to try.

She bit her lip, the softness fading from her face as she frowned at the ground. She could not help but go on to the next logical thought, that how fortunate it was for Summer that Xavier was thoughtful and clever and kind. Summer, who was cradled in his arms.

Then she huddled and shivered under her shawls, and wondered why her face, in contrast to the rest of her, felt so very warm.

Chapter 11

*So foul and fair a day I have
not seen.*

—Shakespeare,
Macbeth

"Bloody hell!" Xavier swore under his breath.

No one chided him, although they were all so close they could scarcely miss the exclamation. If the truth were told it would be seen that each echoed his sentiment exactly.

Genevieve reached up with her one free hand, almost losing her shawls in the process, to use the side of her hand to wipe the large drop of rain from the bridge of Xavier's nose. The course of the large droplet, from his forehead down his nose, had finally been one too many and had caused him to utter his oath aloud.

"You are soaked through," she said miserably.

"The price I pay for refusing to don my hat today," he spoke, not bothering to try and sound at all cheerful. Summer had attempted to return his jacket to him, but he had refused it. Now he could not help but shiver from the effects of the rain and cool wind, with naught but his lawn shirt and waistcoat to protect him from the elements.

One edge of the lap robe was stretched over his head, and soaked quite through, causing his hair to drip moisture down his forehead and cheeks every other minute or so. It was equally as soaked along his arms, which were outstretched at forty-five-degree angles as he valiantly worked to create a kind of tent over the ladies' heads. They were huddled beneath the pathetic shelter, the confines of which were limited by the rather small size of the lap robe, pressed against one another between him and the slight overhang of the bank. Genevieve and Penelope held the opposite corners of the lap robe upward with wet, cold, stiff fingers and arms that were rain-soaked and beginning to ache, in an attempt to assist him.

"It is not going to let up, is it?" Laura sniffled.

Xavier sighed. "I fear 'twill not be soon, ladies. I had hoped it was a passing squall, but it seems we have no such luck today. Tonight," he amended, sighing again. He shook his head a little to clear his eyes of rainwater, only to have more of it seep through the lap robe onto his head and consequently trickle down his face.

He made a sudden decision, "We are going to become soaked whether we go or stay, so I recommend that we commence back to the carriage at once."

"Is it safe?"

"It will not tip any further, but no, 'tis not safe because of the danger that someone will run into it. But I shall stand guard. I think it is a fairly safe wager that at least the rain will keep any other carriages from coursing the road too swiftly."

Summer sneezed, and that seemed a signal for them to begin. Xavier dropped his arms, settling the soaked lap robe over her head and shoulders, for whatever good the sodden fabric might do to protect her, even as he cried, "Right then! On our way!"

Laura squealed as the full force of the rain dashed at her, but she led the way as they all began to run. Genevieve felt the rainwater soak through her slippers at once, and was glad she had left off her stockings and would have some kind of dry footwear, however inadequate, awaiting her in the carriage. She wished she had kept on her bonnet—Miss Wheaton would be scandalized if she knew her charge had not done so against the chance she might have exposed her skin to the sun—and sighed to herself that perhaps there was some kind of merit to such strictures.

It did not take them long to arrive at the tilted carriage, but it was long enough that their gowns clung against their skin, cloying and cold, and their hair ran with rivers of rainwater. Their penciled note was stuck flat to the windowpane by the soaking it had had. Laura pulled open the door as soon as she touched the handle. She scampered inside at once, turning and bracing her hand against the panel, and putting out her other hand to help pull up the next individual in line. Xavier stepped forward, placing his hands on his sister's waist, lifting her upward even as she gripped the sides of the opening and pulled up. As soon as she was inside—making sounds of protest that had something (Genevieve thought she heard through the patter of the rain bouncing off the lacquered roof) to do with being unable to retain a seat—Summer was handed up, sodden lap robe and all. She gave a little squeal, for Xavier's grip on the lap robe turned out to be only lap robe, so that as she lifted upward he was forced to place his hand in the area of her posterior and heft her upward with an apparently effortless shove.

There was a commotion in the carriage's interior as the three ladies vied for handles or grips of any kind to help them not tumble back out the door, so that Genevieve was forced to wait in the rain until they contrived a small allowance by which she could enter. There were hands, large hands, at her waist, waiting to assist her upward.

She slowly turned her head, the rain slanting down into her face, causing her to blink as she gazed up at the dark head above her own, at the face of the man who possessed those large hands. His dark hair was inky black, slick with moisture—reflecting something of the carriage lamps' flames that still flickered in the face of the downpour—and hung around his face in unruly waves. His right eyelashes were frosted with mist, his eyepatch a dark oval on his face, and his shirtsleeves were plastered to his skin, revealing the musculature beneath.

He suddenly noted that she had gone still under his touch, and brought his vision down to meet hers. He forgot to listen to the assorted "oofs" and "ughhs" coming from inside the carriage, forgot that he was cold and wet and miserable. Her dark eyes, darker yet in the night, were on him, her expression sober and perhaps even vaguely expectant. Her lips were slightly parted, and she shivered beneath his hands.

His own lips parted as they stood thus, still and un-speaking in the rain, and he held his breath, unable to move or even think.

"Xavier?" Summer's voice floated from the carriage. "We are ready for Genny."

His head pivoted at the sound, and his shoulders jerked back as though someone had poked him with a particularly sharp stick to the shoulder blades. "Of course," he murmured. His hands started to pull away, but then remembered their task, tightening again on her waist as he prepared to lift her.

"Come inside with us," she blurted out.

He shook his head. "I would never forgive myself if something should happen."

"It is so wet—"

"Go on, Genny," he urged softly, making a motion with his chin in the direction of the door. "I shall be just fine."

He had robbed her of breath, calling her by that pet name. She could not help herself; another shiver ran through her, a shiver assuredly felt by those encircling hands, and she found her mind spinning to think that it might not be the cold and wet that caused this latest shudder. She reached with strengthless arms for the door frame, and tried to pull herself up as he lifted her and said, "Out of the rain then." Thanks to his strength, she found herself inside the carriage, standing stooped and trying not to slide back out the door, which was promptly closed behind her, plunging them into a dark-ness that was scarcely altered by the lanterns' light through the windows. She scrambled to the open seat, near the door, and heard Summer's apology and sigh of relief as that girl released her grip on the leather handle she had been clinging to and slid down to meet Genevieve's side.

"Tell me if you are quite being flattened," Summer fretted.

" 'Tis fine. You are like a cloud. Albeit, a rain cloud," Genevieve answered, finding a smile for the girl.

"Do not be afraid to ask, and I shall pull myself up once more, though I do not promise how long I could hold myself thus."

"I'll do so," she said, hearing the muted tones of her own voice. "But there is something you can do for me now."

"Yes?" Summer asked, starting to half stand as though to reach for the leather loop handle that hung at roughly the level of her ear.

"The lap robe. You may keep his coat, but I think Xavier ought to have the lap robe. It will not keep him dry, but it might help to keep him warm."

"Oh, assuredly!" Summer cried at once, untangling the soaked lap robe from where she half sat on it. Genevieve leaned forward, placing her foot for balance while she pulled the handle to the door. The little door swung outward, striking Xavier on the elbow so that he turned at once.

"Cover yourself!" Genevieve cried through the rainfall, thrusting the lap robe at him.

"Thank you!" he shouted back, taking the offering in his hands and draping it around his shoulders at once, grimacing at the cold touch of the fabric. He went to pull it up over his head, but Genevieve cried, "Wait!" and dragged the silk shawl from her shoulders. "Take this. It is warm enough in here that I have no particular need for it. Put it over your head, and the lap robe over that. Papa always tells us that you will stay warmer out-of-doors if you keep your head as warm as you may."

"Your papa is right," he said, and she saw a grateful smile flash at her through the gloom. She waited until he had donned the shawl, ignoring Laura's pointed comment that the rain was slanting in, only then reaching for the door handle. Just as she pulled it shut, she caught a glimpse of Xavier securing the lap robe firmly around himself as he leaned back against the carriage, only a portion of his face now visible in the cowl-like overhang of the covering, as he took advantage of whatever shelter the tilted vehicle provided.

She sighed, some part of her annoyed at him for refusing to come within—they could have made room for him—and part of her glad for the dimness inside the carriage, that none may see the admiration no doubt shining from her eyes.

Somnolence had stolen its way inside the warm interior of the carriage. The ladies were not sleeping, for who could sleep aslant and half crushed, or while struggling not to crush the one below, yet all of them startled from a drowse when there was a rap on the door. Genevieve moved first, reaching for the handle just as the door was pulled open, letting in fresh, cold, wet air. Xavier stood there, still encased in the lap robe except for where he had put out his hand. "They have come!"

he said. "We've the second carriage back, so you ladies may proceed on to our inn for the evening."

"Thank heaven!" Penelope said as Genevieve bent to place her slippers back on her feet. She grimaced as the soaking they'd had transferred cold moisture to the stockings she had donned. Ah well, they would all be soaked anew in a moment, she knew.

Laura was the first one out, making a face at being back in the rain, however temporarily. The others followed swiftly, Michael greeting each as he handed them up into the second carriage. They gave little cries of delight to find dry blankets and warmed bricks inside, and swiftly shut the door against the elements.

Genevieve looked out the window, the rain splatter making the scene difficult to decipher, but she could see that several men had come back with Haddy and Michael. It was obvious from their actions that they intended to assist in repairing the first carriage, the robed Xavier in their midst.

She pulled down the window and called out. Michael was just handing to Haddy the leading strings of the horses which would pull the first carriage once it was repaired when he heard her call. He moved to the carriage window, and inquired, "Yes?"

"Michael, how many men will it take to repair the wheel? Have you enough?"

"Yes."

"More than enough?"

He glanced over his shoulder, assessing. "I suppose," was his answer.

"I am concerned for Xavier. He has been drenched

156

for well over an hour. Ought he to ride with us back to the inn?"

"Ought he, yes. Shall he allow himself that privilege, I cannot say," Michael flashed a grin. "You know how he gets. But, for you dear lady, I will inquire if that is his desire."

"Please."

"Pull up that window while I ask."

He returned in a minute, pulling open the carriage door. "It seems your suggestion met with the fellow's standard for good sense," Michael announced to Genevieve.

"Is he not coming in?" Her brow wrinkled with a slight frown.

"He is going to drive the carriage. Claims he is already soaked through, so what difference a mile's drive or so? He says he shall be quite slow and careful about it," he said, pointing to his left eye, indicating Xavier was aware his handicap must be compensated for by a lack of speed or coaching finesse. Michael followed this with a dramatically distasteful moue. "Which means, you see, that I am to stay behind and assist with the repairs."

"Oh, I am sorry." Genevieve's frown dissipated as she almost giggled at Michael's obvious repugnance at the thought.

"Do not think I shall forget this," he warned as he closed the door.

It was a moment longer as the men exchanged unintelligible words, but then the carriage lurched forward.

It was not a long drive to the next village, which turned out to be Long Itchington. Just as they pulled up in front of an inn which boasted a hanging sign that read THE KING'S HEAD, Genevieve realized the rain had stopped.

"Can you fathom that?" she exclaimed, pointing out the fact to the others.

"And I believe it is actually still quite warm, once one is out of the wet and the breeze," Summer said.

"Humid," Laura agreed. "Most unpleasant. I can scarce wait to remove these clothes."

Now that they had the promise of dry clothes just moments away, Penelope remarked, "I confess that, now that I am no longer shivering, I am rather remarkably famished."

Penelope was the first through the door of the inn, announcing to the waiting innkeeper's wife that food and hot water were promptly needed, "In that order, if you please." They were hustled up the stairs to a large room with two large beds in it and an area that was meant to serve as a kind of sitting room, where their bags were already waiting for them. The innkeeper's wife introduced herself as one Mrs. Denny, and obviously had a few years' experience at her trade, for she brought a large basket into which she requested they deposit all their wet things while she fetched them some supper.

Mrs. Denny found four bedraggled but dry females when she and a servant brought up two large trays of food. The ladies immediately moved to sit themselves in the various chairs in the sitting area, eyeing the roast beef on thick-sliced bread topped with rich gravy, accompanied by roasted potatoes and candied carrots, with an avarice that in years gone by would have set their nannies to scolding. "Do serve," Laura encouraged the servant who had come up with Mrs. Denny.

As the girl began to fill the plates, Mrs. Denny inquired if the ladies would care for either tea or chocolate. Both were promptly requested, but before the woman could leave to fulfill this request, Genevieve caught her arm.

"The gentleman? Is he being served as well?"

"O'course, my lady, and fair famished he were, too."

"That is well," Genevieve settled back with a sigh, accepting a plate with willing hands.

In a room downstairs, Xavier, now dressed in warm, dry clothes, with his dark hair still wet yet once again neatly combed, a dry eyepatch now in place, motioned to the boy who had brought him a bottle of port. "Can you tell me, are the ladies being seen to? Have they received a meal as of yet?"

"Aye, m'lord."

He flipped the boy a small coin extracted from his vestpocket, which the lad was quick to catch, as he further asked, "Will they . . . did they say . . . are they set for guests this evening?"

"I dunno," the boy shrugged.

And that was all the answer I deserve, Xavier thought with a painful smile at himself, at his selfishness. Hoping to just be near her, he was, it seemed, capable of wanting her time and energy even when it was foolish to think she would wish to offer it. Even after all she had gone through tonight, he wanted her to be available to him, just so he could beguile himself with the sight of her.

159

He took a swallow of the port, unsure if it added to or took away from the hopeless feeling that he was little better than a beast.

Chapter 12

I know my life's a pain and but a span,
I know my sense is mock'd in every thing;
And to conclude, I know myself a man,
Which is a proud and yet a wretched thing.
                    —Sir John Davies,
                        "Nosce Teipsum"

"My eye?" Xavier cried, coming to his feet. "Yes, I will tell you how I lost my eye!"

The stable boy before him half cringed, his eyes wide, but as much with eagerness as fear, for it was obvious the gentleman was playacting. The toff's motions were oversized, his one good eye rolled dramatically as he took in his audience, and he propped one foot on a chair in the classic storyteller's pose.

Kenneth leaned forward, though his expression said that he was not hopeful of hearing the true tale. Haddy passed Michael a pouch of tobacco, and the two proceeded to stuff and light their pipes.

"It was a dark night, like tonight, but cold, bitter cold.

The land was gripped in a terrible, lasting ice storm. No man nor beast ventured out on this night, for the wail of the wind was like the cry of the dead. Women closed their shutters to that wind, hearing it speak of a frozen death for any of the foolhardy who thought to step out of the safety of their homes. They knew their cattle would be frozen by morning, but none dared to brave the elements. None, save my brother."

A murmur ran through the crowd, and someone was heard to say they remembered the year of the ice storms.

"Even so," Xavier nodded.

Kenneth sat back, knowing full well that Xavier had no brother, nor ever had.

"He was a big lad, and promised to be bigger yet when he had grown to full manhood. He had never been bested in a wrestling match, and he was the one they always called when an animal or a man needed to be held down for the purposes of doctoring. He could lift ten stone, and he only fifteen years of age. He had never been ill a day in his life, and had never had reason to know fear.

"When he saw that one of the horses—a favorite of his, as not many of the horses could carry such a big, strapping lad as he—had been left in pasture, he was determined to bring the animal in.

"Mama begged him not to go. Papa told him he was being foolish, but my brother wished to go, and there was no stopping him once he had made up his mind." Xavier paused, then said in a lowered voice, "I cannot swear to it, but when he opened the door to leave us, the wind blew in the storm, and I thought I saw icy tendrils shaped as arms reach out and seemingly pull him forth."

"Wot 'appened?" the stable boy asked in wide-eyed expectation, an appreciative grin almost forming around his mouth.

Xavier stood up straight, allowing his jaw to tighten as though from strong emotion. "He was dead, of course, next morning. We found him, his arms raised and frozen before him, as though he had tried to shield himself from . . . something." Xavier lowered his foot to the floor, nodding at the murmurs and hesitant laughs around him.

"But wot of yer eye, guv'ner?" the boy pressed, now openly grinning.

"Ah yes, my eye. You see, it was so very bitterly cold, that as soon as I saw my brother thus, tears welled into my eyes and froze as they fell, freezing my face and leaving the resultant scar you see today."

"Blimey!" the boy laughed, and others laughed with him as Xavier returned to his chair, putting out his hand toward Haddy, who promptly passed over his glowing pipe.

"That was a grisly tale," Kenneth commented as Xavier puffed on the pipe, and handed it back to Haddy.

"It seemed the night for a grisly tale."

"I must agree with that," Michael said around his own pipe stem. "This night I knew me cruel labor, and dark, and a soaking such as I have not had to endure in years. And my best velvet cutaway ruined beyond redemption! The only thing that kept me from promptly hiring a chaise back to London was the fact you had this very gratifying port awaiting us as soon as we came through the door." He lifted his glass, making a dip of a salute in Xavier's direction.

Xavier inclined his head, which then promptly rose, his one eye round with surprise. He rose to his feet, and the others followed the direction of his gaze, seeing as he did that the ladies had come belowstairs. The other three gentlemen rose to their feet as well.

Genevieve led the ladies, her head held high so that Xavier had to grin despite the sudden pounding in his chest, not doubting for a moment that this venture had been her suggestion, for even Penelope looked a trifle sheepish at their daring. The impropriety of ladies coming into the common room created a buzz of muted exclamations, but Genevieve refused to acknowledge it by looking about, coming directly to their table. She stopped before them, hands demurely folded, and announced, "We are beyond bored, and do not care to sleep."

Michael shook his head, removing his pipe and setting it in a glass bowl, saying directly to his fiancée, "Summer, this is most—"

"Irregular, yes," Genevieve cut in. "But, you see, we have decided we do not care." She blinked twice, silently daring her brother to refuse her. Summer's color was high, but she did not speak, nor turn to leave.

Michael glanced around the room.

"There is no one here who knows us," Genevieve assured him.

"But there are plenty to tell tales—"

Xavier pulled out a chair for the lady, even as he said, "Three days ride from London? Who would bother, Michael? Come, ladies, take your chairs and join us. Cards?"

"And claret," Genevieve said, giving him a gracious

164

nod that was made all the more pronounced by the twinkle in her eye. It was in direct contrast with the demure way Laura held herself, obviously less comfortable with this act of bravado than was Genevieve.

"And claret," Xavier confirmed, waving down Michael's obvious protest before he could utter it. He knew exactly how to win Genevieve's approbation by adding, "Let this be something we recall of our youth when we have grown old."

He gained the bright smile he had wished, and felt momentarily dizzy as he raised his hand to signal the innkeeper for service.

"As you will, then," Haddy muttered, not as approving as his friend. "But I will not be putting out my pipe."

"That seems equitable," Summer said, though she made a point of sitting on Michael's far side, away from Haddy.

Michael glanced down at his own pipe, which had ceased to burn, and then glanced at Summer, who gave him a wide-eyed look of appeal. He sighed with apparent annoyance, but the pipe remained in the bowl.

Cards were provided, which Haddy, as usual, inspected, though this time a trifle more discreetly than he had inspected the dice in Wycombe. Satisfied, he suggested, "Cassino?"

"That is for groups of four. We do not wish to be divided, do we?" Xavier said quickly.

"Oh no!" Summer said at once.

Genevieve watched Summer through her lashes, but the fair-haired girl did not look up at Michael. Was he still the reason Summer wished to stay, or were there other considerations . . . ? Had her attention focused on another member of their party?

"I should not care to separate into groups," Laura said, her mouth tight. "If we are to do this . . . this public appearance, I would just as lief be surrounded by numbers."

"Pish!" Penelope said, tossing her head. "Laura, sometimes one cannot have a care for convention."

"Brava!" Genevieve nodded.

"I would expect that of you, Penelope, as you always did prefer the company of these ne'er-do-wells over that of the ladies."

"Yes, I always have. One is not required to stitch as many samplers or paint as many watercolors in the presence of men. I always thought I was quite clever for realizing that advantage."

Laura made a deprecating noise, but it was a low one that could not be heard beyond their table.

"That means whist is out as well," Haddy went on. "What then?"

"Cométe," offered Summer.

Michael looked down at his betrothed again with a modicum of censure, but then heaved a sigh and gave in. "We might as well. 'Tis a mindless game, which might well suit this group."

"It will leave us free to chat," Genevieve approved as Haddy made a growling noise.

"What shall we use for markers?" Penelope asked.

Just then the innkeeper brought over a tray with the claret and a number of glasses. Xavier motioned to him as the man placed the articles on the tabletop, "Do you have some beans we might purchase?"

"Nothing wot's cooked up, m'lord—" the man's eyebrows shot up at the unusual request.

"No, my good man. I mean dry beans. To use as markers."

"Oh, aye! I kin get ye some o' that, sure enow."

The beans were brought and paid for—Haddy guffawed at the first requested price, grunted dampeningly at the second, and finally nodded that the third suggestion was the one that could be added to their charges for the morning—and were distributed evenly among the participants.

As they played, the beans exchanging piles regularly, they recounted the day's experiences. Michael told them how his foot was nearly run over, and Haddy explained how many men it took to hold the carriage up while the new wheel was fixed on the axle. Kenneth laughingly told them of the assistant who could not keep his feet under him in the mud of the road, falling no less than twelve times, and ended up coated with filth from head to toe.

The ladies then explained their own disasters, complete with descriptions of the "joy" of sitting inside a tilted carriage.

"I only wish we could have talked Xavier into joining us inside," Genevieve said, turning to him. "Although I must admit you do not look as though you have taken the experience amiss."

" 'Twas only a bit of warm rain."

"It did not seem so warm then, not to me," Genevieve asserted. She reached for her glass. "Ladies," she announced, "I think we owe this gentleman our thanks. I suggest a toast."

The others picked up their glasses, murmured their thanks, and drank a swallow in commemoration. Xavier colored slightly, and shook his head, saying, "Common decency, ladies, 'twas all."

"Decency is uncommon enough," Penelope informed her brother. "Now take your 'thank yous' gracefully, and allow us to think you most honorable."

He made a half-bow from his seat, one corner of his mouth lifting. He did not turn to acknowledge Genevieve directly, for he knew he could not quite keep his ever-growing regard from showing, not if her eyes met his own.

He gave himself over to playing the game mindlessly, lost to his own increasingly murky daydreams, until someone called his name.

"Xavier? Have you a guess?" Penelope was asking.

He rallied, finding all eyes on him, and that the game had ground to a halt. He laid his card down. "Pardon me? A guess?"

"He was not listening," Penelope said to Kenneth. Turning back to her brother, she said, "Really, Xavier, you were the one encouraging tonight's assembly. The least we might expect from you is that you would care to participate in it." Before he could respond, she went on, "Ask your riddle again, Kenneth."

Kenneth obeyed, "This region of our fair country was, in the seventh and eight century, part of another kingdom. What was the name of that kingdom?"

"I have no thought as to the matter," Xavier confessed at once.

"I think I do," Laura said, obviously still ill at ease in

the common room, for she kept her voice low. "Mercy, or Mercury, or something like that."

"Close enough. It was actually Mercia. But, Laura, how did you know that?" her brother cried.

"Well, Kenneth, you *do* go on forever about your studies. Despite my best efforts, I am afraid some of it must lodge in my head occasionally," she said crisply.

"Then I shall continue to do so, for if some of my wonderful teachings have found their way into your unstudious head it proves there is hope for the larger efforts I make."

Laura made a face at him, and replied, "Do not think you shall have a kiss from any of the ladies, for you are a pompous oaf, as they can now plainly see for themselves."

"And whom shall *you* kiss?" Summer asked, dimpling.

Laura looked around the table, her eyes sliding from her brother at once, and over Haddy nearly as quickly. They lingered on Michael, but then transferred to Xavier.

Penelope said, with something of a challenge in her voice, "No one. She has already been seen in a common room, but she will not allow herself to be seen kissing a gentleman here as well."

Laura lifted an eyebrow at the taunt, and half turned to Genevieve. "Did you not say something about this being a 'last trip of our youth' and 'something to remember in our old age'? Far be it from me to spoil that effect." She rose and stepped around the table, stepping next to Xavier, where she bent and gave him a hasty kiss on the cheek.

He winced inwardly, for her upper lip had brushed

169

the strand of his eyepatch, but otherwise he thought he had taken the salutation with some grace. At least it caused no flutter in his breast, no constriction of his air passages, so it was easy to put a mild look of pleasure across his features. It seemed he was developing a talent for receiving kisses from ladies.

Laura returned to her chair, her face a bright red at her own daring.

Haddy turned to Kenneth. "We must be toads. These fellows have had two kisses apiece, and here are we, still lacking any."

"I will bid you both a good night then, little toads," Penelope said, pushing back her chair and rising to her feet. "I am nearly deplete of markers, and therefore find I am ready for my slumber." The other ladies rose as well.

"I shall bring these with me, in case we wish to wager again," Haddy replied, beginning to scoop the various bean piles into one larger pile in the center of the table.

Good nights and sleep wells were exchanged, and Kenneth yawned as the ladies exited the room. "I'm for bed myself," he declared. "I received far, far too much fresh air today."

The men made their way to their rooms, all mouthing their agreement.

As Xavier crawled into bed, it was of Laura's kiss that he thought. He noted with some satisfaction his growing ability to allow such familiarities; perhaps this journey had been a fortunate exercise after all. Although he knew he could not listen to the clarion call his heart insisted on trumpeting through his soul all-too fre-

170

quently these few days past, for the first time he accepted that he could perhaps reach a smaller, less lofty goal.

He dared to let himself think—not merely dream— how it might be that he could gain new kisses, not from just any lady, but from one specific lady in particular.

Chapter 13

If we do not find anything pleasant,
at least we shall find something new.
                    —Voltaire,
                        Candide

Genevieve turned from the impressively tall spire of St. Michael's and said, "But we are not here to admire Coventry's architecture. We are here to solve a new clue. 'Tis Haddy and Laura's turn again. Do please read the clue!"

"It is medieval, you realize. As is Holy Trinity, there. The priory was founded in 1043," Kenneth said, still taking in the sight of the ancient structures before them. The sun had already chased yesterday's last straggling clouds from the sky, and the day promised to be too warm once again, flooding the scene before them with a light so bright it made them squint as they took in the ancient grandeur before them.

"It has a particularly splendid name, St. Michael's," Michael said.

"Read the clue!" Laura ignored him, echoing Genevieve as she reached for her brother's pocket.

He laughed and dashed her hand away. "I shall, I shall!" He cleared his throat, laughing again when Laura put her hands on his arm and gave him a small shove in pretended irritation. "Here it is then, my dear girl: 'Look for the house of the man who looked at Leofric's lady-wife, known as Godgyfu.' "

Haddy's head slanted back on his shoulders and he made a gesture of surrender with his arms. "I give up. These things are far too obscure for me."

"Are they?" Kenneth grinned, indicating Xavier with a nod of his head. "Look there, you can see that fellow knows."

Xavier made an exaggerated moue of innocence.

"And he stands next to answer if you cannot. You have nine and one half minutes remaining. Laura, have you a guess?"

"That is all we are to know? Look for a house? 'Tis not much of a clue. 'Tis not even a nice little poem."

"No, 'tis not." Kenneth rocked on his heels, awaiting their answer.

"What house? That one?" she ventured unhopefully, pointing to the nearest residence.

"That is your guess, and 'tis wrong. Forfeit!" Kenneth cried, pulling the small bag from his inner pocket, an evil grin on his face.

Laura shrugged apologetically at Haddy, and reached for the bag. "Oh dear," she said after glancing at the slip of paper, which she then read aloud, " 'The partners must sing two stanzas of any song of their choice in the High Street, during daylight hours.' " She looked up,

173

aversion and something bordering on reluctant humor mingling on her face. "Oh, Kenneth, how simply dreadful."

"Yes, I thought so, too, at the time I wrote it. Well, well, well! It seems to me it is daylight, and it seems to me that we are very near Coventry's High Street," he teased.

Laura shook her head. " 'Twould not be fair. By the time Haddy and I have humiliated ourselves, Xavier and Summer will have had an inordinate amount of time to think over the clue."

"Too true! I suppose we must settle that business first, which I believe we will do in short order, for we have seen that Xavier already has the answer." Kenneth turned to Xavier and prompted, "Well? Summer and yourself are next."

"Firstly, Laura," Xavier explained, "you might have had a better chance if your brother had pronounced Leofric's wife's name in its more familiar form of 'Godiva.' "

"Oh!" Laura gave a little squeal of recognition, quickly followed by a black look for her brother.

"But that is not the question, is it?" Kenneth countered.

"No. You asked us to locate the house of the man who looked at Lady Godiva."

"Peeping Tom!" Haddy and Laura cried together.

"Exactly," Xavier said. "But where that structure resides is beyond me." He offered his arm to Summer, "My Fair Summer Rose, methinks we have only about nine minutes to discover something that will point the way for us. Shall we begin?"

Genevieve watched as Summer nodded and smiled, saw how the pink bonnet ribbons were tied in an artful bow to the right of the delicate girl's chin, noted how the lithe form fit against Xavier's side. She looked away, but her ears could not fail to hear, causing her to look again despite herself.

"I never really thanked you . . . for last night," Summer was saying up to the dark head above her own. "Your coat. Sharing the lap robe. Everything." A tinge of pink touched her cheeks, showing the effort it cost her to speak, to remind them all of the enforced familiarity to which he and she had been brought by the combined effects of need and chance.

"It was my pleasure," Xavier said, then seemed to think better of the statement, smiling a little. "Well, a pleasure to be of assistance to such a charming lady, even if the circumstances themselves were not so very pleasant."

"Charming? 'Tis you who is the charmer, I think," Summer shook her head, smiling along with him. "Did Mrs. Denny return your coat to you?"

"She did, none the worse for wear."

Summer made a doubtful face, but she did not challenge the statement, since they all knew he would just deny it. That was Xavier, a charmer indeed, Genevieve thought as the party stepped out as a group. Xavier and Summer led the way, looking for clues.

"You frown, Genny," Michael said at her side.

"No, I do not," she said, forcing her brow to smooth and her mouth to come up to an even line.

"Hmm," he replied noncommittally as they walked along the cobblestones.

" 'Tis you who ought to frown," Genevieve countered.

"How so?"

She wished she had bitten her tongue rather than speak, for now she was forced to explain. "Summer," she said uncertainly. "Xavier . . . ?"

Michael raised his eyes from the road. "What of them?"

"Honestly, Michael!" she cried in a sudden exasperation brought on by his smooth, untroubled question. "Can you not have noted they have become most friendly? Does it not concern you just the tiniest that they may be growing, well, *too* friendly?"

"Ah, yes, as to that sort of thing, Summer is a very affectionate individual. She cannot help herself in that regard. She told me once that her father and the viscountess were particularly close. She rather hopes to emulate them in that regard, and so she is used to bestowing affection wherever it suits her to do so. I accept that fact. It is, in truth, one of the things that makes her so very well-loved." He took her arm, moving her to his other side, for a carriage was approaching. Genevieve took advantage of the moment to put her hand on his arm and hold him back from the group.

"Michael, I know you are not truly this obtuse. I am trying to point out to you that if you cannot show the girl more affection yourself, she may seek it elsewhere," she said in a low voice.

"With Xavier?" he said, his tone reflecting the fact that he was truly surprised. "No, no!" Now he nearly laughed. "You silly goose. No wonder you were frowning! No, Summer adores me. I have no concerns in that quarter."

"Well, I have. You have been affianced for nearly a year and a half now, Michael. No girl will wait forever."

"Summer will," he replied blithely.

"You are steering toward trouble," Genevieve warned in a low, ominous voice.

"Enough, Genny! Do not fret yourself." Now Michael did laugh, taking long strides of a sudden that carried him from his sister's side. He turned, walking backward long enough to call, "See, I go to flirt with my dear betrothed even now. See which gentleman she prefers."

She watched as he sidled up next to Summer, watched as that girl's hand came from Xavier's arm and latched on to Michael's. She saw Summer's face light up as Michael spoke to her, no doubt exercising that occasional and persuasive charm of his.

She knew that he had more of a talent for noting subtleties than he was commonly given credit for . . . and perhaps he saw the signs she saw, but saw them only coming from one party. Xavier. He certainly did not feel threatened. Perhaps he enjoyed having a fiancée who was admired and sought after. Perhaps he liked having someone else devote time to the woman, that he not have to constantly see to her himself. . . . Or, perhaps he really had grown to become an insensitive clod, who loved only himself? Who did only as he pleased? Who truly did not care if Summer's desires were ever met or not? She paled to think it could be true, and some corner of her mind refused to accept the possibility, but another part asked: when was the last time Michael had demonstrated *any* affection for *anyone* other than himself?

177

Well, he *had* just moved her, his sister, from harm's way when that carriage was approaching just now. . . . That could just be long-learned manners, but no, he had been thinking of her well-being. The thought restored the color to her face, and she allowed an audible sigh of relief to escape her lips. She knew, for there was no denying it, that Michael loved *her,* even if it was in his abstracted, careless way. So she had to believe he was capable of loving others as well.

Although, of course, the loose and unexpectant love for one's sibling might be far too little for a spouse, or even a fiancée.

"Oh, Michael," she murmured cheerlessly to herself, "I *do* wish you could fall madly in love with your own betrothed." She kicked at a stone, immediately bruising her toes for her effort, and wished she could limp in the opposite direction, instead of following so docilely behind as her party searched out yet another of Kenneth's tokens.

Xavier stepped forward, pulling the playing card from where it was wedged into a seam between a windowpane and the casing. "A knave of hearts? Does that represent our Peeping Tom, or King Leofric?"

"Both, I rather suppose," Kenneth approved the logic of the question.

Xavier stood up, coming away from the window. "We should not have found it if it were not for Summer's sharp eye."

"You are the one who led us here," Summer said.

"That was simple logic. We know the lady rode from

one end of the city to the other, and back to the castle. We know she was escorted by two knights, so the road needed to support three mounted figures abreast, and therefore our target would probably be on one of the main thoroughfares. From there it was a matter of finding a house with shutters, for all the townspeople were ordered to close their shutters, and no one cracked theirs open but for our Tom. When I saw the pub sign that read THE BLINDED TOM, it was natural to suppose the house, with shutters, would be somewhere nearby," Xavier explained.

Summer gave a twinkling laugh, the others joining her or smiling along as she asserted, "But who could know that so many houses on this street would have shutters?"

"As I said, 'twas your sharp eye that won us the token." Xavier sketched her a bow of thanks.

"And the fact that 'twas the first house next 'The Blinded Tom,'" Summer grinned as she curtsied in return, then said to Kenneth, "Is this truly the house?"

"Who can say?" he replied honestly. "Who can say if Peeping Tom truly existed, or if he was truly struck blind by God for his nefarious curiosity?"

"Good gad, let us hope not," Michael said in an aside to Haddy, who chortled quietly.

Xavier handed the playing card to Summer, who tucked it in the back of her glove as she had not brought her reticule with her. "We now lead in tokens," she told him, dimpling.

"Our two to Laura and Haddy's one, and also Michael and Genevieve."

"And none for us. Yet. But we are next," Penelope said, glancing at her partner, Kenneth.

"Exactly so. But that must wait a while yet."

"Ah, yes. It seems to me there is a duet that has yet to be sung," Penelope said.

Haddy sighed, "I shall lead the way."

The group discussed which song ought to be sung as Haddy led them to the High Street, and some of the suggestions had to be whispered in his ear, for even the titles of such ditties could not be spoken aloud before the ladies, let alone truly considered for public display.

Haddy countered every suggestion with the firm words, " 'Praise God From Whom All Blessings Flow,' " until of course it was quite clear that this was what they would sing. Laura was unsure of the second stanza, so they had to talk their way through the words twice.

"Enough!" Kenneth cried good-naturedly. "If we go on this way, before long Haddy and Laura will have talked us into an eight-part harmony. Let us be on with it, I say."

As the two unfortunates began to sing, carriages rolled by with curious faces staring, and strollers paused to see whatever could be happening, as it certainly was not the season for carolers. Children pointed, and shopkeepers came from their shops to see what the noise was all about. Laura's face was stained a bright pink, but her voice stayed true, which could not be said of Haddy's bass. At the conclusion, there was scattered applause, and a few coins were tossed at their feet. Haddy looked up from the sight of the coppers in the road, and flashed Kenneth a flustered, hostile glare as he hissed, "Do you see what you have brought us to, fiend? Singing for pennies?"

Kenneth responded by roaring with laughter, which continued even as he was forced to take to his heels as Haddy came after him, hands outstretched.

Children darted forward to retrieve the abandoned pennies as the rest of the party followed, at a far more leisurely pace.

"Only look at Kenneth! He has quite lost his dignity," Laura sniffed as they saw the laughing man disappear between two buildings, Haddy fast on his heels. The color was finally beginning to recede from her face, perhaps in part due to the fact that the townfolk's attention had shifted from her to the two darting gentlemen.

"Have you only just noticed?" Genevieve grinned.

"Noticed?" Laura echoed.

"That we are all quite losing our dignity."

" 'Tis the nature of the journey we are on," Xavier said, following Genevieve's lead at once.

Genevieve nodded at him. "We might as well give in to it and enjoy ourselves."

"Give in to it? I was right yesterday: you did strike your head," Laura said crisply. "Just because we are on an adventure, as you so care to think of it, does not mean we must behave as complete nodcocks. Look you, Michael, *you* would never behave so foolishly, would you?"

"Oh no," he assured her at once, "not unless there was a wager involved." He then grinned from ear to ear.

Laura gave him an exasperated look.

Genevieve grinned. "I am merely saying that I do not think we have a choice."

As though to punctuate her statement, Kenneth came

from an alleyway, spotted a stalking Haddy, and disappeared with a large whoop back the way he had come.

Laura stared after him, grimaced, and said, "Perhaps we could abandon them?"

"I suppose," Genevieve dimpled, "but I think it would be so much easier to abandon our dignity instead."

"I am surrounded," Laura conceded when she met smiles all around. "I see the way of this crowd. I have been made to sit in a common room—"

"And therein kissed a man," Summer said, her eyes twinkling.

"Yes, I have been placed in a situation where my personal honor superseded society's dictates, and I hope I lived up to that challenge." She nodded at Xavier formally. "So," she added, smoothing her skirts with both hands and lifting her chin. "If I must forsake propriety, I must." Then she gave a sudden, impious grin, and cried, "Last partner to the carriage purchases our lunch!" She then grabbed her skirts with both hands, and began to run the length of the High Street.

"I cannot believe it," Genevieve cried, astonished, even as she began to run in pursuit, her laughter trailing her, as did Penelope. Xavier followed the dark girl with his eye, catching glimpses of half boots.

Summer looked up at Xavier, drawing his attention downward. "Oh dear, we shall lose now, because of me. I am so slow."

"Not at all!" Xavier responded, wrapping an arm around her shoulders. "If we hurry, we may win out over Kenneth and Haddy, who, after all and greatly to our advantage, do not know a wager is on." He then tugged at her shoulders, and they hurried forward, his arm holding her tight and half carrying her as they ran.

When they reached the carriage, Michael was already up on the box, and had already paid the two young boys they had set to watch the horses. One of the two still held the head of the leader on the second carriage.

"Get in!" Michael cried. "I mean to find Kenneth first, and allow Haddy to be our host for lunch."

"Who shall drive the second?" Xavier asked up at him even as he handed a breathless Summer up into the carriage. "I dare not attempt it in town."

"We shall come back for it. We have no idea of our destination, after all, until we solve another clue."

Xavier glanced back down the street. "We need to find them soon, I think, before the local magistrates take offense at our public and disorderly ways." There was a chorus of giggles from inside the carriage. "Ladies! Running in the streets," he tsked his tongue, but his eye was filled with amusement.

"Our dignity is forsaken, by virtue of committee vote. We shall not be taken to task for it. At least, not until we have returned to civilization," Penelope told him, leaning forward to pull the door closed.

His smile faded and he almost scowled, for that return would be all too soon, measured by his way of looking at it.

"Up, man, or wait behind! Your decision, at once, if you please!" Michael urged, recalling Xavier to himself. As Xavier reached up to mount the box, Michael turned to the boys who were still standing and staring openly, and offered, "Here then, another tuppence for you both if you watch that carriage one more time?"

The boys nodded eagerly, the one moving to take the head of the second horse, next to his mate, as though to demonstrate their continued reliability.

Xavier was up on the box beside Michael in a trice, and it was nearly that quickly that they located Kenneth, who hailed them from the doorway of a candlemaker's shop. He chose to go inside the carriage, wherein he produced a bulky paper-wrapped package. "See what I bought?" he said as he lifted a rectangular shape from the package.

"A lantern?" Laura asked. "Whyever would you purchase a lantern?" There was an edge to her question that might suggest the expense was a foolish one.

He looked at Penelope for a moment, then back at his sister. "I thought it was attractive," he shrugged.

Laura looked at the lantern a second time, her eyes narrowing. "It just looks like a lantern to me."

"But see how well made it is! Sturdy, reliable. See this metalwork here? See how there are horizontal marks at even spaces? Now that is subtle, but it is craftsmanship all the same."

Laura hmmphed, but chose not to pursue the subject, and Genevieve was glad she let it go. Even a man with little funds available to him needed the occasional expression of his independence, and this was a small and reasonable enough way to find such a little pleasure, surely.

Haddy was located a minute later, sitting on a large rock, obviously waiting for someone of his party to make an appearance.

"What? Gave up on the chase?" Michael teased.

"Got tired of being gaped at by the locals," Haddy explained.

"Sitting on a rock on a main road will certainly end that, I should think."

Haddy pulled a disapproving face at this teasing. " 'Tis most ordinary to sit on a rock."

"Oh, most."

"Never mind him, Haddy. We have all decided to give up on our dignity anyway," Xavier said, offering a hand down.

Haddy took his hand, using his other to help pull his stalwart frame atop the carriage. "Have we?"

"We have."

"Might as well."

"That is the general consensus."

"Just so we do not slouch into frivolity," Haddy warned.

"Heavens, no. We could not have that."

"Dreadful stuff, frivolity. People say and do the most doltish things when they think they are being light and humorous."

"It is my experience, old boy," Michael said after clucking to the horses, "that people say and do the most doltish things regardless of their humor or the lack of one."

"You are quite right, of course. Which is why we do not need silliness on top of everything else."

"So, we are to have no decorum, accompanied by a lack of buffoonery?" Xavier questioned. He shook his head, grinning. "Sorry, Haddy, it cannot be done. I am afraid you are in for a torturous time, for the ladies are determined to be gay."

"Egad!" Haddy groaned as the carriage pulled next to the second.

"And, just so you know, you have lost a wager by being the last back to the carriage. You owe us all lunch."

"Devil you say! How can I lose a wager if I did not even know it existed?"

"You must ask Laura that question, although I doubt she will ever admit that she rather supposed all along that you would be the unfortunate loser."

"Laura? Cheeky to bet against her own partner, I say!" Haddy crossed his arms over his chest in a silent protest against either fate or his partner, as Michael tossed the boys their coins. They ran off with their new-found riches, with cries of "Thankee, Lord!" echoing behind them as Haddy unfolded his arms and climbed down, only to mount the second carriage and take up the ribbons.

"Hold up! We have yet a clue to solve," Kenneth called, coming from inside the first carriage.

"Not my turn," Haddy answered from his high seat.

"But you still need to know where to go. It is, in point of fact, Penelope's turn." He pulled a white note from his pocket, saw it was the wrong one, and pulled another, blue one, forth. He made a half-bow to Penelope and leaned inside the carriage to place the note in her hands. "If you will, please."

The ladies all leaned forward in their seat to hear the clue.

"It is in the black country you find me.
Once second only to Canterbury.

186

Out of the castle, in the moat went one:
Richard fled me, but then his time was done,' "

Penelope read, and then at once cried, "Oh, I know it! Kenneth, I know it. It is Lichfield."

"Correct!" he said, making an exaggerated swipe of relief with the back of his hand at his brow. "You have saved me from a forfeit!" He smiled at her, and she smiled back, and for a moment each of the occupants of the carriage fell silent, each quite aware that something more was going on than was being said.

Genevieve interrupted the sudden silence, leaning forward even more to ask, "But, Nelly, how did you know?"

"I am sure I do not know how it is that I remember, but I do recall that my tutor once said that—oh, hundreds of years ago—Lichfield's see was second only to Canterbury's, in power and prestige and all else that matters, I suppose. But I confess, I do not know of which Richard the poem speaks."

"The second, actually," Haddy called from his perch. "Richard the Second. He jumped over the castle wall and made his way through the moat to make his escape. Unfortunately he was recaptured and hence carried to his death."

As Kenneth pulled a playing card from his pocket, he glanced up at Haddy with satisfaction. "You see, good fellow? Not all my clues are too obscure."

"All the ones *I* have to answer," was the acerbic reply.

Kenneth grinned. "I wish I could say I had arranged it that way, but it is merely fate's fickle touch, you know."

187

"Fate is telling us to hie ourselves to Lichfield," Haddy said dryly. "It has grown quite warm, and the hour grows late, so let us be on our way."

Penelope accepted the playing card, turning it over to expose that it was a queen of diamonds. She looked up at Kenneth, her expression questioning.

"Because the next clue has to do with the acquisition of knowledge," he told her without further prompting. "The diamond represents riches, although these riches are of the mind rather than the purse," he explained.

"And why a queen?" she asked.

Genevieve lifted her eyes from the card, glancing between Penelope and Kenneth, for the woman's voice had gone unusually soft.

Kenneth made no reply for a moment, and the two sets of eyes held across the space of the carriage, but then he gave a small but eloquent shrug, murmured, "No particular purpose," and quickly turned away.

Genevieve rounded on Penelope, but that woman's eyes were set on her reticule where she was tucking the playing card.

"You have been given a hint for the next clue," Summer informed Genevieve. "You already know it has to do with the acquisition of knowledge. You must be sure to tell Michael when next we stop."

"Yes, I must," Genevieve murmured, dragging her attention back to Summer. "Of course." Then she looked back to Penelope, who was sitting quietly watching out the window, her hands serenely folded, her expression only mildly thoughtful.

"Nelly?" she heard herself ask.

Penelope turned to her. "Yes?"

"What . . . I mean to say, is everything well?"

"Well? Why yes. Although, 'tis a trifle warm today, is it not?" Penelope said.

"Yes, it is, but I really meant . . . with Kenneth . . . ?"

"Kenneth?" Penelope blinked, expressionless except for a very slight tightening around her mouth.

"Are you two getting on? Do you need to exchange partners . . . perhaps . . . ?" Genevieve finished lamely, faced as she was by that smooth set of features.

"Why no," was Penelope's simple response as she turned back to the window.

Was I quite mistaken? Genevieve thought. Had there been no tension in the carriage just a minute ago? Or if there had indeed been some kind of tension, some wordless exchange occurring, what did such an exchange mean? Was it the natural response to a relationship gone sour . . . or something else? The only thing Genevieve knew for sure was that it was *not* indifference, and that whatever it was was brewing and bubbling and getting set to expand rapidly at some unknown moment.

She only hoped that no one would be hurt in the explosion of emotions that seemed to wait just beneath the surface of what was, quite clearly, practiced cordiality on both their parts.

Chapter 14

It is one thing to show a man that he is in an error, and another to put him in possession of truth.

—John Locke,
An Essay Concerning Human Understanding

"They are burning the fields," Haddy said as he swung down from his saddle horse, pointing the way with one solid arm. "Both sides of the road. We shall have to wait until 'tis passable, and even then we shall have to drive easy lest the smell of smoke spook the horses."

"How long d'you think?" Michael asked from atop the first carriage, squinting into the sun to see the thick, dark plumes of smoke on the horizon before them.

Haddy shrugged. "An hour? Maybe two?"

"Surely not so long as that?"

"The fire's a large one. We daren't risk a dash along the road, not with two teams to handle. Better to wait until the fire's been quite beaten back. The good news is: we can rest the horses for a spell, and then they shall be good for a few more hours this day, perhaps all the way to Lichfield."

"Hmmm, a two-hour wait? That puts us in Lichfield no sooner than six, and that only if the roads improve. It has been quite some while since I have seen holes these big. Fair challenged me, they have," Michael said as though the roads had intended to purposefully annoy him.

"If we must wait, we must. If it grows too late, we shall find something on the way for the night," Kenneth said, passing the ribbons to Xavier. "Here now, you hold the cattle as I unharness."

"If we had known, we could have waited to have our luncheon now, instead of stopping in Coleshill," Xavier replied as he adjusted the reins in his hands.

"But it was refreshing to buy a fresh, hot luncheon, you must allow," Kenneth answered, moving to open the carriage door. "If you would be so good as to step down, ladies? We are halted in our forward progress by a field fire."

"Oh dear, is it dangerous?" Summer cried.

"Not at all. We simply must wait for the flames to work away from the roads. For now, we rest, or at least as best we can, given that the scent may disturb us some."

"Anyone for whist?" Haddy called from where he was draping his horse's reins over a shrub. "I purchased some playing cards from our host last evening." He moved to begin unharnessing the team from Michael's carriage.

There was a general chorus of, "No, thank you".

"No meal, no cards—what else is there to do?" Haddy complained as the right front leader blew air at him. He stroked the soft head and neck, and all but cooed, "You would play cards with me, would you not? Sure you would, if you could, you handsome fellow."

"So it has come down to talking to animals, has it?" Michael said with a critical lift of his eyebrows.

"Better than some recent company I have known," Haddy replied without a pause.

"Now, gentlemen, we must not be at daggers drawn," Penelope scolded as she climbed down from the carriage, followed by the other ladies.

"Hardly daggers. More like needles," Michael said.

"Not even needles. Pins," Haddy agreed.

"They do it for sport," Genevieve explained to no one in particular.

"Sport!" approved Haddy. "Now, there's a thought. Let us have a bit of sport, as in the age-old pursuit of game. We are but hours from our suppers, so let us add to our host's—whosoever he shall be—bounty. This seems to me an open field, upon which we do not infringe unnecessarily."

"Would that not be poaching?"

"My dear Genevieve, not if we are not caught at it."

"Hadrian Aubrey Dillonsby!" Summer exclaimed. "What would Father say?"

"He would say 'shoot true and make a hasty departure.'"

"Haddy! He would say no such thing!"

"Any man who would name his daughter after a flower, and his son and heir after a wall, most certainly would."

"You were named after the emperor, not the wall."

"And the dogs are named Bob and Jane. Plain, ordinary English names—for the dogs. No, Summer, it won't wash. The man's an eccentric, and so I feel safe in saying he would not begrudge me a grouse or two, given the rural setting in which we find ourselves. Not to mention that we have all agreed that we are now living under the rule of pure revelry."

Summer put up her hands, giving up the argument. "I shall not play the damp blanket. You must do as you wish. However, I promise to weep floods when you are brought up before the local magistrate."

"That would do very nicely, thank you," Haddy replied just as the last harness buckle was undone.

While Michael and Xavier climbed down from the carriage boxes, Haddy and Kenneth led the horses under a tree, attaching their leaders loosely that the animals might graze. That settled, they turned back to the carriages, finding their various long guns and ammunition.

"Who is with me?" Haddy called as he loaded his weapon.

"I am," Michael and Xavier replied unnecessarily, their weapons already in their hands.

"Not me, I think, lads. I shall stand guardian to the ladies," Kenneth said.

"You needn't," Laura told him, "now that we know Summer is quite prepared to defend us." She gave Summer a nod of acknowledgment. "Just leave her a pistol—"

"Summer?" Kenneth asked, his eyebrows disappearing under a lock of the light brown hair that fanned across his forehead.

"I am a more than fair shot, I assure you," she replied in her soft voice.

"Come now, Summer, admit you could not fire upon a flea, let alone a man."

"Oh, but I could, Kenneth," she replied, her eyes serious.

Michael stepped next to Genevieve, and whispered in a very low voice, "There is more to Summer than meets the eye."

Genevieve turned toward him at the words, and would have asked him to elaborate on that statement, but Haddy called the hunters to order. Instead all she got from Michael was a wink of his eye as he stepped away from her.

"I shall lead out and act the part of hound, flushing out the prey. I only ask that you do not fire upon *me*," Haddy said dryly to the huntsmen.

"Unless a man might mistake a bird for a bull, I think you need not concern yourself," Xavier said with a laugh.

"There is no danger of that," Laura spoke just as dryly as her brother.

"If there is pheasant to be had, there shall be none of that treat for you," he told his sister firmly, resting his rifle against his shoulder.

Haddy led the men into the grassy field, where they fanned out in an inverted V, Haddy taking the lead point, Xavier on his right to compensate for the blinded left eye, Michael on the left.

Kenneth indicated the shade of a tree removed from

the horses, and the ladies sat upon the grass, which was dry so that none of them felt the need to fetch a spread from the carriage.

"Perhaps we should begin tearing our petticoats to make bandages," Laura mocked.

"That would be to suggest that they shall be so lucky as to come across some fowl and need to fire their guns," Kenneth drawled.

"You should have gone with them, Kenneth. You are usually keen for the hunt," his sister said, untying her bonnet strings and running her fingers through the light reddish brown bangs that had stuck to her forehead in the warmth of the day.

"I've no desire to traipse in the sun."

"What are we to do while we wait? Perhaps I should have persuaded Haddy to leave his playing cards."

"We shall probably play tonight," Kenneth shook his head. He rose to his feet, putting out his hand directly before Penelope, who looked up, startled. "Come," he said, "why do we not go for a stroll?"

Penelope glanced around at the other ladies, her lips pressing into a thin line.

"I thought you did not care to traipse in the sun—" Laura began.

He interrupted, ignoring her, saying down to Penelope, "Just a little stroll?"

"I will go—" Laura began to rise.

Kenneth spun to her, speaking in a suddenly rough tone, "I did not ask you. I am asking Penelope."

Laura sank back to the ground, struck mute and patently offended.

Penelope shook her head, a small, quick shake.

"Penelope," he said, his voice now dropped low, "surely you can spend a few minutes with me? To talk? Alone."

Penelope glanced from under her lashes at Genevieve, who suddenly found herself nodding at the woman. Whatever was wrong between the two of them, perhaps Kenneth was right to want to talk it through, and perhaps settle it, once and for all. Genevieve nodded again, a discreet, tiny nod of encouragement.

Penelope's shoulders momentarily slumped in surrender, and then she offered her hand to Kenneth, and was assisted to her feet. He did not release her hand, instead pinning it to his sleeve with his own, larger hand.

"We shall be back within the hour," he said to no one in particular, and led Penelope away, in the opposite direction the hunters had taken.

"Well, I never!" Laura said to his retreating back.

"Do not refine upon it, Laura," Genevieve told her.

"Yes, do not," Summer spoke. "He did not mean to be insulting. He just needed to speak with Penelope alone for a while, and there was no subtle way to do that." She exchanged knowing glances with Genevieve.

"That is all very well; I can understand that they have unfinished business to attend to, but he really need not have spoken in such a harsh manner to me." She fanned herself in agitation with her bonnet. "And we must also consider that 'tis improper to let her be alone with him. And we have allowed it!" Laura persisted. "We are supposed to be chaperoning one another."

"I hardly think one thing is more improper than the next," Summer said.

"What do you mean?" Laura's eyes narrowed.

"I mean, is not running in the High Street just as terrible, if not more so, than taking a stroll with a long-time friend?"

Genevieve raised a hand to her mouth, as though to stifle a cough, but really to hide her smile.

"Summer Rose Dillonsby, I would point out that I was not the only one to run through the High Street!"

"No, of course," Genevieve soothed. "But is that not just the point? Conventions are meaningless until we reach Brockmore. We no longer concern ourselves with them. Kenneth and Penelope will be the better for having talked, I feel sure, and that is all that matters to us now."

The ladies fell silent, until Summer proposed that they braid some of the taller grasses around them into garlands and necklaces, a task that busied their fingers, if not their minds. Summer coughed a few times, making them all aware of the occasional gusts of acrid air that blew over them when the wind shifted, adding to the discomfort of the overly warm day.

A shot rang out, followed by a second, making the ladies jump.

"Let us hope it is not Haddy who comes back trussed," Summer said, making the other two laugh quietly even as another shot was fired.

Kenneth and Penelope had not returned by the time the huntsmen reappeared. As the three approached, Haddy triumphantly held up a brace of grouse.

"The Mighty Providers return!" Michael announced as Haddy made small bows of self-congratulation.

"Who would have thought it?" Laura asked, leaning forward to peer at Summer. "Now you may marry Michael, my dear, as he has proven he can keep dinner upon your table."

"Not true, alas!" Michael admitted without any real sign of regret. " 'Twas Haddy and Xavier who brought down these fine specimens. So you see, I am worthless."

"Hardly," Summer said, a smile lifting the corners of her mouth. It warmed as Michael turned to her. He etched her a bow, handed his long gun, equipment, and his hat to Xavier with the words "Would you be so good, old chap?" stretched out on the ground, and laid his head in Summer's lap without so much as a by-your-leave. Her hands went at once to his hair, running her fingers through the damp sandy-colored hair at his temples.

Genevieve frowned, thinking her brother far too presumptuous by half.

Xavier collected Haddy's accoutrements as well, as that gentleman said he would ride down the road a bit and see what was the status thereof.

When Xavier returned from stashing the firearms either in the carriage or with the extra horse gear, he put his hands on his hips, glanced about, and asked, "Where are Kenneth and Penelope?"

"They have taken a stroll," Laura answered, doing a poor job of stifling a yawn.

He glanced around again at the gently rolling hills and the increasingly numerous clusters of trees toward the horizon, and reached up to rub his jaw. "Which direction?" he asked when he saw no sign of any strollers.

Laura and Summer pointed the way they had gone with nods of their heads.

198

"I suppose we ought to see if we can locate them, as I expect Haddy to come back with favorable news. That rise there is a likely place to begin," Xavier said, volunteering himself to go and look.

"I shall go with you," Genevieve declared suddenly, rising to her feet.

"Hmmm," Laura said dampeningly at her side, causing Genevieve to glance down at her.

"Really, Laura, you do have a problem with being informal," she snapped, moving at once to take Xavier's arm.

They had not gone far when she had to remind herself to slow her pace, that the movement of her feet need not match the racing of her heart—due to Laura's censure, no doubt, or perhaps the suddenness of her rise from sitting for so long.

"How long have they been gone?" Xavier asked at her side.

"About an hour. Kenneth said they would be returned by now, but I suppose one loses track of time . . . on such a beautiful day. Did you enjoy the hunting?"

"Oh, yes. It is one thing at which I am not particularly disadvantaged by having sight in only one eye, you must know. As long as the creatures are so unlucky as to fly not too far to my left, I can usually get them in my sights and bring them down right and tight enough. No need to squint one eye, you see, and I already know how to adjust for depth." He spoke lightly, but there was an undertone of something deeper in his manner, as though it was a subject he did not care to pursue.

"I rather suppose you would." She wanted to erase

some of that discomfort, so she went on, "It does not stop you from doing much though, does it?"

"No," he answered simply. As though the words were pulled from him, he added, "There are only a few things that are beyond me. Town driving. Some dances, if I do not care to harm those around me. That manner of thing." He stiffened beside her, trying to make his arm remain relaxed under her touch, but it was a costly effort. It made his words come out clipped. He knew what was coming. This was how it began: a light discussion, a few words to relax his guard, and then . . . ! And then, they asked. The women always asked: might they see it? Might they know what was under that patch?

He could not bear it. He could not endure having her see him so very naked, so ugly. He would have to refuse her, of course. The only trick of it was, though, to refuse her gently, kindly. To not cut her. To not make her feel horrid for her natural curiosity.

"Do you think we shall travel on to Lichfield tonight?" she asked.

The agony of suspense was broken, and he all but sagged at her side. Somehow, magically, she had not asked. She had not made him resent her. She'd had the opportunity, and had let it go.

Now his arm did tense, for he had to do something to keep from shuddering with relief, and that was to allow every muscle in his body to tighten almost painfully.

"Xavier?" she asked, slowing her steps, her delicate brow wrinkling as her mouth formed a small frown at the change in him at her side.

" 'Tis nothing. A chill, perhaps."

"I knew you ought to have come inside the carriage last night," she scolded.

He merely nodded, unable to speak. He indicated with a movement of his head that they should continue walking, up the slight incline before them.

They reached the top without further conversation, although Genevieve made a pleased sound at the sight that spread before them on the other side. A large field slanted away from them, covered with the fuzzy green carpet of new growth. The burning of the adjacent fields had left an uneven veil of smoke hanging in the air through which sunbeams poked, striving to reach the ground. It created a crazy quilt of light and shade, making the new crops glow bright green, in contrast with the gray-green areas where the sun's rays did not strike. Leafy birches stood in a long row that bordered the right side of the field, sentinels against the wind that surely blew here some seasons, now like silent guardians awaiting the time of their duty.

"Beautiful," she breathed, her face aglow as she stood washed in one of the afternoon's sunbeams. Her lips were slightly parted in appreciation of the sight before her, her eyes filled with dark gleams of wonder.

He did not bother to look away from the sight of her enthralled visage, instead drinking it in and thinking his legs must surely have gone too weak to carry him another step, or even to hold him upright. He responded, his voice equally a sigh, "Yes, beautiful."

"I am so glad we came on this journey," she said. Just as she began to turn to him, just as he struggled to clamp down his emotions, to hide away his secret yearnings, and knew in a moment's panic that it was not possible, a voice sounded, crying out faintly, "Hallooo!"

They turned as one. She released his arm, turning her back to him, and he closed his eye, hidden from her sight as she discovered the location of the voice.

"There they are!" she cried, raising her arm and waving at Kenneth and Penelope, who had just emerged from between two of the birches. Penelope's hand was on Kenneth's arm and she walked close to his side, so perhaps their stroll had done its task and a new harmony had been achieved there.

Xavier used the moments of their approach to stand still and silent, carefully tucking all his responses behind a calm facade, refusing to look at the lock on his heart, afraid the pain in his chest meant the hasp had been broken.

He could only be grateful that Kenneth and Penelope had saved him from revealing that fact to Genevieve.

Chapter 15

Love is blind, and lovers
cannot see
The pretty follies that
themselves commit.
　　　　—Shakespeare,
The Merchant of Venice

"Why do they burn the fields?" Summer asked, swaying against the side panel of the carriage as it took another dip through a pothole in the road. Genevieve peered out the window, but could see very little of the blackened fields, for the lanterns on the exterior of the carriage obscured her vision almost as much as did the night itself. She turned her attention again to the carriage's interior, dimly lit by the lanterns without, to see that Summer's dainty nose wrinkled in distaste at the caustic smell that still hung in the air.

"The ash is good for the soil. And besides, it clears the field of weeds," Penelope answered.

"Is that what you and Kenneth were doing?" Laura

asked, her mouth forming a slight, not entirely pleasant smile. "Looking at the soil?"

"Yes," Penelope said, frowning. "Among other things."

"What manner of other things?"

"Maybe this is not the topic for the moment," Genevieve interjected. It had grown dark an hour since. They were all tired, and a little concerned that they had not found an inn for the night. Everyone was growing a little testy.

"Not at all. What else have we to do but talk?" Laura countered. She leaned toward Penelope. "I hope you settled your differences."

"What differences?"

"You need not pretend we do not know. Kenneth was quite upset the day your father denied his offer. No, Genevieve, do not say a word; we all certainly know it happened, and I see no reason to pretend otherwise, now that she and Kenneth went on that stroll today. All I want to know now is this: have you and Kenneth settled your differences?"

" 'Tis a foolish question," Penelope snapped.

"Foolish? In what manner?"

"How can we settle 'our differences'?" Penelope cried, her voice rising. "Either we may marry or we may not, and Father has said we may not. There is nothing to settle." She looked out the window, her arms crossed over her breasts.

Genevieve bit her lip, hearing the wound that still lingered there.

Laura sat back. "Ah. That is well. I mean to say, I for one cannot bear to have people mooning about. Get on with the business of finding suitable partners, I say." At Genevieve's belligerent glare of reproach, she added, "I am only thinking of them both. Kenneth is the sort to . . . well, to have hopes, even when they are plainly idle hopes. I had hoped this 'talk' of theirs today set him quite straight on the matter. I have every reason to think you, Penelope, are not the sort to . . . well, to lead a fellow along the primrose path."

"Laura!" Genevieve hissed.

Penelope shook her head, saying in a cool and brittle voice, "No, Laura. You may rest easy on that account. I am not the sort to lead a fellow along."

"Then all is well, and you all may cease looking daggers at me. Sometimes it is all that much more pleasant once the air has been well and truly cleared. Do you not find that to be true?"

No one answered her, not even Summer, who vainly fanned the pungent air inside the carriage with her handkerchief.

The carriage slowed to a halt at the next village, and the next, but both times they were told there was no room to be had. It seemed there was a local fair set to occur the next day, and all the rooms for hire were taken long before dark.

"What do we do?" Summer asked of Haddy out the carriage window, which they had finally opened with relief once they were clear of the smell of smoke.

"We drive until we find a place," he answered gruffly. "Lichfield is only another four miles or so, and there is bound to be room there, if not along the way."

They purchased some more lantern oil, replenished the level in the lanterns—while Haddy made terrible

growling sounds when some of it spilled onto his boots—
and set out on their way once again. Summer fell asleep
in the corner against the squabs, and Penelope nodded
off as well. Laura kept her own counsel, except for the
occasional sigh of extreme boredom.

For herself, Genevieve worried her lower lip, wondering why the world sometimes seemed so very unfair.
Michael's betrothal to Summer was on shaky ground;
Xavier was distracted and seemed to be caught in some
silent passion; and Kenneth and Penelope were struggling to accept that they could not fight against fate, or
at least her father's dictates.

And she, yes she, was infatuated with the man who
threatened her brother's future happiness. If she was
honest and did not wrap up the truth in clean linen, she
had to see she was drawn to Xavier. She found herself
watching him, seeing the way he behaved with the others, especially with Summer. The way he was always
there when the fragile blonde needed assistance. But,
too, she noted more: his grace of movement; the way he
cocked his head, the better to see, sometimes; the way he
put himself forward, trying to help or to soothe when
matters became agitated. There was a certain timbre to
his voice sometimes that made the hairs on the back of
her arms stand up, that made her want to lean toward
him, to pretend that the warm voice was intended just
for her ears alone. There was a light in the back of his
gray eye that held her in place, did not let her breathe
easily, that confused her more than she cared to admit.
She was drawn to him, yes, despite the evidence of her
eyes, those eyes that saw how he solicited Summer's
attention, how he placed himself in situations where he

could aid her, how he attempted over and again to win the fair girl's approval or appreciation.

And, worst of all, she had long since come to the conclusion that it was not her place, nor even within her ability, to change any of it. All she could do was ride it out and see where the days took them.

It was beyond exasperating. It was past worrisome. It was a kind of hurt that went too deep for examination. It was making her head ache, and she longed for a bed, that she might hide in slumber from the thoughts that plagued her.

Nearly an hour later they drove into Lichfield. The main street was dark and unwelcoming. Summer and Penelope stirred when the carriage halted, and they all waited together in a miserable silence as Haddy went within to attempt to find a room. They startled when the carriage door was yanked open, and Haddy loomed into the darkness of the interior. "We have rooms!" he declared, the relief obvious in his voice, echoed by Summer's audible sigh. "We shall be crowded, but at least we've beds for the night."

There was little conversation as they moved inside the inn. Laura did not even demand that her large case be brought within. Genevieve trudged after her up the stairs, at the foot of which she heard Xavier request that a simple meal be sent up to the ladies, and one to the men's room belowstairs.

The four women found they had been assigned one large room, not near so large as the one they had shared in Long Itchington. Two beds were pressed right against each other, leaving just enough room at the foot for one person to pass along the wall; and opposite the outermost bed, just enough room for one long dressing table and four elbow-to-elbow females to stand. The single window was closed, and the air in the room was too warm and stagnant.

"We shall have to dress and undress one or two at a time, at the most," Penelope declared sourly.

"Oh dear," Summer said, "but at least it is only for one night."

"How many more days is it until we come to Brock-more?" Genevieve asked, not quite able to keep a tartness from her voice.

"If we travel no faster, and the roads do not improve, as much as four days," Laura replied hollowly.

Everyone made a face, except Summer, who said, "Michael will not take so long as that. He is quite a creditable whip, in case no one has noticed." Her face glowed in the candlelight.

Genevieve frowned at that glow, then reached out and took Summer's arm. "There is no room to take a meal in here. We will need to descend to the common room once more, unless by some miracle a sitting room may be hired. Summer, let us crawl upon the beds and leave room for these other two to change into something suitable for dinner."

They crawled over the beds as Penelope moved to open the window against the warmth of the evening.

Penelope and Laura changed with unaccustomed haste, donning simple muslin dresses, not too sadly wrinkled once they were pulled free of their cases. They brushed out their hair and pulled it back into simple falls to save time and energy, completing their toilettes just as there was a knock at the door. Laura opened it to find the inn's mistress with a large tray in her hands, an assortment of foodstuffs arranged thereon.

"My good woman, have you a sitting room where we might dine?" Laura asked.

"No, mum."

"Then we shall have to take our meal in the common room."

"Oh, aye mum?" the mistress questioned, doubt reigning in her wide eyes.

"Aye indeed. Our brothers will be joining us, I feel sure."

"Brothers, mum? Oh aye!" the woman cried doubtfully, then of a sudden her face cleared and she gave a broad wink. "That's the way o'it then? Right enow. T'common room it be." She turned and shuffled under the heavy load toward the stairs.

Laura looked at Penelope, faintly alarmed. "What do you suppose she meant by all that?"

Penelope was obviously uncertain whether to frown or grin, but finally the grin won. "Why, my dear Laura, she means she does not believe those are our brothers at all. She thinks we are fancy pieces!"

Laura's hand flew to her chest as she cried in horror, "No!"

"Oh!" Summer said from the bed. "Oh dear! Do we dare go down now?"

"Yes, we dare," Penelope said with a lifting of her chin to go with her chagrined smile. "We ought not be punished for the fact the creature is daft." She stepped around Laura, exiting the room to follow behind the innkeeper's wife.

Laura looked to Genevieve and complained, "That

one always bucked propriety to remain with the men. But, this is certain folly."

"That is probably quite true. But I do not care. I am having my dinner belowstairs. You may choose what you wish to do."

Laura drew herself up, her chest expanding in irritation. After a moment, the air went out of her in a noisy sigh of capitulation, followed by a warning, "But each lady must sit with her own brother, and there must be only conventional conversation. Summer, that means no hand-holding under the table with Michael."

Summer blushed, but did not deny that such had ever occurred.

Laura gave them each a hard, speaking glance, then exited, closing the door behind her.

Genevieve sighed with relief when she was gone, but not because of Laura's dictates; rather, because she wished to speak alone with Summer. As she stood still, allowing Summer to undo the multiple buttons down the back of her gown, she opened her mouth to speak, but was interrupted.

"Genny, what do you think of Xavier?" Summer said in a quiet voice.

"Xavier?" Her voice was hollow, for her heart had started to pound wildly at the sound of that name on Summer's lips.

"Yes."

"What do I think of him?"

Summer made a clucking sound with her tongue, and pressed, "Yes. What do you think?"

"He is very cordial."

"Yes, I think so, too. What else?"

Genevieve frowned fiercely, since Summer could not see her face. "He is polite. Congenial. Gentlemanly."

"Oh, indeed! It was so very good of him to look after me during the rain, was it not? He is very thoughtful that way. Do you not think so?"

Genevieve made an assenting noise, although every nerve inside her body was tingling, just as it did when she thought she was just about to fall off her mount. She wanted to tell Summer to cease, to leave the subject be, to not reveal that she had become aware of a man other than Michael. That the man was Xavier.

Summer went on, "And handsome, too, if one discounts the scar and the patch, although they do lend an air of mystery, do they not? Of course, he cultivates that effect by never admitting what really happened. And he has a plump pocket as well. Not as plump as does Michael, but—"

Genevieve spun around, disregarding the fact that her last few buttons were not yet unfastened. She cried bluntly, "Summer, do you love Michael?"

"Oh yes," Summer said, one hand lifting to her throat in a defensive gesture.

"Completely?"

Summer blushed a deep red before she said, "I rather suppose, yes."

"But . . . do you ever . . . ?" Genevieve's voice caught as words failed her. She cleared her throat and began again, "I mean to say, do you ever think what it would be like if you did not love him, and you were not betrothed to him?"

"What an odd question, Genny!" Summer laughed,

an unsteady sound. "No, I do not think about that, not really."

Genevieve met Summer's eyes for a moment before the blond girl turned decisively and presented her own buttons to be undone.

"Not really?" Genevieve asked uncertainly.

"In point of fact, I am not sure what you are asking," Summer clarified.

Genevieve began to undo the buttons before her. "I suppose what I am asking is . . . what I am saying is . . . ," she finished quickly, "do you ever wonder what it might be like to kiss someone other than Michael? Or hold someone else's hand? Or marry someone else?"

Summer looked over her shoulder, just beginning to frown. "Do not tell me that you do not wish me for a sister-in-law?"

"Oh no! That is to say, no, I do not mean that at all! I know we will continue to get on famously. I think Michael is most fortunate that you accepted him. It is only that, well, I suppose I have been wondering if you have regretted having accepted him?"

Summer turned her face away again, staring out into the room somewhere above the beds. "You mean, because it has been so long since the banns were read."

"Well, yes." Genevieve stared at her fingers as they worked the buttons; they were almost as clumsy as her tongue.

"Yes," Summer said quietly.

"Yes?" Genevieve echoed faintly.

"Yes, sometimes I regret having accepted him. Michael is not tractable. He is stubborn—sometimes to a fault." She turned to face Genevieve, her dark eyes

212

sparkling with something perilously close to tears. "In all this time, he has yet to tell me he loves me. Not even when he proposed. He said it would be a 'fortuitous arrangement resulting in the blending of our affections.'"

"Oh, Summer, no, he could not have."

"He did. At the time, I thought it rather charming. But now . . ."

"What are you going to do?" Genevieve whispered, for her throat was tight with tears that echoed Summer's threatened ones. She heard the dread in her own voice.

"Do? Why, nothing. I have accepted him. I shall go to the altar with him, of course."

And that was right where she ought to leave it, Genevieve knew. She had no business interfering, and indeed, was afraid of more than one consequence if she did. But there were tears glittering in her friend's eyes, and it seemed there was heartache just around the corner, no matter which way they turned.

"But what . . . what if there were another? What if someone did love you?" Genevieve closed her eyes, to hold back the tears and so that she need not see any new truths on her friend's face. And, too, she wanted to hide from her betrayal of her brother, as well as a betrayal of a secret corner of her own heart.

Instead, Summer gave no answer at all, so that Genevieve was forced to open her eyes. She found Summer staring at her, hard, or as hard as those doe's eyes could stare. "What are you talking about, Genevieve?"

"Love. Real love. We all deserve it, surely," Genevieve went on a little wildly. "Papa says the notion of choosing a marriage partner only based on affection is poor management of one's estate, but I find I happen to agree with the poets. I find I cannot bear the thought that . . . you . . . or Michael . . . need marry for anything less. For happiness. For joy. Am I too terribly foolish?"

"But, Genevieve, you know I must love him if I have waited so long."

"Do you? Is there no one else you could feel an affection for?" Her fingers curled into fists, as she said the final words of betrayal aloud, "Does, or will, Michael come to love *you?*"

Summer turned away, shrugging out of her dress with sharp movements. "I cannot think why you would say such things to me. You are out of sorts today, Genevieve. Why is that? What is it about the idea of marriage, or love, that has set you at me like this?"

"I am not—"

"Is it because of Xavier?" Summer cried, pulling from her bag a gown, which unrolled toward the floor, her hands automatically moving to smooth the packing creases as she stared at her friend.

Genevieve froze. "Yes," she answered in a hollow voice, now aware beyond doubt that Summer had not missed Xavier's approaches.

"Because he is my partner?"

"No." Monosyllables were all she could manage.

"Because he has seen to my needs sometimes?"

"Yes."

Summer stared at Genevieve anew, her hands idly stroking the dress before her. "He is very sweet, is he not? I mean to say, all one could wish for in a gentleman."

Genevieve nodded, unable to trust her voice.

214

The blond girl's eyes searched Genevieve's face for a long minute, and by the time she turned away, she had lost all signs of anger in those eyes and in her stance. "Oh, Genny," she said on a sigh that had the faint edge of a laugh in it. "You have some very pretty little romantic notions in your head. We were not talking about Michael at all."

"What—?"

"Please do not fret. Everything will be fine. These things always work themselves out for the best, often in ways that surprise us." She pulled the dress over her head, and tied the strings at the neckline and under her bosom, fitting it to her lithe form. She glanced in the mirror, and declared, "My hair is quite well enough. Do hurry down, Genny love, or we shall not leave you a bite."

"But—!"

Summer did not wait, lifting a hand in a delicate wave of farewell, then ducked out the door, closing it behind her with a decided click.

Chapter 16

*The heart has its reasons which
reason knows nothing of.*
　　　　　—Blaise Pascal,
　　　　　　　　Pensées

Genevieve was the last to arrive at the common room.
If anyone but Laura felt restrained, they were doing well
at disguising the fact, although Kenneth's sister had
obviously ruled supreme when it came to the seating, for
each gentleman had his sister on his right. Still, they ate
freely, giving a call of salute when at length the grouse
they had brought with them were served, exchanging
stories of the hunt thereof, and otherwise belying the fact
that a mere hour earlier they had all been exhausted.
Genevieve sat next to Michael, who leaned back in his
chair to say to Kenneth, "Where were you off to this
evening, old fellow?"

"I was arranging the solution of our clue, should we
be interested tonight."

"Oh, a clue at night!" Summer breathed, her eyes

shining in the candlelight. "That would be most novel."

"I agree," Penelope said at once.

"Is that acceptable to everyone?" Kenneth asked.

Everyone nodded, although Genevieve did so with no real enthusiasm. She was still more than a little distraught and perplexed by Summer's conversation earlier, and by her own questions of the girl. Now she stared from under her lashes at Summer, as though to look at her hard enough would be to comprehend what the woman was thinking, feeling, planning.

"But in the meanwhile, might we have a Little Riddle?" Summer asked, and Genevieve saw the dark eyes flutter first to Michael, then to Xavier, and lastly to Genevieve's own, where she immediately dropped her gaze, as did Genevieve herself.

"Certainly," Kenneth responded, reaching for his pocket as usual. He read, " 'Here in Staffordshire, in 1487, the Battle of the Stoke brought about the end of one fellow's ambitions to wrest the crown from Henry the Seventh. Who was he, how did he call himself, and what was his eventual fate?' "

"Simple!" Haddy cried, leaping to his feet as several heads bobbed knowingly around him.

"Go ahead," Kenneth grinned, responding to Haddy's pleased expression.

" 'Twas Lambert Simnel, who called himself one of the two missing princes in the tower, son of Edward the Fourth. He was captured and made to turn the spit in the royal kitchens. Am I right?"

"You know you are."

"That was too easy. Do let us have another," Laura complained.

"Not till I have had my kiss," Haddy said, hands on hips as he gazed around the table.

"There goes any shred of reputation we had hoped to maintain," Laura grumbled.

Haddy grinned, and leaned down to plant a wet, noisy buss on her cheek, and said loudly, "There you go!"

This did not go unobserved, for a murmur ran through the room, at which he added loudly, "May I have another?"

Laura glared up at him. "If it were not for the fact that I wish to be present when the next clue is read, I would leave this table at once. Let me further say, that if you do not sit down immediately and behave yourself entirely, I am leaving," she said frostily. "And, if such is the case, there will be no clue tonight."

"Haddy, that was really too bad of you," Summer tried to scold her brother, but she could not force down her smile completely.

He sat down, totally unabashed. " 'Bout time Laura was kissed, I say."

That lady rose to her feet, her face quite flushed, and it was only by physically putting hands on her and uttering half a dozen soothing comments, that she was persuaded by the group to remain.

She sat very straight in her chair and said, "At the next inn, I insist, Kenneth, that you and I be registered under false names."

At that the group could only burst into laughter, but amid the mirth Kenneth agreed he would fabricate a name. This seemed to soothe her more than anything else had done, and the group turned to Kenneth. He was requested to present the next clue, which he handed to Genevieve.

She held it up before herself and Michael, but before she read it aloud, she told him, "I am reminded that earlier today Kenneth told Penelope that this next clue has to do with the acquisition of knowledge."

"Acquisition? At this time? We would be fortunate to find a church unlocked, let alone a place of commerce."

"Acquisition does not always mean making a purchase, Michael."

"It does in our household."

Haddy chortled his agreement.

"Let us see what it has to say." She held the paper closer to a candle that was stuck in a wax-dripped bottle on their table. "It says: 'I am the son of a bookseller. I was born the eighteenth of September, in the year of our Lord 1709. I was friend to David Garrick, the actor. I wrote a book entitled *Historical Voyage to Abysinnia*.' Hmmm, I do not know it, do you?"

Michael shook his head.

She went on, " 'I am buried in Westminster Abbey. I was known to be slovenly in my appearance and in my habits, but am better known for the fact that I was compassionate and generous. If you guess my name, you must find the work I am perhaps best remembered for: my 1755 publication.' " Genevieve lowered the paper to the tabletop and looked at Michael, her expression revealing she was utterly perplexed.

In answer to her mute inquiry, he replied, "No, dear Sister, I have no thought as to whom, or what, he means."

"We know it must be somewhere here in Lichfield," she countered.

"And we know it has to do with publications. Some sort of proclamation, or deed, or book, perhaps."

"Whatever it is, you shan't find it here in this inn," Laura said, her tone still cool.

"Quite true," Penelope said, rising to her feet. "I suggest we ladies find a shawl. It may be cooler out-of-doors than we think."

The shawls were fetched, lanterns were secured from the innkeeper, and then Michael and Genevieve led the way out into the night.

"Oh, it is not cool at all," Summer remarked as she stepped out into the evening air, lowering her shawl so that it merely draped low across her back and on her forearms.

"Far more pleasant than that common room," Penelope agreed.

"Whatever are we looking for?" Genevieve asked her brother.

"The obvious thing is a bookseller's establishment."

They looked at each other in the glow of the lantern he held, and said together, "The High Street!" and then grinned at one another for their mutual insight.

"It hardly seems likely we shall find anything other than a dark walk for all our trouble," Michael added.

" 'Tis only a stone's throw," Genevieve said as she pointed the way, taking his arm to lead him forward.

As she had promised, it was only a matter of walking the length of a row of houses and then they all saw it at once: a lighted building with an open door. It was the only shop with the curtains still drawn open and candles obviously burning within, not to mention the open door that invited admission. Michael led the way, stepping back at the threshold to signal that his sister ought to go in before him.

"Good evening?" she called into the candlelit room as she stepped over the threshold.

A man, small in stature, came from behind a hanging curtain, and inclined his head. "Good evening, my lady. Might I help you?" He moved behind a lectern—obviously a relic from some church remodel or other—and settled on a high stool behind it, folding his hands before him atop the wood.

"Well, I do not know precisely. We"—she indicated the others that filed in behind her—"are on a treasure hunt, and desire to find the next item in our hunt."

"I see. And what would that be, my lady?" he asked.

"I do not know. That is part of the problem." She turned to Kenneth, "I can only presume this is the correct gentleman for our task tonight?"

He nodded, as Michael said under his breath, "I should think so. He's the only bookseller open in the entire shire at this time of night."

Genevieve ignored her brother. "Is he allowed to help us? Or will we forfeit our token by doing so?"

"No, not if you ask the right questions," Kenneth answered. He lifted a hand in the shopkeeper's direction, "This is Mr. Leamer. Mr. Leamer, may I introduce Lady Genevieve, and her brother, Lord Herland." The necessary introductions completed, he explained further, "Mr. Leamer has already been informed that you are indeed, as Michael suggested, to find a certain written item, but he is not free to tell you what specifically it is. He may, however, answer any 'yes' or 'no' questions you may think of that might allow you to find it for yourselves."

"With only about five minutes to spare, I believe," Michael said as he consulted his watch. To Genevieve he urged, "Ask away!"

"Is it a book we seek?" she asked the bookseller.

"Yes."

"Published in 1755?"

"Yes."

"Is it large?"

"Yes."

"Do you have a copy here?" Michael interjected.

"Yes."

"Is it readily apparent? By that I mean, is it lying about where we can see it easily?" Michael went on.

"No."

"Is it on the shelves?" Genevieve asked.

"Yes."

"Is it by someone famous?"

"Yesss," the smaller man hedged. He glanced at Kenneth, then added quickly, "Though I believe he ought to be more so. A clever, good man, who did much for—"

"Ah-ah!" Kenneth warned, wagging a finger. "Be careful what you say, Mr. Leamer."

"Oh, as though we shall ever come to know what it is!" Genevieve scoffed in a mock frustration that showed she was truly enjoying the pursuit.

"I've a thought," Michael said, a light beginning to dance in his hazel eyes. He walked up to a shelf, placed

222

a hand on the bindings there, and asked, "Is it on this shelf?"

The bookseller smiled at the ploy, glanced at Kenneth, who shrugged, and replied, "No."

Genevieve flew to the next set of shelves, and between the calls of the brother and sister as they touched one shelf after another, Mr. Leamer's head was forced to swivel back and forth as he called out rapid negatives.

Genevieve's hand had already gone down to the shelf below before she realized that, for once, his reply had come back, "Yes."

"Oh, Michael! 'Tis here somewhere!"

He crossed to her side and they began at opposite ends, touching individual spines, asking, "Is this the one?"

Finally Mr. Leamer merely nodded with a smile, and Michael pulled the thick book from the shelf as Genevieve clapped her hands in triumph. *"Dictionary of the English Language,"* Michael read, his finger running over the embossed printing. He looked up, "Ah! By Johnson, of course."

"Samuel Johnson," Kenneth nodded. "But, I do not know if it ought to count. You both all but cheated! You were supposed to ask questions about various authors, and dazzle us all with a list of scholarly wits and your knowledge thereof."

"Could not do it that way, old fellow. Don't know any."

"It counts! It counts!" Genevieve cried, squeezing her brother's arm in excitement.

"Of course it does. We cannot help it that we are too

clever, in a nonbook-learning sort of way, by half for our dear Kenneth."

The argument never went any further, for Kenneth reached out and spread the book open in Michael's hands. He flipped a few pages, unsuccessfully, and then explained, "Your token is in there somewhere."

As Michael fanned the pages until he came to the playing card, Genevieve announced, "It shall be a diamond, perhaps the king," as indeed it proved to be.

"How did you know that?" Kenneth grinned.

"Because when you gave Penelope the queen of diamonds, you said it stood for the riches gained from knowledge. And a dictionary of our language must surely be useful for the gaining of knowledge. And it seems fitting to deem Mr. Johnson the King of Knowledge."

"Socrates or Solomon might argue the point. But, as for ourselves, we gained a token, at least, for our trouble," Michael said as he handed the card to his sister.

"And a book," she said, making a motion with her head that indicated the tome in his hands.

He did not try to argue with her, merely sighing, knowing that Mr. Leamer needed to be rewarded for having stayed open for them. He purchased the dictionary and included a bit extra for the man's trouble. His sister dimpled up at him as he handed the weighty book to her. She told him, "We are tied with Xavier and Summer, at two tokens apiece."

"We? Then how is it that I am the only one out of pocket?" Michael grumbled good-naturedly as they exited the shop. Mr. Leamer was quick to pull his curtains and shut his front door behind them.

"But now we do not know where we need to venture," Xavier said as they gathered in a semicircle on the High Street. He looked away from where Genevieve laughed, for to watch her was to have to join her, and he did not think the others would find it so very irresistible, and he would make a spectacle of himself.

"Should we have that clue now or in the morning?" Kenneth asked.

"Now," Haddy and Laura said together, for they were the next team to play.

"Two in one day!" Kenneth chided, but gave in at once by saying, "Very well. However, I have not written it down. You shall have to have it from me orally. Is that acceptable?"

They agreed.

"Let me think a moment. . . . This is plain stuff, but, uh, let me say that this town was purportedly built by a giant. There is a bit of poetry that goes with it . . . and it is very like this, if not exactly so: 'His name was Leon Gawer, a might strong giant, who built caves and dungeons, many a one, no goodly buildings, ne proper, ne pleasant.' That is very close to it anyhow. Now, you must tell me the name of the town."

"I do not even know which shire you mean," Laura cried as Haddy rolled his eyes. "It could be here in Staffordshire, or in Cheshire, or Derby, or even Nottingham. Come, Kenneth, you must tell us more than that!"

"Very well," he agreed. "I realize that was fairly small as clues go. Let me add this: 'tis north of Nantwich."

"Well, that does help," Haddy conceded. "At least we now know we will be out of Staffordshire and into Cheshire." Then a calculating grin spread over his face, and he reached into his pocket, extracting the map he carried with him. "Let us have a look, shall we?" he said to his partner as he unfolded the map.

"Not fair!" Michael cried, even as he laughed with appreciation at this duplicity.

"I should not talk after the trick you and Genevieve just delivered," Haddy said in his best sanctimonious tones.

"No one said *how* we must find the book."

"And no one has said we may not look at a map."

"Come into the light," Laura urged.

Kenneth said nothing, his thumbs in his vestpockets.

"It appears they are to be allowed," Xavier commented. Genevieve acknowledged the comment, where no one else bothered, and he found himself smiling at her, unable to take his eyes away until she looked down at the map, too.

"Look you, we shall want to stay on the mail roads as much as we may," Haddy pointed to the slender line. "That takes us up through Newcastle." His finger followed the line upward. "Then we are into Cheshire and the first town is Church Lawt, which is east of Nantwich. We know it is north of the latter." His finger followed along as he spoke, "Hmmm. See here, Middlewich is north of Nantwich, and that makes a kind of sense. Sounds the sort of place a giant might build dungeons and whatnots, eh?"

"Sounds believable to me," Laura agreed, albeit not wholeheartedly. Still, she raised her eyes to meet Kenneth's and asked, "Is it Middlewich?"

"Sorry. Ha! And that after cheating!"

"Oh, Haddy!" Laura sighed, giving her partner a lowering glance.

"You agreed!" he defended himself.

"Forfeit!" Michael cried, earning for himself another of Laura's dark looks.

Kenneth went to reach for his forfeits bag, but Genevieve stopped him by saying, "That can wait until we are returned to the inn. For now let us solve the clue."

"All right," Kenneth agreed, stuffing the bag back into his inner pocket.

Genevieve reached between Haddy and Laura, taking the map, which she presented to Xavier. He looked at her questioningly.

"It is your and Summer's turn. I think you should have a chance at the map as well."

"Thank you," he said, suddenly wishing all these people were gone, all but one. There was something stirring deep in her eyes, something deep and unfathomable. Her features seemed faintly sad, making the light in her eyes something that demanded inquiry, that made him want to dash the map to the ground and seize up her hands and demand that she speak to the matter. A friend would, a true friend. But he was no longer that, not when he found himself thinking that a kiss might tell him even more than would her words.

He took the map with numb fingers. Summer came to his side, that girl's face placed close to his shoulder as she peered down at the printed cloth, and he wished with an intensity that almost frightened him that she was not his partner, that he could have chosen who his partner might be, hang the consequences.

He pointed randomly at a town north of Nantwich.

Summer made a small, elegant movement with her shoulders that suggested she had no alternate opinion, so he peered more closely at the old, tiny, cribbed writing and asked Kenneth, "Would it be Chester?"

"So it is."

"Huzzah!" Summer cried. Michael gave his betrothed a quick glance, a sideways smile forming on his lips just as he turned to Genevieve and lifted an eyebrow that spoke volumes.

"I am sorry. I have no token to give you. I shall fetch one when we are returned to the inn," Kenneth said, patting his pockets idly, as if he could conjure one that way.

"Come, my dear, walk with me in the dark," Michael said, offering his arm to his betrothed. He did not relinquish the lantern he held, so his invitation was not quite literal.

"Delighted," she replied, accepting the arm.

Genevieve could not be sure, but she thought perhaps Summer made a point of not looking in her direction.

Laura went after them, apparently disdaining an offer from Haddy, should one have been forthcoming. He, in his turn, gathered up the other lantern and walked sedately behind the three ahead of him. When Genevieve glanced about, she realized that Kenneth and Penelope had already stepped away, the woman's hand on the man's arm as they walked to the right in the far shadows that were not quite touched by the lanterns' glow.

"Shall we?" Xavier said at her side, and she saw that he had offered her his arm. She took it, but her touch was diffident. He felt that estrangement, and his stomach sank into his boots.

They walked in silence, falling behind the others, who seemed eager to return to the inn now that their sport was done. Genevieve could think of nothing to say, nothing that would not be a demand to know the depth of his feelings for Summer.

At length she grew embarrassed for herself, so incapable of light conversation, and looked up to see Xavier's profile. He was staring ahead, his attention focused outward. "What is it?" she asked at that alert posture, turning her own head to see what it was that held his attention so raptly.

"Nelly. And Kenneth," he replied, inclining his head to indicate their direction. "They are not returning to the inn."

She saw that it was so, that the two forms had melded into one dark shadow, that they did not move parallel to the rest of the party. Even as she watched, they slipped between two buildings, lost in the dense darkness there.

"I must go after them. Something is wrong here."

"I will go as well." At the quick shake of his head, she added, "You cannot leave me in the dark, alone."

His jaw tightened, but then he nodded. "I cannot. Perhaps I should take you to the inn first?"

She answered him by moving toward the darkness between the two structures.

He stepped at once to her side, offering his arm anew, which she accepted. "Be careful," he said, "the paths are uneven."

She warmed at his solicitous words, even if they were nothing more than he would offer any female.

They emerged onto a narrow, dark street, which appeared to be entirely empty of life. "Where could they have gone?" he said in a low voice. "Why did I not bring a lantern?" He pointed to his left. "Let us go this way."

The street remained as still as when they first stepped onto it, despite the fact that they patrolled up one side and returned down the other.

"It is pointless. We have lost them," he said, standing in the center of the street, gazing up and down the silent road. "There are dozens of side streets they might have taken."

A faint light came from above them. " 'Oo's there?" a tremulous voice called. " 'Ooever ye are, get ye gone, or I'll set the Watch after ye, I will."

"Come along," Xavier said to Genevieve, taking her arm. "There is no point in staying here."

"Kenneth would not harm her, you know that," Genevieve said as he led her forward.

"I know he would not."

"They just went for a stroll."

" 'Tis a strange time and place for a stroll, without so much as a candle to guide them," he said tightly.

She slowed her steps, coming to a halt to gaze up at him, his face darkly shadowed despite the three-quarters moon in the cloudless sky above them. "You must realize it is possible he is trying to persuade her to defy your father. I think Kenneth is still very much in love with Penelope."

He stared down at her, unblinking, until finally the set of his shoulders eased and he sighed, "I think so, too."

"Do you think she loves him as well?"

"I am afraid so. I do not know. Sometimes. . . ."

"Yes, sometimes I think so, too. She has been so very cool to him, but then she blushes like a young girl the next moment. It all makes sense if you think they are trying to hide their truer feelings. It is really very sad."

"They are playing with fire. Father has already said he will not allow it."

Her head tilted a little to one side. "Perhaps this is their last summer, too, Xavier. Perhaps they are saying good-bye."

He stared down at her again, until finally he nodded. "I think you must be right." His voice went even lower. "But 'tis dangerous stuff—this being together when you know you must eventually part."

Her heart leaped into her throat, only to slide down into her stomach, where it sat and ached so that she wished to curl around it. He meant himself, and Summer, of course.

"Oh, Xavier," she breathed, her voice cracking, because she could not just stand there, so close to him, not without saying something, and the words that came, came from her heart. "Do you love her so very much then?"

He fell very still. "Her?" he echoed blankly.

She gasped and swallowed and forced back tears. "Summer. I know you must love her. I have watched you. I . . . I"—her voice wavered, then steadied as she rushed on—"I think you must not let . . . let Michael stand between you. I am not convinced that his heart is truly engaged. I know you have so much to offer Summer. It is probably for the best. She even said it would work out for the best. I . . . I wish you . . . I hope you know every happiness, and—" she cut herself off abruptly, bringing the heels of her hands to press against her mouth and physically hold back the sob that teetered there.

"Genevieve," he whispered. She could hear that he was stunned.

"Oh!" she gasped, unable any longer to hold back her tears. As they fell, she lowered her hands and gathered up her skirts, backing away from him blindly. She turned and ran, running for a light in the distance, only dimly aware enough to hope that she was running toward the inn.

He watched her go, unable to move, but thankful she was moving in the right direction. He ought to go after her, to be sure she arrived safely. Yes, he would. He would, as soon as his mind stopped spinning, and as soon as he could breathe again.

She thought he loved *Summer!* Oh, how easy it was to see why she would think it. It was all crystal clear in a moment's time. He had ever had a tender manner with Summer, knowing she was the sort who wished, if did not need, to be protected. His own code could allow nothing less than that she be assisted as she demanded, however gently.

But that was not what was most astonishing, as much as it had surprised him to find Genevieve took it to mean something more. No, what kept him rooted now, unable to move for the shock of it, was that having admitted what she thought she knew to be the truth—she had shed tears. She had cried to think that his heart was engaged elsewhere. Genevieve had been brought to tears by the thought that he, this scarred, tortured wreck that he was, might have given his love to another.

He could not believe it, could scarce perceive what it

meant. For a moment he felt as though his entire body was filled with quicksilver, that he must surely glow as he stood in the center of the dark and deserted street.

Then another thought struck him: perhaps she cried for Michael. Perhaps she thought she was witnessing the end of Summer and Michael's betrothal.

The quicksilver turned to lead in his veins, and he shook his head, even more afraid to believe this. Yet, it could be. It probably was. He was, no doubt, the biggest fool alive to have even thought for a moment that her tears had been shed for herself, for some secret affection that she might have felt for him, for the one-eyed beast.

And yet . . . She had said that she did not believe Michael's affections were truly engaged. A subterfuge? But why? Better to say nothing, if she truly hoped that things would stand as they were, if she wished to support her brother's interests. No, the only reason she had to speak of such matters at all was to discover something for herself. But what?

The depths of his own feelings for Summer, of course.

Only she had not allowed him to speak to that at all. She had rushed through her own words, and ran away when words failed her. She had learned nothing. No, all she had done was to speak to her own feelings, her own thoughts. And she had cried, unable not to, though he had seen her struggle to overcome the reaction.

Why the tears? Why the sadness that had rested in her eyes all evening?

He began to move, at first slowly, but then his stride increased, as though to match his tumbling thoughts. In a minute he was running, running the way he had last seen Genevieve go.

He burst into the inn, drawing the attention of all to himself. There sat Penelope and Kenneth, both staring blankly, too innocently, but his eyes passed over them, searching for one face in particular. She was not there.

He bounded for the stairs, leaving the door wide open behind him, taking the steps three at a time. He ran down the short hall, his bootheels stomping, and slid to a stop before her door. He could hear someone crying within, and knew she had returned. He raised his hand, prepared to pound the door from its hinges until she came to him, talked to him, explained it all to him—but then his arm froze. He backed away from the door, colliding with the opposite wall, where he stood still, breathing heavily.

What would he say? And even if he knew the words, what right did he have to say them? What did he really know?

No. He could not bear it if he was wrong. He could not open himself up to that hurt, the possibility that he was so very mistaken. He did not dare, not unless he was so much more sure that he would not be offending her, or inviting her scorn.

He pressed against the wall, using its solid surface to lever himself back to a more or less steady stance. He weaved his way down the hall to his own door and opened it quietly, and then shut it carefully behind him.

Inside, he sat upon the bed, his head in his hands. He felt close to tears himself. He had not been looking forward to sharing a room for the night with anyone other than Haddy, because of the damned eyepatch, as always, yet now that seemed an insignificant concern. After all, he had done it a thousand times before at school. What was a minor humiliation should his patch slip in the night? What was such a thing weighed against the confusion that now seized him? If only he knew what her tears meant! How could he know? How could he dare to hope . . . ?

He lay back on the bed, his arms flung wide, his good eye staring upward sightlessly, his heart pounding. It was a wide bed, intended for more than one occupant. It seemed to stretch on far beyond the boundaries of his own body, his own needs. Just as did his life, his future.

Then it struck him, a revelation of such sharp clarity he gasped aloud: what was more important, truly, a future that was as it had ever been, or a chance to expand it, to fill it, to share it? Was it better to protect himself from harm, or better to dare, to make an effort toward happiness?

His hands curled into fists, as he allowed his vision to rove the room as though to find and pin down an elusive truth, a truth that was in actuality already there before him: would her rejection be any more painful than the wounds he already carried? And, should the attempt fail, would not at least knowing, of seeing at last that every dream was wasted and must never again be pursued, at least numb some of the pain of such an ending?

How could he hope to gain her love if he never offered his own?

He sat up again slowly, straight, his spine stiffened, and held his head up. No. Retreat was no longer an option. The time had come to refuse to fear the pain. The time had come when he had to risk it all, when he could no longer hide behind an ancient scar.

He made a silent vow. He swore that even if it killed

every last human instinct in him, he would finally dare the impossible: he would allow himself to attempt to woo the girl, to see if her tears meant what he so desperately hoped they meant. He would court her, and then ask her to accept him as he was, would insist that she take him without first seeing beneath the eyepatch, without satisfying a natural curiosity. He would ask it of her so that he might know whether such a love as he dared to believe in could exist or not. He knew it was wrong to demand anything of her, but it was the test, the only thing that would show that he himself, the man, not the title, or the wealth, or even the eyepatch that he knew sometimes created a sense of intrigue in the feminine heart, had indeed won her love.

There was no going back, not now that he had seen some unexplained sadness hiding in those dark brown eyes, some deep secret that called him inexorably to discover its meaning—no, no going back, not even understanding that the need to examine that secret imperiled his very soul.

Chapter 17

She never told her love,
But let concealment, like a worm i' the bud,
Feed on her damask cheek: she pin'd in thought;
And with a green and yellow melancholy,
She sat like a patience on a monument,
Smiling at grief.
                    —Shakespeare, *Twelfth Night*

Genevieve did not come down for breakfast. She would have liked to have seen Laura and Haddy fulfill their forfeit from last night—they were to give a penny to everyone, from the grandest guest down to a stableboy, that they came into contact with for an hour, a considerable and annoying task at a busy inn such as this—but she could not bring herself to rise from the bed and dress to go down. It was not until all the other ladies had gone down to find their morning meal that she forced herself to rise and wash and dress for the day. Then she stood at the window, gazing down at the courtyard below and the morning bustle there, letting the morning breezes wash over her, wishing they could cool her thoughts as well as they cooled her skin.

A knock on the door set her heart to racing as a voice announced it was time for the cases to be taken down. She opened the door with downcast eyes, which saw in a quick glance that a pair of less than perfectly polished pumps waited without. She dared to raise her eyes then, for this revealed that it was not Xavier, but rather a postboy that had come for the bags this time. After she admitted him and indicated the baggage, she stepped back to the window, once again watching the activity below, her arms crossed before her although she was not chilled.

Just as the postboy left with the last of the bags, Summer returned and helped Genevieve look about the room to see if they had left behind any ribbons or other small items that could be tucked into their reticules. None were found, but instead of moving from the room, Summer sat down on the bed, patting the space beside her.

"Come, sit, Genevieve. Tell me," she went on as the dark-haired girl sat, "are you not feeling well today?" She reached to touch Genevieve's forehead.

"I feel fine."

"But you had no breakfast," Summer said as her hand dropped, having found no fever.

"I was not hungry."

"Ah," Summer said, and frowned.

"It is the travel, I suppose."

"Oh, yes," Summer said, too polite to argue as always, although there was an undertone of doubt in her voice. She slid off the bed. "Let us be on our way.

Kenneth says that Chester is about fifty-five miles from here, and we must doubt that we shall make it such a distance all in one day, even though he says we will not take near so long a break for luncheon today."

"And hope there shall be no field fires."

"And hope there shall be good roads." Summer tucked her friend's arm through her own and led her down to the waiting carriage.

Xavier was there, handing the other ladies into the carriage. Genevieve could not be sure, but she thought for a moment that his hand hesitated before it reached out to offer her assistance. She took the offered hand, touching it with just the ends of her fingers, for as brief a time as she might, and turned at once to Penelope to utter some inane thing about the weather once she was inside the carriage. She did not watch as Xavier handed Summer up, although she did raise her eyes in surprise when Kenneth entered the carriage as well, finding a seat next to Laura, forcing his sister and Summer to be rather crowded next to him.

The day promised to be cooler, so that they were content to leave the windows closed and thereby keep out some of the dust as the vehicle lumbered along. Summer revealed to the occupants that she and Xavier had earned an ace of clubs—to signify the supposed club that a giant such as Leon Gawer might have possessed—for their token last night. Laura denounced the comfort level of the inn, and Kenneth chimed in about the inferiority of the morning meal, although it was agreed that last night's dinner had been adequate. He then went on to tease Laura about having her breakfast interrupted every other minute as she and Haddy were forced by the forfeit to rise and seek out someone to give them a penny. Laura sniffed and colored, and told them of the elderly gentleman who had obviously thought her quite daft and had threatened her with his cane.

Genevieve found she could not contribute to the dialogue, so she closed her eyes and pretended to sleep. It was not until they had traveled for over an hour that it occurred to her that perhaps Kenneth had chosen to ride within the carriage, that he, too, after last night's disappearance, might wish to avoid Xavier's company.

The miles passed, and luncheon was a simple affair at the side of the road, taking no more than twenty minutes. The ladies sat to one side, the men to the other, and conversation was decidedly scarce. Kenneth murmured something about wishing to arrive at Brockmore as soon as time would allow, and this created assenting murmurs from the group at large, who as if by tacit agreement, all rose, packed the remains of the meal, and crawled back into or on top of the carriages.

They had ridden for over eight hours when Haddy called a halt again to suggest that Chester was only an hour or so away, and as it was not yet dark, would the ladies mind if they traveled on? No one protested with any vehemence, so that the drive was resumed.

Genevieve laid back into the squabs, eyes half closed, listening idly to whatever bits of conversation came along. Her eyes opened more fully, however, when she realized that Kenneth was speaking of Xavier.

"Nelly," he was saying, "do tell us how Xavier came to arrive at that scar and the loss of his eye. I have never heard the story, you realize. I believe I was only about four when it happened."

240

"Oh, he never really says," Penelope said.

"I know that. That is why I am asking."

"'Tis a matter of honor, you see," Penelope said with reticence.

Genevieve looked to her, and found Penelope's eyes had flickered up to find Summer's face.

"What is a matter of honor?"

"Not revealing what happened."

"But why?"

"Really, Kenneth," Penelope said, retreating behind formality, "if you wish to know, you must ask Xavier."

"But he will not say!"

"That is his choice."

The carriage's interior fell silent, a silence Genevieve believed she understood, even though she knew no more than Kenneth: Penelope did not care to say in front of Summer, did not wish to taint her brother's image in any way before the woman he loved.

Her mouth set grimly at the thought that Penelope had noticed the growing attraction as well.

Conversation became general again as Genevieve stared out the window at the gently rolling fields that flourished on the alluvial plains before her.

A nighttime fog greeted them as they rolled into the city, reminding them they were no more than about six miles from the Rivers Dee and Mersey, and the Irish Sea was not so very far to the north. It brought with it a dampness that tended to chill, so that the ladies reached for their shawls, and some of them wished they had a pelisse at hand.

The inn was large and gracious, causing Kenneth to frown where he sat across from Genevieve. He would be thinking of his slim purse, of course, which would be slimmer yet after this night.

"Ought we to attempt to find another inn?" she suggested, only to Laura rather than Kenneth.

"Certainly not!" Laura cried. "I wish to be out of this conveyance at the earliest possible moment."

Genevieve sighed to herself, but did not pursue the matter, as she had no reason but the true one to justify searching for another inn. Haddy returned at that moment, opening the door to offer a hand down, putting a period to any discussion of the matter anyway.

As they moved toward their rooms, Michael complained about having had no company, riding alone atop the first carriage all day while Kenneth sat within, and Haddy and Xavier had brought up the rear. He insisted that everyone join him in a parlor he had bespoken for supper. Laura nodded approval of this plan, as did Summer, so it was agreed to by all.

Dinner was slow in arriving, leaving a group of people alone who had little to say to one another. Only Haddy waxed eloquent, going on about the various hunting that was available in this county.

Michael seemed restless, sitting then standing, moving to a window, then back to his seat. When he ceased pacing to stand staring out at the fog through one of the two bay windows of the parlor, Genevieve moved to his side. She spoke quietly, that her voice not carry beyond their immediate circle. "What is it, Michael?"

"Ennui, quite simply," he said.

"Yes, everyone wishes we were already at Brockmore. It fair makes me shudder to think of the return journey to London. But, of course, that will not be until after we have rested for a week or better at Kenneth's estate." He nodded, his hands thrust deep in his pockets as he continued to glower out the window, as she prodded herself into continuing, "Michael?"

"Hmm?"

"What did you mean when you told me there was more to Summer than met the eye? And that look you gave me last night, when she said 'huzzah!' what did that mean?"

"Again I say, 'tis quite simple: my look meant 'see, I told you so.' 'Huzzah' indeed. *You* would not say such a thing, and yet Summer dared it. She is all that is delicate and sweet and charming and good, but she is more than those things as well."

"Do you mean you do not care for her character?"

"Oh no, that is to say, I like her character very well. I am just saying that she is also intractable, stubborn, and determined to have her way."

Genevieve stared at him, almost smiling. "She said the same of you."

"Did she?" He turned to face her, surprise on his face. "Well, I'll be dammed, though I cannot claim I am shocked to learn it." He rocked on his heels, then uttered a short laugh, and shook his head.

"Do you love her, Michael?" She reached up one hand, touching his sleeve.

"Quite."

"I mean, truthfully. Do you really love her? I . . . I do not believe I have ever heard you speak in such terms."

"But a gentleman does not," he said, drawing one hand from his pocket to tweak her nose. "Not to his sister."

She grabbed his hand. " 'Tis important, for her, Michael, to know."

His eyebrows danced once, his hazel eyes almost serious. "Ah, you two have been talking, I see. No, not another word, Sister dear. You are quite right to think that moment of confrontation is approaching. Know that I am aware of it. But it is not for now. Brockmore, I think. That would be logical. Bide your time, as I must bide mine."

When she parted her lips, he held up a warning finger, halting her, and turned to the room at large, speaking loudly. "Let us dance! We have the room, we have the music-maker"—he signaled Haddy, who nodded—"and we have the time, if not the energy. Something slow, maestro?"

Haddy nodded again, extracting the piccolo from his inner pocket, which he blew upon several times until he was satisfied and began to play in earnest.

Michael turned to Genevieve and told her, "I do not care to dance with either you or Summer." He walked away, leaving her face stained a frustrated pink, and seized up Penelope's elbow. They swung into the dance at once, as Xavier turned to Laura, who was beside him, and Kenneth to Summer. Genevieve stood alone, stepping back into the curtains at the window, turning her head away from the dancers. She stared at the blackness, ignoring her own reflection to peer into the night, more than a little angry with her brother's smug dismissal, acutely aware that Xavier held Laura's hands in his own, and feeling the fool for being resentful of such a familiarity.

The music changed, and a hand touched her elbow,

causing her to jump. She spun to find Xavier there. Laura was no longer at his side.

"A dance, my lady?" he asked, offering the hand that had touched her.

"I am rather weary," she said, shaking her head ever so slightly. At least it was the truth.

"One dance."

She almost shrank back into the curtains, to physically hide behind them, but from somewhere came the sense to stop acting so missishly. "As you please," she said, taking his hand. She noticed then that the music suggested a waltz, and that Kenneth held Penelope in his arms and that the pair were the only other couple now dancing.

She pulled back a little, but Xavier did not release her, instead turning around and placing his other hand at her waist. Reluctantly she brought her hand up to lie along his arm, her fingers nearly touching his shoulder, as the dance demanded. In a moment they were moving. She stared over his shoulder, getting flashes of the sight of her brother, Laura, and Summer where they sat to one side, sipping wine and talking quietly.

"Genevieve," he said, his voice very quiet, a deep rumble in his chest, which was far too near to her own.

"Yes?" She glanced up briefly, meeting his gray gaze, then looking away again.

"Will you be my partner?"

"What?" She stumbled in his arms, coming against his arm. It did not waver, holding her upright as she found the tempo once more.

"Will you trade partners, so that Summer might be Michael's?"

"Oh." For a moment she could not think what to say, and struggled against the confusion that filled her. She looked up at him then, searching his face. "Do you truly wish to do that?"

"I do." He smiled.

A smile? What did that calm, coaxing smile mean?

"I do not see how we might. You and Summer have one more token than Michael and I."

"I would be happy enough to surrender the extra token to Summer."

"But why?" she burst out, her hand tightening along his arm.

"They need to be together more, do you not think? We have already seen that absence does not make Michael's heart grow fonder, so perhaps immediacy will. He is ever pleased when she solves a clue, you have seen that for yourself."

"Yes," she said slowly, seeing that smile still, the steady gaze from his good eye, the calmness of his features. For a moment she said nothing as they danced past her brother, and her gaze fell. As they danced away from the subject of their conversation, she whispered toward his second button, "Do you mean to worsen the situation there?"

"Not at all."

She did not look up, frowning at his button, for he did not sound offended. "For I fear that scheme will work in the reverse of what you wish. I fear that if Michael and Summer are much in each other's company, that sooner than later a decision will be reached. And it might not be to your liking," she whispered urgently.

He said nothing, merely pulling her along in the form of the dance.

"Xavier," she said from between clenched teeth, her eyelids once again rapidly fluttering to force back tears, "if you love her, you must be most direct about it."

Still he did not answer. She dared to lift her eyes, for the briefest moment, to glance at his face, which she found to be still very calm, though now there was a softness there. Perhaps his hand tightened at her waist. Perhaps he pulled her just the tiniest bit closer.

"Genny," he said.

"What?"

"Genny, look at me." His low voice had grown thick. She looked up, unable to resist the pull of that voice.

"Genevieve Leatrice Cadby, I do *not* love Summer."

Perhaps the music ceased, perhaps she no longer danced. She could not say, for all she knew was his face before hers, peering down at her, demanding that she believe him.

"No?" she heard her unsteady voice ask.

"No."

"What's all this then?" a voice asked at her elbow. She slowly turned her head, and equally slowly became aware that it was Michael who spoke.

Xavier's hands fell away from her, and she realized she had not only ceased to dance, but also to breathe. She began again suddenly, with a little gasping sound.

"You two have quite forgotten your steps," Michael went on. "Here is the proof then that it grows late and 'tis time for slumber. We are too forgetful by half."

There were sounds of agreement all around them. Genevieve felt Summer slip an arm through hers. She stared at the girl for a moment, as though she had never seen her before, her senses returning to her slowly, as though she were just waking from a dream.

"Good night," a deep, familiar voice said above her. She looked up at Xavier once more. He gazed down at her unblinkingly, and she suddenly wished nothing quite so much as to reach up and touch his face, just to see what his reaction would be to such a caress, just to see if his mouth would turn into her palm as she suddenly, fiercely wished it might.

"Good night," she said automatically, and then, too soon, far too soon for comprehension, Summer pulled her away toward the stairs.

She undressed silently, and crawled into the bed next to Summer, who was not inclined to chat either, leaving Genevieve, gratefully, in peace. The other girl was soon fast asleep, but Genevieve lay awake as her faculties began one by one to function again. Xavier had said that he did not love Summer. There was something in the way he had said it that made her want to believe it, made her want to conclude that he had *never* loved the girl.

Or was he just being noble? It would be very like him. He would see that he must not interfere in Summer's happiness, and he would step away, would extinguish his own longings. . . . But, then, why tell *her?*

There had been something else in the way he spoke also, something of warmth and encouragement—or was she mistaken about that as well? Was she wishing for and hearing things that were not there?

She did not know. It was impossible to say. Yet she lay in bed, unable to sleep, feeling a tingle that started in her toes and crept up her body to the very top of her head, only to trace back down again, leaving her breathless and trembling and eager for the morning's light, for there was a muddled hope in her mind that morning would make it all seem clear.

Chapter 18

Not all that tempts our wand'ring eyes
And heedless hearts, is lawful prize;
Nor all, that glistens, gold.
                    —Thomas Gray,
        "Ode on the Death of a Favourite Cat"

"Do you agree?" Xavier asked, the morning sun creating a gleaming line along his beaver hat.

Michael's shoulders moved under his jacket and he pulled a face. "Don't know if I care to."

"Michael!" Genevieve scolded, her heart rising and falling in her breast repeatedly. One moment she was filled with the desire that her brother would answer that she was now to be Xavier's partner, the next she recoiled from the idea.

Instead of clarifying anything for her, the morning had brought severe doubts that she had interpreted anything correctly last night, and doubts had brought a terrible reticence into her manner. Reticence had tied her tongue and locked her eyes to the floor, so that now she could not even meet Xavier's gaze. He had told her that he did not love the girl, yet she had seen them together, folded into one another under that blanket, and it had stung to see how well they had looked together, how solicitous of Summer he was. Yet . . . he had denied it meant love. Denied it, and she had looked in his eyes, and for those moments had believed it.

Summer interjected, "Please, Michael, it would be such sport. After all, we are betrothed, and you yourself said you did not wish to be partner to your sister."

"That was before we ever started. Now it is too late. 'Tis unfair."

"I have said Summer, and yourself, may have the extra token," Xavier repeated patiently.

"But that is not right, is it?" Michael argued. "You earned the token as a team, and ought to keep it as a team, that you might win the wager. It makes no never mind to me to fund a prize for the winning couple, but there are others who would feel the pinch dearly enough, and would argue the unfairness of a change such as you propose. No, I think things must remain as they are."

Genevieve heard a small sniff to her side, and lifted her eyes long enough to see that tears were turning Summer's brown eyes into dark pools. The tears spilled over, running down Summer's cheeks.

"Oh, Michael," Genevieve breathed, gathering up her friend's arm, alarmed by the tears, and further alarmed to find that she was faintly pleased to see them, to allow them to perhaps mean that if Xavier loved, he loved alone. Her dual responses confused her, so in her confusion she berated her brother, "Only see what you have done!"

Michael eyed his betrothed dispassionately, and said dryly, "What's fair is fair. No use turning into a watering pot over it."

Summer raised a handkerchief to her mouth, attempting to stifle the small sounds she made.

"Come, old man," Xavier said, frowning. " 'Tis merely a game. No point in upsetting the lady, is there?"

Genevieve stiffened, new doubts threatening to reach like tendrils into her mind. Last night she had been so sure, so shocked by the sincerity of his denial, but last night seemed very far away, and increasingly uncertain to her in the morning light.

Her thoughts were interrupted when Michael said sharply, " 'Tis a ruse."

"Michael!" Summer said on a sob.

" 'Tis, I tell you. Listen and hear the truth, for it has become quite clear to me that none of you know it! Summer set her cap at me the day she left the schoolroom. She believes she may snap her fingers and that every gentleman must come running, and I did, just as a good puppy ought. I even was so under her spell I asked her to marry me, did I not? Yes, but now I have seen it so very clearly. I have been made to play the game she set into place. We are very alike, we two, and I can see exactly what she has done. Well, that is the end of her manipulations! I shan't be told what and when and how I may behave. I shan't be made to dance to her tune by the mere existence of a few tears. I shan't, I tell you. Summer, I will *not* be your partner, not for the purposes of this treasure hunt. That is final." He crossed his arms over his chest, staring defiantly at the girl.

The girl gave two more terrible sobs, then drew herself up. "Very well, Michael. I release you. You are under no obligation to me any longer. I wish I could say I wish you well for the future, but the truth is"—she sobbed once more, then cut off the sound ruthlessly, and finished—"the truth is, I hope you rot in Hades!"

She turned, gathering up her skirts in one hand, the other pressing the kerchief to her mouth, and ran back into the inn.

Genevieve watched her until she disappeared, then turned with large, incensed eyes to face her brother. "Michael!" she hissed harshly.

But instead of looking abashed, or even mildly repentant, he was grinning from ear to ear. He reached down to tweak his sister's nose. "I thought that would not happen until Brockmore," he told her.

"You were expecting that . . . that scene?" she cried.

"Or something very like it. Genny, I know you think me mad, but I am not. You just do not truly understand Summer. You have to see that she has been catered to all her life, and little surprise that, with her sweet, mild ways. But underneath her sweetness there is an iron will, my girl. She is used to absolute obedience from her devotees, her brother, her younger sister, and of course the servants. She is, in fact, quite spoiled. I only thank God I saw it before we married. Only ask Haddy, here. Haddy, is Summer spoiled?"

Haddy did not hesitate, saying, "Terribly, I am afraid."

"See?" Michael beamed.

Genevieve snuck a glance at Xavier, finding he looked on with a faint frown. A slow throbbing ache began in her chest, one that told her clearly that if Xavier had been noble and let the lady go to her love, the noble act had been set aside by this latest turn of events. Summer had just become untethered, free, accessible.

"But at heart a very loving creature," Haddy went on. "After all, she did set her cap at you quite because she fancies you so much. She always said she would have a love match."

"Quite."

"But you realize I cannot allow you to have led her on this way. Even if she did release you of her own accord, I am afraid the Dillonsby name has been besmirched."

"Oh, of course," Michael agreed, waving a hand in the air. "Honor must be met, and all that. But as dueling is illegal"—Haddy grunted a resigned acknowledgment of that fact—"I think perhaps I have a better thought."

"Say on."

"I will marry the girl after all."

Xavier cocked his head to one side, shifting his weight from one foot to the other as he listened, and the slow ache in Genevieve's chest grew to a pounding pain.

Haddy hesitated, frowning quickly, then his brow cleared. "Daresay that would do the trick. Though Summer will put her heels down and refuse to have you back, I have no doubt. Ah well, when we have returned to London, I shall see if perhaps her old nanny might be able to convince her of the wisdom of continuing such an attachment."

"You will do no such thing! Adle-pated nodcock! No

one will ever convince Summer unless Summer wishes to be convinced."

Haddy shifted his weight from one foot to the other, much as Xavier had done. " 'Fraid that may be true," he conceded. "What then?"

"I shall have to convince her myself, as I am the only one she wishes to persuade her," Michael said complacently.

Genevieve stared from one gentleman to the other, not sure whose announcements startled her more, not sure if everything had changed or stayed the same. She cried, "How shall you ever do that, Michael? It is quite clear you have mortally offended her, and without doubt broken her heart. She would rather marry . . . anyone but you!" Genevieve said, bitter disappointment in her voice.

"Not a bit of it! Do you not see? Now that it is quite clear, to both of us, that I shall be my own master, I am quite free to pursue this arrangement. She has wanted me to pursue her for the longest time. She shall come around, make no mistake, though she will lead me a merry dance before she succumbs and owns to it."

Genevieve's mind spun at his audacity, at the shifting of her hopes and fears, and the true ring of logic that sounded through with his confident words, and she cried the first thought that came to the fore, the thought that was of paramount importance to her as of late, "But you do not love her!"

He turned to her, his expression as surprised as it had been yesterday. "Of course I do. Utterly! Who would tolerate such a little beast if not for the love of her?"

"True, true," Haddy muttered.

"Michael," Genevieve cried, struggling to understand, refusing to look toward Xavier. "I do not comprehend—"

"I can see you do not. That is because you are one thing Summer is not: generous. You give of yourself, not caring if you get back. You cannot understand that she wants something so very much—namely myself—that she has tried every trick to get me. She adores me, no doubt because I adore her as well. It has been dashed difficult, you know, playing the part of the callow, heartless, uncaring youth. And shame on you, Genny Cadby, for believing it of me! Oh, I am every bit as spoiled as she, but not callow, even you must own to that. But you see, I *had* to tell her I was not to be had, not under the terms she dictated." He laughed then, shaking his head and smiling widely. "Who knows, perhaps this is her cleverest trick to date? Perhaps I am still being manipulated by the little minx. But I shan't mind. 'Tis time to look forward to the chase."

"But what if you are wrong? Terribly wrong?" she asked, her hand at her forehead.

He laughed again, and Haddy nodded beside him. "I am not wrong. You will see for yourself, Puss, when I win her back." He stepped around his sister, heading for the inn, whistling a carefree tune as he resettled his hat at a jaunty angle.

Kenneth and Penelope exchanged mystified glances.

"Has he gone mad?" Genevieve asked blankly, her hand falling to her side.

"No. But thank goodness the two of them will finally be getting on with things," Haddy said. He paused, cocking his head to one side, and added, "Although, she may well make him play the pretty for quite some while yet. Just to prove she has as much pluck as he."

"I think that point has already been well proven," Xavier said. Genevieve spun, turning to look up at the dry tone with wide, uncertain eyes. She met his amused look, and did not know what to make of the fact he smiled after the retreating Michael.

"What a curious courtship!" she cried, just to cover the fact that she could not quite remove her gaze from his, and then could have bitten off her tongue for the words.

"Not the first in this group," he answered quietly.

Her heart flipped, and she shook her head ever so slightly, utterly bewildered. She parted her lips to speak, to ask some outrageous question about his feelings—and could only regret that Kenneth stepped forward, interrupting the moment before she could quite bring the words to her lips.

Kenneth held up a blue sheet of paper. "I see no need to wait upon Summer and Michael to read the next clue, as it is Penelope's turn, and we must get on with collecting the next token. Preferably soon," he said, casting a dubious glance toward the inn.

Penelope took the paper and said, "We may have to abandon Michael. It is difficult to believe Summer would wish to travel in any wise near the man."

"I think you are wrong there," Xavier said to his sister, turning at last from the steady gaze that had been locked with Genevieve's, his one gray eye filled with a cross between gravity and amusement.

"We shall see soon enough."

"You think they are in love, despite all their words,

their . . . confrontations?" Genevieve asked Xavier, her voice low and uncertain.

"The clue," Kenneth prompted Penelope.

"I believe it entirely," Xavier said, seemingly without regret.

She shivered again, and something in her broke loose and refused to dwell any longer in uncertainty. She could believe that whatever his feelings for Summer were, or had been, he had put them away, forever. If there had been anything, it was now only dust, never to be resurrected. She ought to grieve for him, for the loss of a dream, or a hope, but there was a new ringing in her ears, a sound very like song, and she found it took all her concentration not to break out in a silly grin as she closed her eyes and felt something very like a sigh move through her.

> " 'Four miles northeast of Chester am I.
> The remains of Price, where I did die,' "

Penelope read, then shook her head. "It is too easy, Kenneth. You have given me his name, and everyone knows James Price was hung and that his bones remain still on Trafford Heath."

He took the paper from her fingers just long enough to turn it over, and said, "Read the back."

"Michael was right. You *do* change the rules. Though it is your own forfeit you risk by doing so."

"Just read it."

"It says, 'You must name James Price's crime exactly and must recite the poem his remains have inspired.' " She lifted dancing eyes, and cried, "I have not been

258

caught out, dear Kenneth, and so you are saved, for I have heard the words from your very lips. James Price robbed the Warrington Mail, and was hung on the Heath for his crime. Years since, in his skull has been found a robin's nest, and I am afraid a chant grew from that unfortunate occurrence."

"But how does it go?" Laura challenged, stepping forward, glancing at her brother to warn him he would not escape his forfeit unless the entire clue was solved as stated.

But Penelope knew it, for she said at once, " 'Oh! James Price deserved his fate, Naught but Robbing in his pate.' "

Genevieve opened her eyes at last, finding that all were staring at Penelope, although she could not say why; she was lost to her own thoughts, thoughts that only allowed her to see that Xavier was also looking at his sister, smiling slightly.

At the stares, Penelope defended herself, "I did not compose it, I only repeated it."

"Not fair! Kenneth has been providing her with the answers. Is that why you two went off alone last night?" Laura challenged.

Penelope flushed a dark red, and Kenneth reached to straighten his cravat. "I should say not! We misstepped, is all. It was dark," he said.

Haddy offered a disbelieving snort.

"We were back very soon, once we found our way," Kenneth continued, then pointed at Xavier and Genevieve, the latter of who was suddenly drawn away from her own vaulting thoughts, forced once again to awareness of others around her. She blinked rapidly, struggling to recall what had last been said, and why her name had been mentioned.

"We were back before you two were," Kenneth accused.

"We were looking for you," Xavier said and almost smiled, visibly undisturbed by the accusation.

Genevieve felt several shades of pink creep up her face at Kenneth's insinuation, a fact that caused Penelope to fix her eyes briefly on the smaller woman as an awkward silence fell.

It was Penelope who ended it. "Water under the bridge," she said after a long moment. "And I have not cheated. I have merely paid attention sometimes when Kenneth spoke." She put an end to the discussion by suggesting, "Shall we be on our way to the Heath to find the token?"

"I shall notify Summer and Michael," Xavier offered, moving toward the inn.

The others did not climb to their respective seats, quite uncertain when and if either of the once-betrothed couple would be accompanying them. Genevieve waited with them, feeling detached, as though she might float away on the next breeze. She arranged her face to reflect a mild interest in her surroundings, but in truth she was once again lost to her own thoughts, thoughts not easily categorized. She only knew she felt a sense of keen relief, and something close to giddiness.

To everyone's surprise, Summer was accompanied from the inn by Xavier within three minutes, pulling on her gloves, her face as calm and sweet as ever despite the faint signs of recent tears. Behind them came Michael, carrying one of her hatboxes in one hand and the picnic basket in the other.

The ladies turned, wordless at the sight of Michael performing even such a minor task, and with rounded eyes lined up to be handed into the carriage as Michael placed his burdens in the second carriage.

Xavier lifted his hand, offering assistance into the carriage. Genevieve felt perhaps his fingers lingered just a little longer than truly necessary, but she could not actually swear that he pressed her fingers with his own before releasing them.

Summer was just about to be handed up when Michael called out, "Summer, do say you will ride atop the carriage with me. It promises to be a lovely day." He closed the door of the second carriage, and crossed the cobbles to stand near her.

"I am Lady Rose to you," Summer said in her quiet voice, now firm with resolve. "And, no, I shall not sit with you."

"You will. One day you will," Michael told her, grinning, moving to step around Xavier and offer her his hand.

She disdained it, reaching for Xavier's instead. "Whyever would I?" she asked as she settled in her seat, not bothering to look at the man.

"Because I love you. Adore you. Desire you. Need I go on?"

She sniffed, and said to Xavier, "Please close the door."

The door was duly closed. Michael stepped back, looking through the window at the woman who studiously ignored him.

"She will give you a very hard time of it," Xavier observed as he mounted the box and leaned down to present an arm up to his friend.

"Yes. She is quite determined to play hard to catch. Delightful, isn't it? I confess, I am the happiest man alive today," Michael answered with a contented sigh as he settled beside Xavier and gathered up the ribbons.

Inside the carriage, Summer was silent but Genevieve found her tongue and began to chat happily, unaware that when she turned to speak with Laura, Summer and Penelope exchanged a speaking glance with one another.

Chapter 19

As lines so loves oblique may well
Themselves in every angle greet
But ours so truly parallel,
Though infinite can never meet.
        —Andrew Marvell,
        "The Definition of Love"

"This was too bad of you, Kenneth," Penelope said sternly as she picked her steps, with the delicacy of distaste, away from the weather-bleached bones that were all that remained of James Price.

"Somehow it had seemed more clever, and less gruesome, when I thought of it at home. My apologies to everyone. It never struck me how disturbing such a sight might be."

"I know he was a thief," Summer said, "but it seems so cruel to leave him here this way." She walked at her brother's side, quite deliberately avoiding being anywhere near Michael.

"Cruel, yes, but perhaps necessary. It certainly tells

any footpad who passes by what the locals do to those who dare to rob a man, or the mails, in this county," Haddy said.

In her hand, Penelope carried a five of clubs playing card. Kenneth had explained that it had been twenty-three years since James Price was first set to swinging on the heath, and he had added the numbers two and three to arrive at five.

"And why a club?" his sister asked as they made their way back to the carriages.

"For the club a footpad often carries, you see."

When they had returned to the carriages, Penelope said, "It seems that there is another clue to be revealed, if we are to know our next destination."

Kenneth pursed his lips in thought as he drew out a piece of blue paper. "Let us see . . . whose turn is it? I confess I am a bit confused on the matter. It ought to be Genevieve and Michael, but . . . was there an exchange of partners?"

"Oh, yes!" Michael said eagerly, just as Summer said, "Indeed not!"

"Well, which is it?"

"As I recall, the last thing Lord Herland said on the matter was that he absolutely refused to be my partner," Summer said in her quiet voice.

"Hasty words," Michael acquiesced, breezily adding, "Now rescinded. But what do you say, Xavier, Genevieve? Are you still in mind to take a new partner?"

"I shall allow Genevieve to choose," Xavier said softly.

Genevieve felt a pins-and-needles shiver run up the nape of her neck at the steady gaze he turned upon her, and started to shake her head. The idea of extending the reasons for enforced social contact with Xavier now seemed extremely inviting, so inviting that she had to doubt her own eagerness. It suddenly seemed more than awkward, rather blatant, this exchange of partners, as though she opened a secret door into her innermost thoughts, allowing others, and perhaps even him, to see some of the crazy fluttering that ran through her at the idea. But before she could shake her head, she stopped herself. After all, there was more to be considered than just her own wishes. The purpose of agreeing to this journey had always been that Michael would learn to appreciate his fiancée, and that he and Summer would come together at last. The former had been accomplished, but now the latter seemed an even more unlikely goal. Would Summer have anything to do with Michael unless she was forced to it?

For a long moment Genevieve stared at her friend, at the buoyant angle at which she held her chin, at the dark eyes that shone in a kind of contrast to her denials, at the pretty face that showed no sign of alarm or discomfort, and she suddenly understood that Michael was surely not so very far from wrong. Summer was hardly distressed. Angry, oh yes, there was that in her eyes, as well as a deep, silent emotion that seemed rather like . . . well, like satisfaction, but certainly not any true distress.

Summer met her gaze, blinked calmly once, and waited as did all the others.

"My dear people . . . ," Kenneth prompted.

"Summer already has her three tokens in her reticule," Genevieve spoke slowly, not looking toward

Xavier. "No cards need exchange hands. I see no impediment to trading partners."

Silence met this pronouncement, as all waited for an outburst of some kind from Summer. It did not come.

"Summer?" Kenneth asked uncertainly.

"Summer wishes to be my partner," Michael said, moving to her side. "Is that not correct, love? You surely wish to play the game with your betrothed."

"Lady Rose to you. And you are no longer my betrothed. I released you, if you recall."

"I can correct that," he said, his hands in his pockets as he rocked on his heels, a grin on his face. "Lady Rose, will you marry me?"

"I certainly shall not."

"What if I take your hand?" He extracted his hands from his pockets and grabbed her hand, which she did not pull away.

"Lord Herland, I should like my hand back."

"What if I go down on one knee?" He promptly dropped one knee to the dirt.

"Then you will get a dusty knee," Summer said crisply.

Genevieve stared, smiling despite, or perhaps because of, the sight of her brother so willingly making a fool of himself; Haddy grunted and went to check the teams; and Penelope crossed her arms and put one hand to her mouth to hide a smile. The remaining members of the party merely watched with faintly puzzled or annoyed looks on their faces—with the exception of Xavier, who had a smile lingering around his mouth which Genevieve looked up in time to discover. It was a strange little smile, one that she could only classify as being somehow

. . . well, tender. It sent another shiver coursing up her spine, and she tore her vision away, that he might not look up and see her just as the shiver reached the back of her eyes.

"But what if I make a flowery speech?" Michael went on.

"I could wish you would not—"

"Could wish it, but do not. Ah, yes, my dear, my own, my heart! It will make the sun rise each morning for me if you would be so good as to say you would be mine. Birds shall not sing for me until you have promised to wed me as soon as may be. The leaves on the trees shall not dance until you have—"

"Oh, posh!" said Summer, staring off at the horizon as though in extreme boredom, but she made no attempt to move away.

"Shall not dance until you have whispered those golden, blessed words."

"Partner," Xavier said near Genevieve's ear, causing her to spin toward him a bit too rapidly, so that she almost reached out to touch him, to steady herself. He stood very near as he went on, "Would you ride with me, instead of in the carriage?"

"Yes," she answered simply, although she did not wear a riding habit, nor would she ask that one be unpacked. No one would appreciate the delay, least of all herself. If she delayed, she would probably change her mind.

"Give me a moment to find the sidesaddle," he said, slipping away from her to raid the second carriage.

As he readied the horse, she had time to begin to regret agreeing to ride anyway. There would be no one to interrupt their conversation should it grow awkward. No one to fill in any silences that might fall. No way to pretend to be ignoring his presence, the presence that caused her eyes to be unable to meet his, that tied her tongue, and made her feel all muddled inside.

It did not soothe her nerves that Michael spoke on, mindless of his fellow travelers, declaring his undying affection. Summer allowed him to hold her hand, even though she delicately yawned twice behind her other hand.

As soon as Xavier stepped back, thereby declaring the horse was saddled properly, Kenneth frowned deeply, and made a dismissive motion with his hand, walking away from the scene of the proposal. Speaking loudly, to override Michael's proclamations, he said, "I declare it Genevieve and Xavier's turn. Here is your clue. And oh," he said, pulling the paper back out of her reach momentarily, "before you may have it, understand that you are not to look at Haddy's map."

Genevieve lifted her eyebrows briefly, her soft smile indicating acceptance, and reached to receive the blue sheet of paper. She read, " 'My Guild Festival dates from the time of my charter in 1179, and is celebrated every twenty years. In ancient times, I was the capital for the Duchy of Lancaster. I was occupied by the Old Pretender in 1715, and by the Young Pretender in 1745.' " She looked up at Kenneth and needled him lightly, "But it does not rhyme."

"I should care to see you get anything to rhyme with '1715.' Believe me, I made the attempt, and it was the wartiest piece of poetry you would ever see."

"On this journey that is saying something," Penelope teased.

Kenneth turned to her and gave an exaggerated frown, and she giggled. Genevieve's eyes widened at the sound, for Penelope was the one female she never thought of as being capable of giggling. They widened further when Kenneth began to stalk the woman, causing her to squeal and dash around the group of people and around to the other side of the carriage. She came around the other side as Kenneth pursued her, her eyes glittering, her cheeks flushed, and she moved quickly behind her brother, crying, "Kenneth! Do stop! Kenneth. Xavier!"—she giggled again as Kenneth reached around the taller man—"make him stop!"

"I say, old man, my sister says you are to stop," Xavier said dryly, though there was an edge to his voice that made Genevieve glance up at him and remember last night.

Kenneth took one more lunge for Penelope—another giggle—and then abandoned the chase, tugging his waistcoat back into place in an effort to restore his decorum.

Xavier then ignored his sister to say to Genevieve, "Our time is running out. Have you a guess?"

She shook her head, feeling the shyness creep back into her manner, causing her to not quite meet his eye. "I am afraid the farther north we go the less my knowledge of the land and its local history becomes. Although, I've a thought as to the duchy. I think it must be Lancaster. That must be north of here, for we are undoubtedly going to travel through Lancashire, and one is named for the other, surely?"

Xavier rubbed his chin. "And talk of the Pretenders does not bring a different picture to my mind. It might be easier to say where Pretenders were *not,* rather than where they were! Very well. Kenneth, we say it is Lancaster."

"Sorry!" he said, his tone of relish taking the place of any true regret. "Time for a forfeit."

Genevieve snuck a glance up at Xavier as Kenneth pulled the forfeits bag from his pocket. Xavier did not appear particularly upset by the turn of events. She chose to model his behavior as Kenneth presented the bag to her.

She pulled out a neatly penned slip and read it quickly to herself. She felt a flush creep up her face, and wished she could somehow force her body not to give her away so easily, for the forfeit demanded a scene of public intimacy she did not think she could enact with any easiness of spirit. She licked her lips once, nervously, thought about asking to draw another only to reject the idea as blatantly cowardly, and she read, " 'The parties of this forfeit shall feed to one another their next meal.' "

There were groans of sympathy mingled with grins all around, although Genevieve noted Xavier said nothing at all, only nodding once.

Laura clapped her hands, laughing. "Oh, Kenneth, you do have a way with little bits of fiendishness, do you not? I am so glad that at last you are showing your true colors to everyone, that they may know I have not exaggerated all these years."

" 'Tis a far lesser cruelty than being made to sing in the High Street," Haddy grumbled good-naturedly to Genevieve. He turned to Laura and announced, "But, good lady, do not fear that you shall be made to sing or sup in any wise uncomfortably this day, for it is now our turn, and I have the answer to our clue."

"Last night he solves a Little Riddle, this morning a treasure hunt clue. 'Tis a miracle!" Kenneth cried, grinning widely.

" 'Tis, my friend!" Haddy rejoined. " 'Tis always a miracle when anyone can glean anything from these rambling, nonsensical clues of yours. But the fact of the matter is, I happen to know that you mean us to go to Preston."

"Bravo!" Kenneth cried, in some surprise.

Haddy made a deep bow to the group at their scattered applause for finally answering a clue himself, then stood and gave a rare grin. "I happen to know that the grouse hunting is particularly fine around the ancient Duchy of Lancaster."

Laura gave him an approving nod. "I care not how you knew it; I only care that we have won our token." She put out her hand, into which Kenneth pressed a playing card: a two of diamonds. She looked up at him and asked, "What significance does this card hold?"

" 'Tis a bit obscure. We shall we passing moors and mountains on our way there—that is the two—and the area is rich with coal, which as you may know is the beginnings of diamonds."

Laura made a face that said she was pretending to be impressed with this logic as she smiled and said, "Ah, my brother, so clever! If only your wit extended beyond your scribblings to the time you keep company with your friends and family."

He refused to rise to the bait. "Enough! Let us away.

271

We've miles to go before we find our beds this day." He made shooing motions at the ladies in the direction of the carriage as he said to Haddy, " 'Tis forty miles to Preston if 'tis one. The day is already half done. Shall we try to make the full run of it?"

"We could have arrived at Brockmore in two and a half days, if we had but put ourselves to it," Michael scoffed, stepping forward to provide the hand up for the ladies.

"Aye, if we followed Michael's desire for neck-or-nothing driving. Personally, I've a care for my hide," Haddy said. "And given that the coming roads are bound to be uneven and hilly, we shall be fortunate indeed if we come the forty miles this day."

"I shall drive the luggage carriage before you all," Michael said, offering his hand to Summer. She did not refuse it, but neither did she look at him, stoically climbing into the carriage without a word. He grinned at her, even though her face was averted, offered his hand next to Penelope, then resumed his commentary. "I shall drive at a pace I perceive to be most proper, and since you will have the advantage of seeing whether or not I overturn as you come behind me, you will be able to feel confident to follow in like manner and pacing. But, fear not, for I shall bring us to Preston, hale and well, ere the night is upon us."

"When it comes to the hills, we shall have to stop and exchange horses more often."

"So we shall do, and yet still spend our evening in the town to which we aspire."

Haddy lifted his hand in a surrendering, if doubtful, salute. "Lead on!"

"Do you still care to ride?" Xavier said at Genevieve's side.

It would be easy to say no, to explain that if the pace were to be swift she might be better situated in the carriage, but she did not. Instead she said, "I should enjoy that."

"Then, dear lady, please meet Farmer George," Xavier said, taking her arm and leading her to the horse that he had readied for her, now tied to the back of the baggage carriage.

"Farmer George?"

"I did not name him. Haddy did, for our poor benighted king, and because it turned out this fellow was rather lacking despite his deep chest, and might have been better used behind a plow than in the traces."

"Oh dear, do you mean to tell me my horse is easily winded?"

"I am afraid so. But do not fear. We shall need to allow the carriages to outpace us at first, but eventually we shall pass them, when they are bogged down in moorland or creeping up an incline."

She almost changed her mind, almost blurted out that she might be better served to ride in the carriage than alone with him, but she bit back the comment. Of what was she afraid? Having to make conversation? Having to pretend she thought no more of him than she thought of just another friend? That he might see that sometimes she trembled at his nearness? And if he saw it, would that be such a terrible thing?

The other ladies were settled, after making dubious remarks regarding Genevieve's choice to ride, and Michael did as he had proposed, setting out at once at a rousing pace, leaving Haddy behind, not even yet upon his box, much to that gentleman's annoyance.

"Up," Xavier said to Genevieve, as Haddy climbed atop his box, offering cupped hands to assist her.

She slid her slippered foot into his hands and was hoisted on to the sidesaddle, and felt a wrench of loss when his hands were taken away. She turned her eyes to watch her own hands as she hooked her knee around the horn and arranged her nearly inadequate skirt so that it hid all but the tip of her one slipper, just as Haddy settled on his seat and called to his team, setting them in motion. It was only a moment more and then Xavier was in his saddle. "Ready?" he said to her, causing her to look up at him again.

The sun was nearing its midday height, picking out the silver threads in his waistcoat, and making his beaver and boots shine with a high polish. He looked well upon a horse, his back straight, his seat true, his deep blue coat and paler blue inexpressibles well matched, giving him a slight military air. He truly had a fine face, with that strong chin that reflected a sound character. For a moment she could think of no other visage that would command respect and admiration as did his, down to the eyepatch that gave him a faintly mysterious air.

He waited patiently upon her reply, his gaze steady and subtly flattering, his attention not on the carriages that left them in the dust, nor the horse beneath him, nor the heat of the day, but rather centered exactly on her, so that at some primal level she knew utterly that he was prepared to wait an hour, if she only said that he ought.

In that moment she wanted nothing so much as to

announce to him that she had fallen quite madly in love with him.

Her hands tightened on her reins, making her horse dance beneath her a bit, as she struggled to overcome the impulse. What if she were terribly wrong? What if the attraction lay only on her side? She bit her lip, and looked down the road, and clucked gently to her horse, urging the animal forward, though not too fast, for she felt no particular need to catch up with the others, no need for haste at all. If anything, she might have desired complete solitude, wherein she might weigh all that had been and judge it anew.

She watched the scenery pass by, faintly exhilarated by the freedom that riding always gave, yet also, reluctantly, saddened by it. She could not make the horse go slow enough to suit her. It seemed they were all in such a hurry to be done with their last summer together. It did not matter that it had been a long, uncomfortable, disturbing time, not when she thought that when it was done, it would remain done and over forever. No more chances to flout society's rules; no more foreign locales shared with favorite friends; no more seemingly idle opportunities to gaze up into a friendly face, a gray eye that glimmered with shared amusement . . . or even, perhaps, something just a shade deeper than that.

"Do you know that you are quite alone with me?" Xavier said, just loud enough to be heard over the trotting hooves of the horses.

"So I am," she said, surprised to find it was true, that her brother had left her thus. Her brother, lost to his own pursuits, that topsy-turvy betrothal, if betrothal it was. "Ought I to be concerned?" she asked, and was embarrassed to find that she said it in a very flirting manner.

He sucked in his breath; she heard it. "No," he said soberly. "You should know I would always see to your care."

She said nothing in reply, for she did not trust either her voice or her words, for they were both threatened by the abrupt pounding of her heart.

"Genevieve," he said, after they had ridden nearly a mile without words. He said nothing more for a moment, and she saw that he was struggling for the words. "Do . . . do you ever wonder about my eyepatch?"

She could only be honest, for something had happened between them that robbed her of the ability to equivocate with him. She wanted to tell him it was a strange question, that an eyepatch was meaningless, but he seemed to need to know something from her. She gave the only answer she could, "Yes."

He sucked in his breath again, and stared straight ahead. "Do you ever wish to see beneath it?" he asked. His mouth tightened to a grim line.

Again, only honesty would serve. "Yes."

"I see."

They were silent again, so that she glanced at him and saw that his mouth was still grimly set. He glanced at her also, then looked away. " 'Tis hideous," he said, his voice raising a little, as though the words were torn from him. "You would find it hideous."

There was no answer to make to that, so she did not attempt to do so. To say "No, I would not" would be to call him a liar, and to deny a response she could not be certain of; yet to say "But, I would" would be to deny the injury, the scarring, and perhaps the natural human response to that which was different. He had asked her, and it had been terribly important, and she had given him the truth, but in doing so, apparently no joy.

Then she began to ache for him, because she saw that he had no further words, no charming banter, no teasing ways. His wound, and her honesty, had taken something from him, had left no hope remaining in his averted face. Now he was stiff and cool and troubled, and she knew with certainty that she could not say anything that would not make the matter even worse.

His constraint became her own, made her lips draw together wordlessly, made her eyes stare straight ahead as did his. For a short while, a very short while, she had thought perhaps they were becoming something so much more than friends, and now it seemed they were not even to have that. She had said what he did not want to hear—such a little truth that she had difficulty believing it was that which had hardened him against her—and upon hearing it he had locked his emotions away.

She wished for solitude again, but now she wished it that she might cry in private. Alone together, they had no way to move past the barrier of pain and doubt, no remaining path but silence and swallowed tears.

He had dared it all then. Dared and lost. She had not accepted him, had needed more than he had to offer. How big was the eyepatch? Perhaps two inches by two? Such a small thing, and yet how large it loomed. Large enough to come between them, large enough to create an impassable wall.

Chapter 20

Poor intricated soul! Riddling,
perplexed, labyrinthical soul!
          —John Donne,
          LXXX Sermons

Michael lifted the bottle and proposed a toast, "To the excellent time we have made prior to our luncheon!"

"To the excellent time!" the others echoed, raising their glasses and sipping at the dark red wine.

"I told you I would set a smacking good pace, and I did. And we are all in one piece, to judge by what my eyes show me," he crowed to Haddy.

Haddy shrugged, obviously more interested in the contents of the picnic basket than he was in Michael's achievement.

"To the glasses," Laura further proposed, admiring the way the afternoon sunlight sparkled on the goblets she had persuaded Haddy to buy from the master of the inn where last they had stayed.

"Most definitely to the glasses"—Michael made a

bow in her direction as there was another round of sips in salute—"for now we all may drink at once, without waiting." He tilted the bottle to his glass, then handed it to Laura. "Come, Genevieve, drink," he chided his sister when he saw she did not lift the glass balanced in her hand.

"No, she may not!" Haddy said. "If she is to have a sip of wine, Xavier must present it to her, and the other way round, I might add. The forfeit, if you recall."

"Ah, yes. But what is this? You shall never have a meal, you two, if you do not sit near one another. Or else your method is one I personally do not care to witness! No, it is one thing to be all that is gay, but I say we must draw the line at throwing food and thereby destroying the mantuamakers' best efforts. Come along, Genevieve. Move next to Xavier there," Michael urged.

For a moment she thought she would plead she had the headache, but she knew it would only be a temporary reprieve. The party would see the forfeit went forward, if not this meal then the next or the next after that. She rose to her feet, moving silently and without looking at him, to sit next to Xavier. As she settled beside him, he was equally as silent.

"I think we may all see that we shall reach Preston at just about nightfall," Michael went on.

"I wish to offer a toast," Haddy said, perhaps to change the subject. "I think we should drink to Kenneth, for is this not the coolest, most pleasant spot in which we have yet dined?"

"Quite, quite!" Penelope agreed.

"Then, to Kenneth, for proposing this tour to the cool and beautiful Northlands."

"To Kenneth!" came the cry.

"See here, Genny. Summer and I shall show you how best to feed one another," Michael said when Genevieve still did not lift her glass.

"We will not," Summer said clearly.

"At least let us entwine arms as we sip our wine."

"No."

"Oh, prithee, my lady. We must show this sorry pair how such things may be done. A mere moment of your time to set these two in the right direction."

Everyone expected another refusal, but it was not forthcoming. "For Genevieve, I will do it," Summer said primly, no smile near her mouth.

Michael smiled enough for the two of them, and stooped down near her. He put out his arm, around which Summer wrapped hers, and each of them brought their own glass to their lips, their faces very near.

"But that is all wrong," Haddy pointed out. "They need to drink from each other's hands."

Michael did not answer, holding Summer's gaze. She gazed back, coolly, but did not move away immediately.

Xavier sat stiffly next to Genevieve, not moving, just as she sat next to him. As Summer at last untangled her arm from Michael's, perhaps looking up at him through her lashes, Genevieve waited to hear Michael reprove her again that she did not drink or allow Xavier to do so. Her hand began to shake from the anticipation of not knowing how she would answer that scold. Five seconds passed, then ten, and then thirty, and Michael settled next to Summer. He talked a great deal, but said nothing to his sister, did not even look her way. All around her several conversations began, as Laura leaned over the basket to bring out the luncheon offerings.

Genevieve began to realize that her breathing was becoming uneven in agitation, that she would soon make a fool of herself if she did not do something.

Her hand lifted the glass, and then her other hand was there at the base, steadying it where it shook. She raised it, even as she raised her eyes, until the glass was before Xavier, an offering.

His gray eye met her own dark brown, too steady to reflect any gentleness or benevolence toward her. She felt her face grow pale, but she did not lower the glass, for somehow the moment must be got through.

Finally he gave a faint, nearly imperceptible nod, and leaned forward slightly. She tilted the glass, slanting the wine toward the edge of the glass, and moved it toward his mouth. His lips parted slightly, meeting the goblet, waiting as she tilted it still more that the liquid might reach his tongue. He sipped, quite possibly receiving very little, and then lifted his mouth from the glass. She lowered the goblet to her lap to help her support its small weight, for her arms felt heavy and nearly useless even as they trembled.

There was a subdued cheer from the others at the sight, but then they went back to their various conversations, their need for playful vengeance satisfied.

Then Xavier raised his glass before her, tilting it, guiding it forward, until the wine flowed into her mouth. She was getting too much, and so her hand automatically came up and touched the glass and consequently his hand, to signal that the glass must be taken away.

Her hand leaped from his at the touch, settling on the base of the wine goblet in her lap.

Cold meats, crusty bread, and sliced cheeses made up their nuncheon, accompanied by almond tarts and the Bordeaux. Genevieve found that the act of consuming a meal with nothing but one's fingers was all the more awkward if one must select a thing and then place it in another's mouth. There was so much to consider.

"Do you prefer the roast beef or the sliced goose?" she asked timidly.

"Either," he answered civilly, if shortly.

"And of the cheeses?"

"I prefer the soft white to the yellow cheeses, usually." He paused, then asked, "And you?"

"I have no particular preference," she said in a very small voice.

"Very well," he said, although he made no move to reach for the parcels that circulated through the gathering.

A loaf of bread came from Kenneth's hands into hers, and she was glad of it, glad to have something to do. She tore off a large chunk, then realized it was too big. She tore it in half, paused, then handed the other half to Xavier, and then reached for the sliced goose that was just passing in front of them.

When she had assembled a selection and set it on a serviette before them, they both looked down at it, neither moving to begin the process of feeding one another. The moment of pause grew too long, and became achingly awkward.

At last he reached for a thin slice of roast beef and rolled it like a cigar. He raised this toward her face, and she leaned forward, gratefully, and took a bite. The ice thus broken, she then reached for a bit of bread and put it to his mouth.

Occasionally their companions laughed and pointed out that Genevieve's lap was dotted with crumbs, or that the piece of cheese Xavier had meant for Genevieve's mouth had ended up in the goblet of wine, but after a short while the sport grew tiresome, for the two parties involved chose not to react or banter. The companions turned to discussions on the improved weather, the likelihood that Michael would bring them to Preston this day, and a somewhat heated discussion on whether or not Haddy's most recently purchased pipe tobacco was too pungent for mixed company.

Eventually Genevieve's nerves settled and her hands ceased to shake, much to her relief. She sat back, sighing and shaking her head when Xavier raised another slice of goose. "I am replete," she said quietly.

"I am not," he answered.

She said nothing, reaching for the meat and lifting it to his mouth. Her finger touched his lip, and she snatched back her hand, causing him to have to raise his own hand and push the morsel into his mouth or else have the meat land in his lap. "I am sorry," she said.

He shook his head, dismissing the occurrence.

She fed him more of the meal, careful to see that her fingers were never again too close to his mouth, a fact that caused her to have to pay particularly close attention to that very mouth. A well-shaped mouth, with even white teeth. A mouth that she had once wished would turn into her palm and lay a kiss there.

"Wine, please," he said. She lifted the glass, grateful

to hear that his voice seemed perhaps a trifle less resentful. He sipped the wine, and nodded a thanks, and then looked at her. His gaze wandered away, and came back. "This is truly absurd," he said and almost smiled.

" 'Tis," she agreed, allowing a small smile to form in response.

"Did you get enough to eat? To drink? You did not take much."

She could hardly say that the forfeit had cost her her appetite. He was making an effort to be civil, as must she. She said, "Perhaps a little more wine?"

He lifted the glass. The level of the liquid was low, so he had to really tip the goblet for the wine to reach her lips. It tipped too far and too much came into her mouth all at once. She sputtered as he pulled the glass quickly away, a dribble of wine running down her chin.

"I am sorry," he cried, reaching into his pocket for a kerchief.

As he handed the linen to her, from its fold fell one of his extra eyepatches, landing on her lap. It was impossible to ignore the black fabric against her pale pink gown. Her eyes flew up and met his, and she saw the new hardness return to his features as he reached to retrieve the patch. "Wipe your chin," he told her gruffly, coming suddenly to his feet. He lurched away, calling some mumbled excuse to the group as he strode out into the countryside.

When he returned a quarter of an hour later, Genevieve did not ask if she might ride beside him.

Chapter 21

And this the burthen of his song,
For ever us'd to be,
I care for nobody, not I,
If no one cares for me.
             —Isaac Bickerstaffe,
                "Love in a Village"

"It was here, in Hoghton Tower, that James the First so enjoyed the loin of beef he was served for his supper, that he dubbed it 'Sir Loin,'" Michael said, looking sharply at Kenneth to see if his answer was correct.

"In 1617," Kenneth agreed as various faces turned to admire the sixteenth century fortified house. "But however did you know that? I was sure I would confound everyone in our gathering with this clue."

"Pure luck, old fellow! Your clue said the building had some significance to James the First. I remembered me nothing of that monarch other than that one tale, the only tale, I daresay, that might be comprehendible or recollectable to a young lad made to suffer in an extremely stifling class of Historical Instruction."

"Bravo, Michael," Summer said, and when he turned to her, beaming at her praise, she added pointedly, "we now have four tokens, and I doubt we shall be the ones to lose this treasure hunt, as no others have more than two."

Kenneth handed Summer the card of which she spoke: a nine of clubs.

"Significance?" Michael questioned as Summer placed the card in her reticule.

Kenneth colored. "There is none, I am afraid." He went on as some of the gathering grinned at his confession, "I own I could not divine any symbolism from a sirloin by which to match a card to the clue."

"It matters not," Summer assured him, "so long as it is a valid token."

"Quite valid. In fact, there are only two more tokens to be won."

"What if, by some long chance, there should be a tie?" Haddy asked.

"I do not know——" Kenneth began, but was interrupted by Summer.

"It should be decided by a Little Riddle, of course."

"That makes good sense to me. After all, the purpose of this excursion was to obtain knowledge, so let knowledge be the deciding factor," Kenneth agreed.

"And speaking of Little Riddles, we have not had one in quite some while. Have you one for us now?" Summer asked.

Genevieve looked at her friend, able now to see some of what her brother saw, for she had noted that Summer no longer insisted that Michael call her Lady Rose, a subtle softening of her stance against him. Even now, one knew that she meant to please Kenneth by suggesting he supply one of his beloved Riddles, even as, perhaps, she hoped that she, or Michael, might offer the answer and thereby earn the right to bestow a kiss on one of their party. What a complex creature she was! Genevieve could not hope to enjoy, let alone play, such deep games. No, not she, for she could not even maintain a simple friendship with a man.

"Very well. A difficult one, then, I think. You must name all the rivers in Lancashire." At the blank stares he received, he added, "I shall tell you there are six."

"Well, the Mersey, of course," Summer said.

"And the Lune," Michael added. He lifted his eyebrows at Summer, encouraging her to go on. She seemed to be ignoring him as she frowned, one finger to her chin.

"The Ribble, near Preston," Haddy said.

"Wait now! Who shall answer? Say no more aloud unless you may name all six," Kenneth warned.

"I may do it," Penelope said. "After all, Xavier has come north on occasion with Haddy for the hunt, and it seems to me they also fished in every stream or river they found, and then bored me with recitations of their exploits."

Xavier gave his sister a cool look, faintly amused, but he offered no resolution. Genevieve would have been surprised if he had, for then he would need to kiss someone, something she did not doubt he had no interest in, even though she had no doubt that the someone would ever be her.

"Let me see . . . ," Penelope ticked off the count on her fingers as she named the rivers, "the Mersey, the Lune, the Ribble, the Calder, the . . . uh . . ah yes, the Hodder, and . . . and . . . It is just on the tip of my tongue. Oh, it starts with a 'W.' Wynde . . . or Wyle . . . Wyre! 'Tis the Wyre!" She looked up and smiled, sure she was correct.

Kenneth nodded. Michael made a disappointed motion with his hand, and Summer looked up from under her lashes at him, her expression benign. Penelope laughed, pleased with herself.

"The kiss," Summer prompted.

"Whatever you say, my love," Michael said at once, reaching for her hands.

"You have hardly earned it," Summer scolded, dancing away. "And I was not speaking to you. I was speaking to Penelope."

Penelope glanced around, coloring slightly. For a moment she met her brother's eye, but then she looked away at once. Genevieve saw how still he stood, his face calm but not relaxed. Again his sister looked at him, and then her chin rose, and she stepped to Kenneth's side. She went up on tiptoe, her hands circling his arm to steady her thusly, and placed a kiss on his cheek, very near his mouth. Perhaps she leaned into him more than her precarious position on tiptoe required, and perhaps her hands lingered a moment too long on his arm once her feet were again flat to the ground before she released him to take half a step back. She looked at her brother again, and her chin did not lower.

"Enough of this," Michael said, a bit irritably. "Where are we off to now? What is the next clue?"

288

Kenneth produced the requisite blue paper, handing it to Penelope. "Our turn again."

She read,

> " 'Go to the land a'west o' the moors,
> And there the prized token can be yours.
> 'Tween Yorkshire and the River Kent,
> 'Tis where my presence will next be lent.' "

"I own the next clue—when we arrive at our destination—will be most obscure," Kenneth explained. "I thought perhaps it would be more helpful to provide a kind of verbal map, that we may at least come to the proper town before we are befuddled."

"Let me think," Penelope said. "For the Little Riddle, I almost said the River Kent, but then I recalled that 'tis truly just north of the bit of Westmorland that separates the two sections of Lancashire."

"Her tutor was especially fond of geography," Laura leaned over to say to Genevieve, who nodded.

"But not very far north at all, that is a certainty. Yorkshire runs all along the eastern border, so that is no help. Oh, I wish I could look at a map."

"He never said you might not," Haddy said, standing and reaching for his pocket.

"Genevieve and I were not allowed to do so," Xavier objected quietly. Haddy withdrew his hand from his pocket.

"It could be Milnthorp, for that is very near the river, but . . . that bit about Yorkshire makes me think it must be more centered. Not Preston, for we have just come from a Preston in the last county, and I know you,

Kenneth, better than to think you would wish to have a name twice. No, no, it must be one of the Kirkbys, so I shall guess the more southern of the two: Kirkby Lonsdale."

In answer, Kenneth handed her a playing card: the queen of clubs. "Because Kirkby Lonsdale is a beautiful place, as is any man's queen."

She smiled at him, and Genevieve startled to see how soft that smile was.

"It shall be a very pleasant day. Would you care to ride with me?" Kenneth asked Penelope.

Xavier stepped forward and took his sister's arm. "She is not wearing a riding habit. Let us away to Kirkby Lonsdale," he said as he pulled her toward the carriage.

"I wish to ride," she said, pulling back.

"No, you do not." He spoke firmly.

"I tell you, I wish it. Genevieve rode with you without benefit of a habit."

"Very well. *I* shall ride with you. Kenneth, you have the box on the ladies' carriage, with Haddy to ride guard. Michael, you shall take the baggage carriage before us, and be so good as to set the pace again, if you will. Haddy, what must it be? Forty, fifty miles from here?"

"Closer to fifty, and rough country."

"Michael?" Xavier said, pulling his sister to the left side of Farmer George and offering her his cupped hands. She gave him a dark, piqued look, then allowed him to hand her up to the saddle.

"Oh, aye, I shall set the pace anew, but only if Summer will drive beside me."

She shook her head.

"But if you drive with me you shall not be in the dust. You shall have fresh air, and my splendid company. Does that not tempt you?" he argued pleasantly.

"It does not."

"Then I shall not lead the way. I shall creep behind Haddy, at his usual tortoiselike pace, and then we shall have to spend the night in some provincial little town with only rough cloths and mediocre food to serve us. The rooms will be drafty and full of smoke, for they ever have fires year-round in such places as these, regardless of their guests' comfort, and we shall be forced to spend our night listening to the master and mistress of the house quarreling for hours on end, their tongues and tempers loosed by the Blue Ruin they have in place of their suppers. We shall—"

"Enough!" Summer cried, her frown clearly not reaching her eyes. "You have convinced me that it behooves me to see that we arrive in Kirkby Lonsdale ere dark, for everyone's comfort, of course."

"Yes, for everyone's comfort. You are so good to think of them," Michael grinned at her, offering his arm. She put her fingers on his sleeve, very lightly, and allowed herself to be guided to the carriage.

Genevieve was handed up into the other carriage by Haddy, who then climbed up beside Kenneth. She looked out the window, and saw Penelope looking up at the box. The gaze was long-lived, ended only when Xavier took her horse's rein and pulled the animal forward.

* * *

"There was an old woman," Kenneth began his tale. They stood at the bank of a bridge that crossed over the River Lune in Kirkby Lonsdale. Devil's Bridge, he called it. "Now, at that time there was no bridge here. The old woman's cow crossed the river. The old woman walked to the river to come after the cow, only now she found the river swollen and quite unpassable. The devil appeared to her, and offered to make a bridge appear overnight for her use, only she must promise that he would have the soul of the first living creature that crossed it, thinking it would be her, of course, to fetch her cow. The old woman agreed.

"When she came back the next day, she found the bridge as promised, and the devil awaiting his payment. Instead of crossing the bridge herself, as the devil had expected, she pulled her small dog from under her cloak, tossed a bun to attract the animal forward, and watched as the little creature ran across the bridge to have its treat, thereby fulfilling her promise. Only, according to legend, a dog has no soul, and therefore had none to forfeit and the devil gained nothing. He howled in rage at the old woman, and disappeared, leaving behind the bridge you see before you today," Kenneth finished with a flourish toward the bridge.

"Very amusing, I am sure, but what clue must we solve?" Xavier asked somewhat testily, one hand on his hip as he looked at the sky. He had already mentioned that if they could make quick work of this clue, there was every possibility that they could arrive in Brockmore by nightfall.

"You must find one part of that story."

"One part? Well, I have found the bridge already,"

Xavier said, his tone reflecting he really was not terribly amused.

"Something else."

"What else could it be?" Genevieve ventured. "An old woman? A cow? A dog? A bun?"

"The devil," Xavier growled.

"You need not look far to find *him*," Penelope said, giving her brother the same cold look she had been giving him all day. Xavier returned the look.

"Let us search about," Genevieve suggested.

"Not everyone. Just the couple that are in line for this, the final token. You have," Kenneth consulted his watch, "five more minutes, Xavier, Genevieve."

"Look for rocks, perhaps, shaped like anything in the tale," Genevieve suggested, turning to cross the bridge. She peered into the water below, around at the banks of the river, and up at the craggy hills around them, looking for anything that might resemble a cow or a dog or an old woman.

It was Xavier who found it, by walking past a rise on the riverbank to the hidden setting beyond. He glanced at a man who reclined against a tree near the bank, a man he slowly realized he recognized in some manner, around whom lay four hounds. Two were black, one was brindled, and the fourth was gray, with plenty of aged white around his muzzle. The fellow sat chewing on a grass stalk, a fishing pole propped at his side, until one of the dogs sat up and another barked, and he looked up to see Xavier walking toward him. Then he hastened to stand, the dogs coming to their feet as well. They stood still and stiff, and then the older dog began to ever so slightly wag his tail.

"You are Kenneth's man. Opperman, is it not?" Xavier said as the dapper shorter man dusted his dark clothes with his hands.

"Yes, Lord Warfield, that I am. Are you the one who is to have the final token then, my lord?" All of the dogs around him began to wag their tales now, seeing that their companion had accepted the stranger.

"So it would seem," Xavier said, putting out his hand.

The man handed Xavier a king of spades. "King of death, you see? The devil?" he supplied the logic behind the choice. "I hope it was as interesting as Master Kenneth wished it. The treasure hunt, that is."

"Interesting, yes, I could say that." To the white-muzzled dog, who was inching forward curiously, he offered the back of his hand that it might be sniffed and said, "Who are you then, old man? How shall I call you?"

"This is Cymru, named for ancient Cumberland, don't you see? And these two dark fellows are Keswick and Penrith, and the lady there is Aspatria."

"Fine names," Xavier almost smiled—the first time in more than a day—as the old dog licked his hand.

"Hallooo!" came the cry, announcing that Xavier's discovery had itself been discovered. Kenneth waved from the rise, turned to beckon the others, and strode toward the tree.

"Have we kept you long in this field, Opperman?" he called as he approached. The dogs turned to him, poised for a moment quivering with excitement until Kenneth half bent toward them, whistling an invitation, and then they came bounding.

"Only two days, Master Kenneth," Opperman said

as Kenneth tousled the head of each of his joyfully wagging and barking hounds, greeting them with obvious fondness. "I had rather hoped I might have another day of nothing but fishing, sipping beer chilled in the river, and the company of dogs, but now you are here, and welcome for all that it means my days of leisure are behind me. Do we go on to Brockmore, Master Kenneth?"

"Yes. It may grow dark before we reach it, but I am familiar enough with the roads near the town of Carlisle, that I feel safe to travel them even so. Did you give Lord Warfield his token?"

"I did," Opperman said even as Xavier held up the card.

"Then let us be away. I've a mind to sleep in a familiar bed this night," Kenneth said heartily, clucking to the dogs, who fell into step beside him with silly dog grins and lolling tongues.

And I've a mind to leave in the morning for London, Xavier thought grimly to himself as he fell in step behind them.

Chapter 22

Errors, like straws, upon the surface flow;
He who would search for pearls must dive below.
                                        —John Dryden,
                                             "All for Love"

"To Kenneth and his treasure hunt!" Michael raised a toast, which was followed by a muted cheer and a tipping of glasses. "Now you should offer a toast," Michael said to the lady at his left, Penelope.

"To the end of a journey," she said.

Everyone raised their glasses, offered their noises of appreciation, and drank again. She turned expectantly to Kenneth, on her left, who was busy filling the lantern he had purchased in Lichfield with oil.

"There!" he said with satisfaction as he stoppered the oil. "So, toasts are circling the table, are they? Very well. Er . . . ah, I know. To Brockmore; to clean sheets and decent food!"

This created a large buzz of agreement, and then it was Laura's turn. "To the remaining health—to everyone's surprise, I feel sure—of this company of splendid persons!"

Next was Haddy, "To the winners of the treasure hunt."

The mutters of "Here! Here!" were accompanied by nods toward Michael and Summer. The prizes they were promised, a new fan and new snuffbox, would no doubt be selected once they had returned to London, if nothing of sufficient charm could be found in the nearby town of Carlisle.

"To Little Riddles!" Summer proposed, and a few laughed quietly, for she had collected the most kisses of them all, and drank again.

It came to Xavier next to make a toast. He lifted his glass, his face lacking the animation of those around him, who were clearly thrilled to have come at last to Brockmore. He seemed at a loss for words for a moment, then said, "To dogs."

"To dogs!" Kenneth echoed, leaning down to pat the head of the large gray who sat at his feet.

Lastly, it was Genevieve's turn. She, too, felt at a loss for words, her mind blank, her heart sore. She said what she thought would sound well, and then realized it went even a little deeper than that, that, if it were possible, she wished to somehow mend fences, to one degree if not the other. "To friends," she said.

This toast resulted in more calls of "Here! Here!" and even a few "Huzzahs." As he was seated near her, Genevieve heard Xavier murmur some halfhearted sound of agreement, and she turned to him, not lowering her glass until she caught his eye with her own. Only then did she allow the glass to come to her lips, as she continued to hold his regard over the edge of the glass as she sipped.

He stared back, unsure what to make of the gesture. She was clearly telling him something. Was it a castigation for the way he had become so cool toward her? Was it a demand for something more? Did she wonder what she had done that had created the barrier between them?

Did she think the barrier was all of his making?

Was it possible she was right?

He looked away, his mouth tightening in confusion and an undeniable misery, but when he looked up again she was still watching him.

"What do you want?" he whispered fiercely, so low even she scarcely heard it.

She wanted to demand that he explain that question, but it was impossible in this crowd. Instead she whispered, "Simple courtesy would do."

He sighed, and struggled to know what to say next. He had asked her a question . . . no, he had asked her three questions: "Do you ever wonder about my eyepatch?"; "Do you ever wish to see beneath it?"; and now "What do you want?" Her answers had only been straightforward. Surely it was not in her to harm deliberately. She had only given him what he always thought he sought: the truth. Was it her fault if the truth was less than he would have it?

His resentment melted away. She was right, of course. She had done nothing wrong. It was his own inability to accept the world's curiosity that stood in his way. Perhaps it was a fault not of his own making, but it had been perpetuated by him. Had he done so for all these years without purpose? Had he hid so long that now he did not know how to come into the light?

He had told himself he must risk it all, but had not known what "all" meant, that thought came clearly to him as he sat and struggled to understand her strange toast. "All" meant allowing her her curiosity; it meant having to see her recoil from the sight of his deformity . . . for only then could he see if she would come back to him.

Even, he supposed with a sudden, shocked insight, as she did now. He had been all that was abrupt, and rude, and condemning, and still she made this silent attempt to reach out to him once again.

He turned to her, his heart beginning to thud powerfully in his chest. "Genevieve?"

"Yes?"

He opened his mouth to speak, unsure just what the words would be, when Kenneth interrupted.

"Xavier, old man. Now that we are all gathered, and out of the way of the public, so to speak, would you answer a question for me?"

Xavier nodded shortly, his disappointment keen as his heart slowed, returning to normal. Ah well, maybe it was best to save any words for a time when they might be alone.

"I mean, the thing of it is, you never *say*, do you? Your eye, I mean. Oh, you tell stories, but you never say how you came by the original injury."

Xavier's mouth twitched in a smile of tight amusement that Kenneth would ask such a question at this moment, and he shook his head. It was no longer that he would not say, not now that he had realized how long he had held the old wound before him like a shield, but rather that he could not say, not honorably.

"It was me," Haddy said in a low voice, causing Kenneth to spin to face him. Haddy's voice grew, with an edge to it as he pitched to his feet in agitation. "Xavier never says what really happened because he is too much the gentleman to always be casting the fact in my face. 'Twas me who did it to him. With a sharp, pointed stick. We were lads. We were playing pirates, and I would have a sword. My mother had told me not to. Xavier told me to watch out, but too late. I tripped. *I* did it." Haddy paused, taking a deep breath before he rushed on. "*I* gouged his eye. *I* gave him that scar. There! Now you know what happened. Beleaguer the man no longer!" He cast up his hands, then stormed from the room, visibly upset.

Summer rose and went after him, causing Genevieve to think fleetingly that if Summer was spoiled as Michael and Haddy would have them all believe, she also was loving toward those she held dear. No doubt, this was why she was loved in return.

"I am sorry," Kenneth breathed. "I never meant to—"

"It is all right," Xavier said, staring at the floor. "It pains him to know it was his fault. People will always ask, you know."

Kenneth flinched. "Still, I offer my apologies."

"Do not offer them to me, but to Haddy," Xavier said, and then a crooked smile settled on his face. "It does not bother me as it used to do." He looked up from the floor then, directly at Genevieve.

Her brow puckered for a moment, but her mouth

slanted at the corners in response to his own lopsided smile. She met his gaze evenly, and for once he tried not to hide anything from her. If she saw his attraction, or his regrets, or his longings, then so be it.

Her eyes widened, but did not drop away, and he could only believe he saw a light spring to life in the recesses of those dark eyes.

"I will. I will certainly do so," Kenneth asserted. His voice dropped away, then went on, sounding faintly strained. "Know this, Xavier, it is not my wish to hurt anyone. Not with words, not with deeds. I only regret that sometimes things must happen anyway . . . ," he ended in that strange voice, which finally trailed away into silence.

Xavier's eye slanted over toward Kenneth, but then turned back to Genevieve, willing her to understand.

"It appears the time for slumber has come," Michael smoothed, standing and creating a signal for the others to stand also. Kenneth rose, lifting his lantern by the handle. He moved, placing it on a table near the door to his front salon.

Genevieve and Xavier were the last to stand, their eyes finally unable to say any more without benefit of actual words. Her eyes were moist, and she felt she might weep or laugh with relief, for there was that in his gaze that renewed the hope she had nearly abandoned.

"Will you ride with me tomorrow?" Xavier asked, offering his arm to her.

She placed her hand there, that he might escort her to the stairs, and she answered simply, "Yes."

"That is well. We will talk."

"I should like that."

He stopped at the bottom of the stairs, and turned to her, a hand raising to brush back a dark lock from her shoulder. "Good night, Genny," he said softly.

"Good night, Xavier," she answered, only then releasing his arm. Other words must wait, but only until tomorrow morning, as far away as that seemed to her now.

She felt his vision on her back as she walked slowly up the stairs, although she could not feel her feet as they floated upward.

Xavier sat in the library, a book near at hand but never opened, a single branch of candles on the table near his chair. He had meant to light Kenneth's lantern, but had found it missing from the table in the salon, and so he had settled for the branch of candles he had found here in the library, a simple light that suited his mood well enough. He stared into the fire on the grate—for the evening was too cool to do without a fire here in the wilds of northernmost England—not moving, deep in thought. He could not sleep, did not wish to sleep unless it was to bring the morning nearer. In the morning, he and Genevieve would make an excuse to ride alone together, perhaps to tour Kenneth's estate, and he would hide from her no longer. He would tell her how very much he wished her to be a part of his life permanently, how he had come to love her. He would kiss her, not fleetingly as he had only a few mornings ago over the breakfast table, but tenderly and in a manner that spoke louder than words. If she must see beneath his eyepatch before she would have him, then see she would. That minor and momentary disappointment would be nothing compared to the happiness of years to come, if he was not wrong and if she felt for him what he felt for her.

He did not drink—there was no need of liquor for him to feel giddy. His world spun and dipped wildly already, as he anticipated the morning, and as he dreaded the moment when she insisted she had to know the whole of him first, even his most visible imperfection. For it was her right. Surely, once she knew, it would be behind them. He knew this, on one hand anticipating the end of all the years of waiting upon the inevitable moment, and on the other dreading it all the same, for there was always the possibility that it would be more than she cared to live with every day for the rest of her life.

He thought he knew her better than that, but there were all the episodes, all the years, when he had been trained by society to know otherwise.

Tomorrow he would know. Tomorrow was too far away, and too soon. Tomorrow his life started anew, or would become an empty, terrible burden. Tonight he could not sleep, for tomorrow loomed too largely before him.

There were noises in the night, noises he largely ignored, lost to his hopes and dreams and, still, a handful of fears. He paid no mind until it penetrated into his consciousness that a door had opened into the room wherein he sat. He turned in the chair, seeing a murky figure in the shadows of the doorway.

"Xavier?" came Genevieve's voice.

He rose, crossing to her at once, a sudden joy buoying his heart at the sound of his name on her lips. He gathered up her hands and pulled her toward the dim lighting of the candles as he said, "Genny? You are still up?"

She sat in the chair he had just vacated, not removing her hands from where they still lay in his, as he sat on the footstool before her. "I could not sleep," she said.

"Neither could I."

"Xavier?" she questioned again, then went on, her eyes downcast. "Are we friends again?"

"Yes," he answered at once, ardently, squeezing her hands.

"I am so glad," she breathed, her eyes raising to meet his.

Their eyes locked in the dim light, silent messages flying between them. Relief. Pleasure. Renewed trust.

He did not breathe, and did not feel the loss of it. All he knew was that she leaned toward him, her eyes soft and shy but unwilling to leave his. He leaned toward her as well, guiding her closer to him by the pressure of his hands on hers. Closer and closer, so that their mouths were only three inches apart, and then two, and then one, and then his heart somersaulted with joy as she allowed him to press his lips to hers. She did not recoil, did not cause the contact to be broken, but leaned further into him.

The door opened again, with a loud bang as it bounced off the wall.

It was Xavier who pulled away first, looking up, startled, not quite sure what had happened. It was only a moment more before he understood that Laura, in her nightrail and a wrapper, had invaded the moment, loudly, and that even so Genevieve had gone on kissing him for a moment longer until it had been he who startled from the caress. He almost ignored Laura to lean forward and take another kiss from Genevieve's lips, but the opportunity was lost when Laura stormed toward them.

"She is gone!" she announced, thrusting a folded paper at Xavier.

He held Genevieve's one hand tightly still as he lifted his other to accept the paper. "Gone?" he echoed, wishing Laura would go away.

"Penelope. I suspect she and Kenneth have eloped. This note is addressed to you."

"What?" Xavier cried, flipping open the trifolded paper with one hand to find a filled page of petite handwriting. A playing card fluttered from the folds, landing on the carpet at his feet: a queen of hearts.

"We are very near Gretna Green, you must know," Laura said.

Xavier read the note aloud. " 'My dear brother: it pains me to have fooled you this way, but you must be realizing at this moment that Kenneth and I had planned this entire treasure hunt for the sole purpose of eloping to Scotland without raising suspicions or casting doubt on our propriety as we traveled together. We wished nothing to mar our choice to wed. You may recall that very soon after Father denied my hand to Kenneth, I claimed I would elope with him, and although you thought I was merely raging against fate, you see now that I was only speaking the truth. The excessive heat of London, most fortuitously, gave us an excellent excuse. It is but ten miles to Gretna Green, and I have little doubt that we shall be married ere you

305

should find this note. Please, Xavier, wish us happy. We are most uncertain how we shall get on, as I rather suppose Father will deny my dowry, and Kenneth's papa will most probably cut him off entirely, but we are determined to live and love together nonetheless. We shall see you in a day or two, as we plan to return to London to confront our fathers with our news. With love, Penelope.' "

He looked up, pale even in the dim candlelight. "When did you find this?" he asked Laura.

"Just now. I heard horses and a carriage in the drive, and went to Penelope's room to see who could be arriving, as she has a much better view of the drive than do I from my room. But, of course, no one was *arriving* at all. I saw Kenneth on the box, driving away. With Penelope not in her bed, let alone her room, and her wardrobe well raided, it did not take me long to jump to a conclusion. I was just coming for you, when I found the note. You were not in your room, and I have now finally found you here," she said, giving Genevieve a long look that said she was perfectly aware what she had interrupted.

Genevieve merely smiled softly at her.

"I saw it coming, or at least I ought to have done! Their pretenses of indifference grew steadily less believable," Xavier cried, leaping to his feet, reluctantly releasing Genevieve's hand. "I thought Kenneth sounded peculiar over the toasts. He was apologizing for much more than upsetting Haddy. And that night in Lichfield when they disappeared: I thought they were perhaps saying good-bye, but now it seems more likely they were plotting this event. The fools! How will they live?

Kenneth scarce has a ha'penny in his purse. No, I must stop them. They are hardly gone. I can catch them easily, on horseback." He started to move from the room, then stopped, looking back at Genevieve. "In the morning. We will talk in the morning," he said, willing her to respond positively, to allow him to go so abruptly, to take no offense that now his duty lay elsewhere.

"Let me go with you," she offered at once. As he started to shake his head, she went on, "Penelope may need me."

He hesitated, then nodded. "You may be correct. Or, even perhaps, she will listen to you where she would not listen to me. Come, change as quickly as you may to a habit, and fetch a heavy pelisse. It is chill nights here in Cumberland. I will ready the horses. Meet me in the courtyard in ten minutes, no more."

Genevieve flew to her room, Laura in her wake. She put the other girl to work, helping her out of one set of clothes and into the other.

"Perhaps I should wake the others?" Laura suggested. "We could form a search party then."

"No need to search. We know their destination," Genevieve shook her head. "No, better to bring them back quietly, with no one . . . knowing . . . the better . . . ," her voice trailed away as she stared at the sandy-haired Laura, her hands slowing where they buttoned the decorative vest of her habit. "Or," she said tentatively, "or should we? Should we bring them back? I mean to say, it is very clear they have decided this is what they wish. Xavier is right to be concerned about their future, for even though Penelope is the daughter of an earl, it is not the thing to elope this way. She will not

307

be all that is acceptable anymore. Yet, still, I cannot help but wonder. . . ."

"Do not be ridiculous," Laura said. "Of course they must be stopped. Are you going to go with Xavier or not?"

Genevieve stared at her, then rallied herself and pulled her bonnet over her dark hair, securing the ribbon under her chin. "Yes, yes, of course I am going to go with him. Come, help me with this pelisse."

Genevieve was in the courtyard a minute later, Laura at her side despite the fact she was dressed only in her nightwear, where Xavier waited with two horses and a couple of curious stablehands, who stared and whispered back and forth to themselves.

"Damme! You need a chaperone," Xavier said in a low voice near her ear as he helped her to mount. "Laura—?" he started to turn to where that lady shuffled from one slippered foot to the other, shivering in the night's chill, but Genevieve put out her hand to stop him.

"Never mind about that. It would put us that much further behind. Besides, I rode alone with you once before, and my name is not in tatters as a result. This will go no further than Brockmore, which we both know is nowhere near London."

Laura nodded acquiescence, and Xavier did not argue, swinging up into the saddle of the other horse. "I have given you Farmer George, as you are familiar with one another. He is not the one for long distances, but I feel sure we shall come upon them very soon anyway. Ready?" he asked. When Genevieve nodded, he said, "I am all but certain they shall have a lighted lantern with

them. That will give us something to watch sharp for."
As it had always been in Kenneth's mind to enact this
elopement, it was no small wonder he had purchased the
lantern—some sign to his lady love that their plans were
still forthcoming?—and readied it against their departure. Looking back on it, their scheme seemed so obvious, he marveled that he had missed it.

They put their heels to the horses, and bounded into
the night, leaving behind Laura, who waved both hands
at them in farewell as she thought to call, "Did you bring
a pistol? It could be dangerous." She received no response over the sound of the galloping hooves, glanced
briefly at the stablehands, who shrugged their lack of
knowledge, and then called out to the riders without any
real hope that either of them had thought of their own
safety, "Oh, pray do take care!"

Chapter 23

Love conquers all things:
let us too give in to Love.
  —Virgil,
    "Eclogue"

Genevieve urged her horse to catch up with Xavier's. He was a good two lengths ahead of her, protecting her well-being by finding the safest path and risking his own neck over hers. There was a goodly amount of moon-light, but the road was rough and their pace was danger-ously swift. She tried calling to him, now that they were well beyond Laura's hearing, but her voice did not carry forward to his ears. She urged the horse even more, leaning forward into the wind, willing Farmer George to keep his wind. She concentrated so on coming alongside of Xavier, that she missed the fact that there were other hoofbeats that had joined theirs.

"Stand! Stand and deliver!" a voice shouted as a mounted shape came alongside her horse. She looked over, seeing only the outline of a man, but she also saw that in his hand a pistol glinted in the moonlight. She stared dumbly for a moment, but that was a moment too long for his taste, for he reached out and grasped her mount's rein. A hard jerk set Farmer George to dancing sideways at too great a pace. He collided with the other horse, veered sharply to the left, and must have caught a hoof in a hole for suddenly his head went crashing toward the earth, and Genevieve went tumbling over his head, sprawled upon the ground.

She was numb for a minute, the wind knocked out of her. She thought perhaps she was not trapped beneath the horse, but she could not be sure.

Everything happened very fast then, nearly too fast for comprehension. She became aware that the glinting pistol was pointed down at her, that the man—now she could see that he was masked with a dark kerchief, and she began to understand that they had encountered a footpad—was demanding goods from her. She had no breath to tell him she had nothing to give him, but it did not matter, for suddenly the pistol swung up and away. A second later there was a retort and then a mass of horseflesh passed very near her, looking like one gigantic creature with a multiple of legs. She sucked air somehow into her lungs, and rolled away from the flailing hooves, scrambling to her knees. Her bonnet was gone, and her hair fell in her eyes. She dashed the hair back and struggled again for breath; it was growing just a little easier to do so.

Then she saw that Xavier had ridden his horse directly into that of the footpad, that the two men grappled for possession of the pistol, looking in the dark like a two-headed satyr battling itself. Another retort sounded, the footpad uttered a string of curses, and one of the horses snorted in fear.

Suddenly the two sprang apart, the footpad's horse backing away only to have its head cruelly wrenched to one side and a set of heels fiercely dug into its side. The horse screamed and leaped, plunging away from the scene of the battle. Amidst the thundering of its hooves as the footpad made his escape, she heard Xavier cry out her name, "Genevieve!"

He slid from his horse, the pistol dropping from his hands as he slid to his knees and rushed to pull her into his arms, only to thrust her at arm's length and visually inspect her. "Are you hurt?" he demanded, his hands and eye searching her hair, neck, back, and arms for any sign of injury.

"No," she croaked out, taking another, deeper breath that steadied her a little. "Just winded."

"Thank God!"

"Are you well?"

"Yes, I am fine. The shots went wild, I believe."

"Will he be back?"

"Possibly, though I took his pistol. I do not know. Probably not, if he knows what's good for him." He managed a weak smile, then held her tightly to him again. "I would never have forgiven myself—"

" 'Tis all right. 'Tis all right," she murmured, finding the air that now filled her lungs not near so sweet as the feel of his arms around her. She knew. She knew that he had no love for Summer, for his love was all for her. It was in his embrace, in the timbre of his voice, in the way his face had paled even in dim moonlight when he had thought she might be harmed.

He put her from him again, looking down into her face, and then lowered his mouth to hers. It was a scared, hungry, proprietary kiss, which she returned without restraint, clinging to his shoulders where he knelt before her.

Finally he pulled his mouth away, and said shakily, "I am being a fool. That outlaw could return any moment, perhaps with a gang to back him up. We should be going." He stood, pulling her up with him. As he straightened, suddenly he could see a dark spot on the front of his white shirt. His fingers went to the spot. It was not wet, not blood, but a small bit of soft fabric that met his fingers.

His fingers closed around it as he gasped, suddenly recognizing it as the eyepatch, knowing that nothing covered his marred eye any longer. His vision flew back to hers in horror as his other hand left where it grasped her arm, leaping automatically to cover the scarred and ruined left side of his face.

They stood frozen thus, he knowing she had seen it already, had seen it and kissed him all the same, and still he could not bring his hand away, could not voluntarily expose her once again to his maiming.

Her hands came up, closing around his fingers, his wrist, and she gently pulled his hand away from his face. He could not help but resist, but her pull was insistent until she had brought his hand down to his side.

Then her hands rose again, closing on either side of his head, and she pulled his mouth down to hers once more. His hands hung limp at his sides as he trembled at the caress, and he was just about to believe a dream had come true and allow his arms to rise and wrap around her, when she pulled her mouth from his.

It felt like an ending, and his heart plummeted, leaving him weak, touched by a dawning devastation. A farewell kiss, this then, or a thank you for having saved her, maybe. Nothing more.

Only, it was not so, for instead of releasing him, she pulled his head further down, so that now she stood on tiptoe and pressed her lips to the scar below, the scar above, and the lid of the wounded eye itself.

His arms rose then, clasping her tightly to him as he made a gasping sound of relief and joy mixed, as he held her, incapable of words. His heart rose and soared, laughing at him for ever doubting her, telling him that, as she loved him, he had never had anything he must show her other than his own love in return.

After a long time, she unwrapped her arms from around his neck and said softly, "Xavier? Must we go after Penelope and Kenneth? Do they not deserve this as well?"

"Of course they do," he answered simply just before he kissed her again.

Chapter 24
Epilogue

Haply I think on thee,—and then my state,
Like to the lark at break of day arising
From sullen earth, sings hymns at heaven's gate;
For thy sweet love remember'd such wealth brings
That then I scorn to change my state with kings.
—Shakespeare,
Sonnets

"It is not too late," Michael said to Summer where she sat next to him on the box. " 'Twould only take us about an hour to arrive at Gretna Green and have our nuptial day behind us."

"I shall be married in St. George's," she told him, "not in some horrid little Scottish village, over an anvil."

"Ah, well, my love. I suppose I do not care, just so it is me that you marry, wherever. Will that be soon, do you think? Our banns are already posted—"

"We are no longer affianced, if you will recall," Summer replied crisply, a slight smile hovering near her mouth.

315

"Ah, me, yes. I believe I have neglected to ask you today if you will marry me. Will you?"

"No."

"Well, if not today, then how about tomorrow?"

Summer giggled, and Penelope and Genevieve exchanged glances as Penelope picked up a roll of wide, white ribbon.

"Come stroll with me, my dear, and we will leave the old married people to do the work," Michael said, seizing up Summer's hand and pulling her away from the carriage. She squealed in surprise but otherwise scarcely offered a protest as she was taken away to the gardens.

"It will not be long ere we go to a wedding in St. George's, I think," Penelope said, fixing the end of the ribbon to the side of the carriage. She stepped back to observe the effect, then turned the roll in her hand, creating a twist. She handed the roll to Genevieve, who continued the twist as she stepped around the carriage to secure the opposite end on the other side.

"I do not know," she said, leaning to one side so that her voice might carry to Nelly's ear. "Sometimes I believe they enjoy taunting each other too much to ever actually marry. It may well be the longest courtship ever," Genevieve said with a smile. She pretended to pout then, and said, "And whatever is wrong with being married over an anvil?"

"I found it quite to my liking," Xavier said from the top of the carriage, where he was hanging wired bunches of ribbons and orange blossoms. He leaned over the edge to smile at his bride.

She smiled back up at him, saying with a happy sigh, "So did I."

"I am glad you found it an acceptable practice, for I have reason to hope that Father and Sir Roger may not be quite so quick to condemn two over-the-anvil marriages as one."

"That was our hope," Genevieve said.

"It may have been what was in your mind," Xavier said, jumping down from the carriage top.

"Oh, Xavier, watch the dust," Penelope scolded.

He went on. "But I was only interested in being married, no matter where it took place. With this lady." He came behind his bride of four days and slipped his arms around her, hugging her to his chest. She colored at the public display, but did not bid him stop.

"That became obvious," Penelope said dryly, but with a twist to her lips.

"Obvious, you say? At what point?"

"All along, I daresay, but it began to become most clear the night Kenneth and I tried to steal five minutes alone together, in Lichfield."

"I, for one, am grateful that you did," Xavier said sincerely.

Genevieve twisted her head to look up at his face above hers, exchanging a soft smile with him. The eye-patch was back in place, of course, but it served now only as a barrier to the curious, not as a shield against emotions, emotions forever set free the night they each said I do. She leaned into him, and asked, "What opinion do you have about our not-so-joyful pair? Do you think Summer will relent and have Michael?"

"Yes, later than sooner, perhaps, but love will win out, you know."

"I know," she said, and smiled up at him again.

317

"Our wedding coach is nearly ready to go," he noted, bending his neck to kiss her on the nose.

She looked at the coach, hung with ribbons and flowers meant to declare to anyone who cared to see that a wedding party was passing by, and squeezed his arms where they wrapped around her waist.

"Haddy has said he refuses to drive it thusly decorated. I think we may persuade Michael to do the honors." She dimpled and asked, "Do you think Haddy and Laura will ever fall in love?"

"When chickens give milk."

She laughed then, and turned in his arms, and kissed him full on the mouth, ignoring her sister-in-law's presence.

When Penelope made a point of stepping to the other side of the carriage to give them some privacy, it resulted in making them laugh.

Her mouth finally free from its favorite activity of late, Genevieve turned serious for a moment, to ask, "Do you think Lord Ackerley . . . I mean, my papa-in-law, might truly cast Nelly off without so much as a feather to serve as a dowry?"

"It matters not," he shrugged. "I've my own income from my maternal grandfather and some long-standing investments, so I shall see they never starve. And Kenneth is clever. He never had much capital to work with, but I have come to learn that he was putting aside what he could toward this day. If he invests it properly, they should come out all right. He means to go to Sir Roger without apologies, which I think is the best way to handle the man's bluster. We shall see what occurs in that quarter. But, no, I do not think Father will cut Nelly

318

off. He has always had a rather soft spot for the girl. And besides, his heir followed his daughter's suit." Xavier grinned then. "Perhaps we will convince him that it is all the crack to elope. One cannot punish one's children for being fashionable, can one?"

"No, indeed, I should think not." She smiled again, wrapping her arms around his waist and lifting her face for another kiss.

They continued to kiss and murmur words of endearment until they heard rapidly speaking voices, at which they turned curious faces. Summer had come from the garden, and was saying "No!" just as quickly as Michael, trailing behind her, could say, "Please?"

"No."

"Please?"

"No."

"Please, you know you love me."

"I have not said so."

"But you do not deny it. Say you love me."

"No."

"Say you will marry me."

"No."

"Please, my darling."

"I do not think so."

"Please?"

As the two settled beneath a tree to continue their contest of wills, Genevieve turned back to Xavier with a questioning look and asked, "Shall any of us be able to bear having such a display accompany us all the way to London?"

"If it means they find love, we shall bear it," he said, with something serious behind the humor in his eyes.

"It makes me recall what Summer said just a few days ago. I thought she was talking about you and her, but now I see she knew, even before we did, that you and I were meant for one another. She told me that these things always work themselves out for the best, often in ways that surprise us."

"It would surprise me if she and Michael ever truly agree on anything."

"Please?" Michael's voice floated to their ears.

"No!" came Summer's voice.

The newlyweds looked at one another and burst into laughter, holding on to each other, knowing they would never let go.